A COVERT AFFAIR

KATIE REUS

headline
ETERNAL

Published by arrangement with NAL Signet,
a division of Penguin Group (USA) LLC.
A Penguin Random House Company.

First published in Great Britain in 2016
by HEADLINE ETERNAL
An imprint of HEADLINE PUBLISHING GROUP

1

Cataloguing in Publication Data is available from the British Library

ISBN 978 1 4722 3140 6

Offset in 11.6/14.79 pt Palatino LT Std by Jouve (UK)

Printed and bound in Great Britain by CPI Group (UK) Ltd, Croydon, CR0 4YY

Headline's policy is to use papers that are natural, renewable and recyclable
products and made from wood grown in well-managed forests and other
controlled sources. The logging and manufacturing processes are expected
to conform to the environmental regulations of the country of origin.

HEADLINE PUBLISHING GROUP
An Hachette UK Company
Carmelite House
50 Victoria Embankment
London EC4Y 0DZ

www.headlineeternal.com
www.headline.co.uk
www.hachette.co.uk

Dedicated to my loving mom.

Prologue

Collateral damage: damage, injuries, or deaths that are incidental to an intended target(s). Unintended civilian casualties or destruction of civilian property.

"Evacuate now!" Karen shouted through their comm line.

Nathan immediately pushed himself up from one of the pillars of the Metro Station, his gaze locking with Freeman's, twenty feet away. This was fucking bad. They were undercover, but the urgency in Karen's voice told him that didn't matter now.

Freeman was closer to the exit. Nathan could see him pausing, as if he was going to wait for him. "Go!" he shouted at his teammate, already sprinting after him.

Selene was shouting over the comm too, telling them to get the hell out. He'd never heard her sound panicked before.

Adrenaline shot through him like a cannon blast as he ran, his legs eating up the distance between the subway tracks and the nearest set of stairs. He ignored the strange looks he got from people. If Karen or Selene told him to start tap-dancing in the middle of an op, he'd do it. Not because he was a mindless puppet who followed orders, but because he trusted them with his life. He couldn't say that about many people. And if they were telling him to get the hell out, then he was outta here.

That was when he heard it. A familiar whistle and then a whoosh of air. The unmistakable sound of a rocket.

Shit, shit, shit.

They were screwed. Without thinking, he tackled the woman nearest to him. Hell, if he could save one random person, he'd do it. Before she could utter a scream, an explosion rent the air, the roar deafening as a brief blast of heat licked through the station. Keeping her body beneath his, he covered his head with his arm as debris rained down around them.

Something hard slammed into his left leg. He groaned at the shock of pain as the bone snapped. Before it fully registered, something else fell onto his arm, skimming his head. Not as heavy, but his vision blurred for a moment. The edges of his sight went black and he fought to remain conscious as the woman cried beneath him. She wasn't struggling but was huddled up trying to get even closer to him. He succumbed to the darkness dragging him under.

Nathan's eyes snapped open to the sound of groans and crying nearby. Shit, he must have lost consciousness for a couple of seconds. The woman was still beneath him, her body shaking. That was good—she was awake. "You okay?" he rasped out. There was a dull ringing in his ears, his head pounding.

"Think . . . so." Her teeth chattered.

"I'm rolling off you." When he did, he winced as a jagged pain tore through his leg. He glanced down his body and grimaced at the odd angle his lower leg stuck out at. Definitely broken. It would be easy to give in to the pain and lie back, but he could actually hear his former gunnery sergeant telling him to "rub some fucking dirt on it, Marine!" Code for get over it and man up.

He quickly did a scan of the rest of his body. His head hurt, but his other leg seemed fine and he could move his arms and torso well enough as he pushed himself up.

As he scanned the interior of the Metro, he withdrew his weapon instinctively. He could see a few unmoving bodies, some pinned beneath large pieces of concrete, others lying with their body parts twisted at odd angles. Not good.

The woman, still huddled in a ball on the dusty floor, gasped at the sight of his SIG. "What is that?"

What the hell did she think it was? "It's fine. I'm . . . the police." Not true, but he wasn't going to tell her he was part of an elite group of NSA agents the public didn't know about and that he'd been working on a covert op when someone had decided to blow up the place. He tapped his earpiece, seeing if he could turn it on, but he knew it was pointless.

He hadn't heard anyone since the explosion.

Piles of rubble littered the station, and he could see patches of blue sky from where the ceiling had caved in. "Freeman?" he called out.

"I'm good. Broke a couple bones but I'll live," his teammate shouted from nearby, his voice shaky. It sounded as if he was on the other side of twin piles of rubble.

"Same here. Broke my leg, can't move too much without help." A wave of nausea swept through him, but he shoved it back. There was no time for that shit.

"Sit tight. Gonna see if my phone works." Freeman's voice had that thready quality to it, as if talking was a struggle.

His phone. Hell, why hadn't he thought of that? Moving sluggishly, Nathan patted his pants pocket, trying to feel for his cell, when the woman next to him gently touched his arm.

Her eyes were wide and her face and hair were streaked with dirt, probably from when he'd tackled her to the dingy floor. "You're bleeding," she said, still shaking but not as bad as before. She pointed to his head before looking around and snagging her purse, which was a foot from them. "I think I've got some tissues or something."

Her fingers fumbled to open the giant purse, but he stilled her with his free hand. "It's okay. Just sit tight. Help is on the way."

Pop. Pop. Pop.

His blood chilled in his veins. Gunfire. There was too much debris in the way, and the acoustics of the place made it impossible to accurately decide which direction it had come from. But it wasn't right on top of them, which was good.

"Was that—"

Nathan held a finger to the woman's mouth. Eyes growing even wider, she nodded, so he dropped his hand. He pointed in the direction of the stairs. There was a pile of rubble there too, blocking what he knew was their only exit. He'd have to crawl over it with some difficulty, but she should be all right as far as he could tell.

Keeping his weapon in his hand was a difficult feat as he crab-crawled backward, dragging his busted leg as he went. And didn't that hurt like a bitch? But he couldn't afford to let his guard down and he couldn't attempt to belly-crawl. He might not know the exact direction of those gunshots, but he knew the general area. The west side. So he was making it to the east side and not exposing his back to anyone. He needed to get backup, because if there was a team down here, he wasn't fit to engage. He'd do it no problem, but he had only one weapon and he was fighting uncon-sciousness each second that passed. They needed help.

At this point he wasn't sure if the shooter was the dirty DEA agent they'd brought in as part of this op or someone completely new. Didn't much matter. The only thing that mattered was getting out of this place in one piece and making sure no more innocent civilians were injured in the name of greed and power.

He glanced over his shoulder once as he crawled, relief flooding his system as they reached the nearest pile.

"Can you make it over?" he asked the woman quietly. Whispering would carry louder down here.

She nodded. "Yeah. I don't want to leave you, though." Her voice was just as quiet as his.

"It's okay. I'm going to make a call for help. Rescue teams should already be setting up outside. Go as far as you can to the stairs, but don't crawl under any beams or unstable-looking boulders. Don't take any risks. If you have to sit tight, just wait for a rescue."

"You're sure?" she whispered, clearly torn.

"I swear." He appreciated her bravery, but he wanted her out. He wanted as many innocent civilians out of here as possible. For all he knew, there could be bombs planted in the Metro, ready to be detonated. The rocket could have been only the first stage in this attack.

"Okay," she said. "If I make it to a rescue team, I'll tell them where you are."

"Thanks." As she started to climb, he managed to tug his cell free from his pocket—and found it had been damaged. The screen was busted and it was beyond repair. Freaking great.

Sighing, he weighed his options, trying his best to ignore the pain blasting all his nerve endings. He could try to crawl up after her or make his way to where he'd heard Freeman last. He couldn't leave his teammate behind. At this point they couldn't call out to each other, not with an unknown gunman somewhere nearby, so he'd just have to crawl until he found his friend.

Gritting his teeth, he'd started to move when an eerie cracking sound echoed through the tunnel. A thick chunk of concrete slammed down barely ten feet away from him. Pieces shattered out in every direction.

Looking up, he saw more pieces starting to fall. Panic bloomed inside him as he scrambled backward again. He winced as his palms dug into sharp shards of debris, the pieces cutting up his hands. He'd moved two feet when another chunk crashed where he'd just been.

His heart in his throat, he kept moving until he backed up against another pile of rubble. At least he'd made progress.

"Ortiz?" Freeman called out, despite the fact that they shouldn't be talking.

"I'm good." For now. "You?"

"Yeah."

Okay, then. That would have to do for now. As he settled up against the uncomfortable pile to take a short break, the image of Amelia filled his head. The thought of her surprised him, but maybe it shouldn't have. He'd locked up his memories of her for years, compartmentalizing the way he had to in order to attempt to get over her.

For the first time in almost twelve years, he wanted to reach out to her, just hear her voice again. He could have died today. Hell, he still might die. The only thing he was sure of, he didn't want to leave the earth without talking to her again, seeing her again.

Chapter 1

HUMINT—Human intelligence: information gathered from human sources. It is done openly and covertly.

"So, who's the lucky lady?" Selene asked, raising an eyebrow as she straightened her white blond ponytail back into place. With multiple skill sets, most of them deadly, she was one of the best operatives Wesley Burkhart had ever trained.

Right now Wesley decided to ignore her as his two-year-old granddaughter bounced on his knee. "How was the run?"

"Uh-uh. You don't care about my boring run." Tall, lean, and strong, she strode to her refrigerator and pulled out a water bottle. "Spill the deets. I know you're not heading back to D.C. tomorrow for work. And you've been acting weird lately. It's a woman; I know it." She pinned him with a pale blue stare that would have made a lot of people squirm.

But he was deputy director of the NSA. A stare didn't affect him. Even if she was right about it being a woman. But the situation was complicated.

"Spill da deets!" Faith demanded, her little fist sweetly patting his face.

His heart tightened. He'd never been married or had kids. Though he considered Selene like a daughter to him. And now he considered Faith his granddaughter, whether they were related by blood or not. That shit was just unimportant details, because the two females in the kitchen with him were his family. He'd taken Selene in when she was a teenager—after she was rescued from a drug lord who'd kidnapped her—and she'd burrowed her way into his heart without trying.

As he cleared away the knot in his throat, his mouth pulled into a thin line. "You're teaching her terrible slang."

Selene just continued watching him as if she could read his mind. "I'll figure out who she is. You know I will—and I won't use my computer skills either. Just good old detective work."

He snorted, then cringed when he smelled something unpleasantly pungent. Lifting Faith off his lap, he handed her to Selene. "I got the last one. Your turn."

Her lips parted, likely to protest, but she stopped when his phone buzzed on the kitchen table. He was never off the clock, so it wasn't a surprise that he was getting a call after what most civilians considered normal working hours on a Thursday evening. When he saw the phone number of an old friend, he frowned. This wouldn't be work-related.

"Hey," he said as Selene and Faith disappeared from the room.

"You busy?" Matias Deleon, one of his oldest friends,

asked. Former CIA, now living in sunny Miami, he'd been enjoying his retirement for a little over a year.

"I'm free. Everything okay?"

There was a pause. Slight enough, but Wesley didn't miss it. "Are you in Miami right now?"

So Matias was avoiding answering by asking a question. Typical. The retired spook knew that the NSA had a covert base in Miami. Whenever Wesley was in town, he got together with Matias. But he could tell this wasn't a social call. "No."

Another, longer pause. "I . . . need a favor."

"Lay it on me."

"It's small scale for you, but I'm calling in all my favors for this. It's about a girl."

Surprise filtered through Wesley. Much like him, Matias had been a lifelong bachelor, married to the Navy first, where the two of them had originally met decades ago, then to his job. "Okay."

"Before I retired I bought some condos when the real estate market in Florida crashed. Instead of flipping them, I decided to rent them out, especially since I'm living here to manage them. It's been a good investment."

Wesley pulled a water bottle from the fridge and stayed silent as Matias got to his point, which sometimes took a while. They'd been friends a long time and Wesley knew how the man operated.

"One of my renters is—was—a young girl about twenty. She didn't have much of a credit history, but she's had a hard life, so I went with my gut and gave her a chance. She's been the perfect tenant. More than a tenant if I'm being honest. She's become like a daughter to me." He snorted self-deprecatingly. "Or maybe like a granddaughter. Whatever. She's a good kid and she's gone missing. It's been about a month."

Finding missing people wasn't remotely his specialty, but Wesley had resources he'd lend to Matias if he was able. Before he could respond, his friend continued.

"She's been living in the condo almost as long as I've been in Miami. We have dinner together twice a week and sometimes lunch more than that. She's been working and putting herself through college, going part-time. Then out of the blue I get a letter from her— a fucking letter, not an e-mail—with the current and next month's rent, explaining that she's found a new job and will be moving out of the city. The letter read as if it was from a tenant to an owner with no clear personal relationship. Her place had been cleaned out and all her accounts closed. Not that she had many. There's been no activity on her one credit card, and her cell phone has been shut off. By her, or someone claiming to be her. It's not like she lapsed in paying her bills, she just fell off the grid."

"Have you reported anything to the local police?" Wesley figured he knew the answer but asked anyway.

"Not exactly. I know a few local detectives, but she's an adult and by all accounts she doesn't look like a missing person on paper. And my instinct doesn't count for shit with the cops. Not officially anyway. I'd just come off as an overprotective friend. And before you ask, the check was a cashier's check with a return address of her condo. I don't know what happened to her stuff, but it's not in storage anywhere local that I can find. She quit her job the same way, with a letter. She doesn't have a boyfriend, wasn't having any issues with any men, no family, and only a few friends at school. She'd taken a semester off school to earn money, but she was planning on taking a summer class. This just isn't like her and . . . there's more."

Wesley sighed as he heard the garage door opening. Levi would be home now. He figured Selene was giving Faith her bath, since she hadn't come back to the kitchen. "Tell me." He nodded at Levi, Selene's husband and a former operative, as the man stepped into the kitchen. Maybe it was Wesley's expression, but Levi just nodded once, then headed back to find his wife and daughter. Still, Wesley opened the side door to their kitchen and stepped out onto the porch for privacy.

"I couldn't let this thing go, so for the past month I've done all I can to find more. Turns out there are similar instances of other young women in the same age range who have 'gone missing.' Not missing in the technical sense, but they've quit their jobs, then fallen off the face of the earth. Completely going off the grid. I'm talking no e-mails, no phone bills, no credit card or bank account use, no rental agreements anywhere, *nothing*. And the ones I've found so far have all ended their rental agreements the same way, with letters worded eerily similarly to the one I received. It could be nothing, but my gut says it's not. They've all got a connection to Bayside Community Center—"

"Bayside?"

"Yeah, you know the place?"

"I know the owner. She's above reproach." She was newly married to one of his guys and a sweet woman.

"Maria Cervantes?"

It was O'Reilly now, but Welsey didn't correct Matias. "Yep."

Matias let out a breath. "I looked into her as much as I could and she looks clean. She one of yours?"

"More or less."

"Okay. Regardless, there's a connection at Bayside, but there could be more links I'm not seeing. I've done all I can, but I don't have the resources you do."

"Have you asked anyone at the Agency?" Referring to Matias's former employer.

Matias snorted. "No. I can and might, but I'm asking you first. You have more resources than anyone I know, you don't care about bullshit red tape, and you're a friend. I trust you with this."

"I might not be able to help you."

"I know."

Wesley had more questions and he'd get them answered, but for now . . . "Can you send me everything you've accumulated so far?"

"Yeah. I've saved everything online. I've scanned my letter and the copies from the other rental owners. I've got everything uploaded to a private file-sharing site."

He'd been prepared for Wesley's questions. Good. "Send the info to my personal e-mail. I'll look at it tonight and let you know what I find."

"Thank you."

"Don't thank me yet." Miami was a beautiful place to live, but it had a dark underbelly. Drugs, weapons, and women were all sold for the right price. Recently he and one of his teams had helped shut down a huge sex-trafficking ring, but there could be others in Miami. Hell, there probably were. There was a lot of evil in the world, and unfortunately he couldn't stop it all.

But he was damn sure going to try to help his friend. If the girl was being trafficked, he was going to find her and save her.

Wesley glanced up from his computer as his assistant/ super-analyst Karen Stafford half knocked on his open door, already stepping inside. "You got a second?"

He held up a finger, then turned so she could see he had his Bluetooth in. When she started to back out, he shook his head and pointed at one of the cushy chairs in front of his desk. Sleek and polished as always, she nodded and took a seat, setting one of the many tablets she used on her lap. She worked her magic as he hurriedly ended his current call.

As he tapped the earpiece off and slid it out of his ear, he looked at her. "So?"

"*So*, I know why your friend was a spook for so long. It's taken us four days and considerable resources and we've found thirty-five more women to his fifteen. I can't believe he discovered fifteen linked women with basically just doing on-the-ground research."

Wesley wasn't surprised but didn't respond, even as his gut tightened. Thirty-five more women? Not good.

"They've all got almost identical socioeconomic backgrounds—tough childhood, placed either in the foster system or with relatives instead of their parents for long periods of time, all in the lowest income bracket. None of them are under eighteen or older than twenty-eight. None have a history of drug or substance abuse. They had a tough time growing up, but none of these women are addicts, something I found interesting and noted in my files. Ethnic backgrounds vary, but basically they're young, healthy, and from the pictures, pretty women."

Wesley nodded once. "This is good work."

"There's more." Her tone was dark. "Your contact is right, they're all connected to Bayside Community Center one way or another, but there are other connections including the owner of a couple local restaurants. Twelve of the missing women have worked for the owner, Amelia Rios, at one time over the last year. She has a background similar to the women's and according to what I've dug up so far, she's worked very hard to get to where she is. It appears she might have had some dealings with a local loan shark when she started her first business, but she doesn't have a record. With her similar history and the connection, I wanted to note her too. Oh, and she changed her last name when she turned eighteen, which could be for any number of reasons, but again, I found it interesting.

"This is just the tip of what I've found, but after researching I'm convinced your friend is right. Fifty women, all living in Miami at the time they disappeared—that we've found so far—all leave their lives under the same circumstances. They're all basically alone in the world, so no one will miss them, and they're young and beautiful—and a legal age."

They were easy prey was what it boiled down to. To hell with that. This wasn't the type of case he normally worked on, but he was going to make an exception for his friend and because it was the right thing to do. He simply couldn't look the other way, and he wasn't letting another agency take over.

It would be tricky, but he was going to reach out to the local PD and set up a small task force in Miami to figure out what the hell was going on. He had enough discretionary funds to make this happen. It was possible someone thought they could step into Paul Hill's shoes, a man who had run the skin trade in Miami for a long time. A man the NSA and other agencies had brought down—though he'd ended up getting killed in prison not long after. The thought made Wesley smile. He was glad that bastard was dead. "Will you shut the door?" he asked, earning a surprised look from Karen.

But she stood and shut the door before returning to her seat.

He had the perfect agent in mind for this op. "I know you're friends with Ortiz."

She nodded. "Yes."

Nathan Ortiz had been injured in a Metro bomb blast in D.C. months before. He'd recently been cleared for active duty, but Wesley didn't want to make the mistake of sending him into the field too soon. Wesley was the one who'd recruited him as a Black Death 9 agent. Ortiz was now a member of the NSA's elite group who took on covert, off-the-books operations, but this would be his biggest op to date, since he was so new. And he was just coming off bed rest and physical therapy. Still, he was from Miami and familiar with the city in a way that would help him blend with the locals. Not to mention that one of his cover IDs was perfect for what Wesley was contemplating.

"How's he been doing?" Wesley knew what went on under his purview, but Karen likely knew more about the day-to-day workings of their people.

She lifted her shoulders slightly. "He's more than competent, but you need to put him back in the field. He does all his work without complaint and he does it well. While he has the skills of an analyst, he doesn't love it the way Elliott or I do. And if you keep him here too long, you'll burn him out. I think he's starting to feel stagnant."

Surprise flickered through him, but he didn't show it. "He told you this?"

"No, but we're friends. Tucker and I had him over for dinner last week and he said something about wanting to get back in the field. It was the *way* he said it. He's ready."

Wesley nodded, glad her instinct was the same as his. In the end he'd make the decision he thought was best, but he valued Karen's insight. "Thanks. Clear your schedule and hand off anything that isn't a priority."

"We're going to find these women?" There was a trace of surprise in her voice, probably because she knew as well as he did that finding missing women wasn't what they did.

"Women are often used in the sex slave trade, and profits from their sales go to funding terrorism." That was the angle he'd use for getting this operation off the ground. Because he was already involved and simply couldn't walk away. Not when Matias had asked him for this favor and not when all these women were just disappearing without a trace. No one was looking for them.

Until now.

Chapter 2

Blown: discovery of an agent's true identity or a clandestine activity's true purpose.

Two weeks later

Amelia Rios took the tulip-shaped champagne glass from her date, Iker Mercado, with a smile. At forty-five, he was seventeen years older than her and definitely the oldest man she'd ever been on a date with. Not that she dated much, not with her schedule. But Mercado was interesting, charming, handsome, and he didn't have a reputation as a man-whore. If he had, she would have declined his invitation. In her experience, playboy types tended to have little respect for her gender. *No, thank you.*

If anything, the man had practically lived like a saint for the last twenty-five years. She knew from gossip that his wife had died at nineteen during childbirth. He'd only been twenty, yet had raised his daughter and had never gotten remarried or really even dated. If gossip was to be believed, of course. In this case, she believed it.

"You look beautiful tonight," he murmured, his gaze raking over her appreciatively. But not in a creepy way. Everything about him was so polished, from his tailored tuxedo to his genuine smile. When he looked at people or talked to them, he was always engaged, and none of it seemed forced.

"You look pretty good yourself." She smiled, pasting on the brightest one she could muster. She rarely came to events such as the auction Mercado was putting on. She always felt like an impostor at things like this. While no one could say she didn't look the part with her sleek black dress, new manicure and pedicure, and, thanks to a friend, an intricate hairstyle that looked as if she'd paid a fortune to have it done, she still felt like a fraud. It was her own insecurities, something she was well aware of. Didn't change the fact that she felt like a big fake standing around with so many women of Miami's high society, all of whom were decked out in glittering, blinding jewelry. Part of her that she hated admitting existed wondered why Mercado had even asked her to this thing. He'd pursued her decently enough too, asking her out three times before she'd agreed.

She was pretty, she knew that, but so many of the women were wealthy and elegant with the right pedigree. She was none of those things. She'd lived in dumps for years before finally getting her restaurants off the ground. Now she made a good living, but some days she still felt like that young girl working double shifts seven days a week and so desperate to claw her way out of her life that she'd have done practically anything. People who think money can't buy you happiness have never been poor. Not that she actually thought money could *buy* happiness, but it sure as hell paid the bills and gave her stability.

"So, how do you think it's going? Or is it too soon to tell?" she continued, taking advantage of it just being the two of them. Considering he was the one putting on the silent auction for charity and was a well-respected man, they'd barely had more than a minute of alone time tonight. Oddly she wasn't that disappointed. The man was perfect on paper and incredibly nice, but she didn't feel much of a spark.

"I think it's going well." He stepped a fraction closer, letting his hand settle on one of her hips in a loose but somehow still possessive gesture. It didn't make her uncomfortable, but it was surprising. "Though I now see that asking you to this for our first date was a mistake."

Shock rippled through her at his words. Did he not think she was the right kind of woman to bring to this? "Was it?" Her words came out icier than she'd intended.

He blinked in surprise, a small frown pulling at his mouth. "We've had no private time. I'd like to take you out again soon, just the two of us. Maybe I'll cook for you?"

Oh God, she felt like an idiot. She wanted to crush all her insecurities, but sometimes they just flared to the surface with no warning. The clenching in her gut dissipated when it registered he hadn't been insulting her. "I—"

"Iker!" A female voice cut off the rest of what Amelia had been about to say.

Which was maybe a good thing. She wasn't certain

she wanted to go on another date with him anyway. If the spark wasn't there, she doubted it would magically appear during another date. Deep down she wondered if she'd ever feel that "thing" with anyone. She had once, but that was so long ago. Over a decade. And she was pretty certain she'd just built up the combustible attraction in her mind. No one could have been that sexy, that intense, that—

She realized that Mercado was introducing her to someone. Naomi Baronet. A beautiful woman with bright red hair swept up into a simple twist. She was likely in her forties. Her features were sharp, defined, and elegant. Amelia smiled and shook the hand the woman was offering. Thank God she didn't have to do the air-kiss thing so many people had been doing tonight. "It's a pleasure to meet you."

"You as well, Miss Rios." Her eyes glinted with something that made Amelia feel uneasy. The woman watched her like a bug under a microscope.

But she kept her smile in place. "Please call me Amelia."

"And you must call me Naomi. I've been wanting to meet you for a while now." Her smile was easy, her teeth a brilliant white, but there was no warmth in her eyes.

"You have?" Amelia couldn't imagine why. She had never even heard of this woman.

Naomi nodded, her eyes narrowing just a fraction as Iker slid his arm around Amelia's waist, holding her loosely, but still close. It felt as if he was being protective. "Yes, I know you've been working in tandem with Maria and all those . . . unfortunate women."

Disdain laced the last two words, even as she tried to mask it. "I know Maria's father disapproves of all the time she spends at that center, but she's such a giving woman. I don't know how she does it."

Unfortunate women? "That" center? This woman was like a cartoon character. Amelia forced herself to keep her voice even. Sometimes her temper got away from her, and tonight was not the time for that. "She does a great service to our community. And those 'unfortunate' women are basically young girls who had nothing growing up and simply want a better life for themselves. And they're not afraid to work hard for it." Something Amelia could appreciate. Ice coated her voice even as she tried to order herself to keep that facade in place. But people like Naomi, who wore entitlement around themselves like a silk wrap, annoyed her.

The woman blinked in surprise, but before she could respond, Iker's grip on Amelia tightened. "Naomi, I see someone I need to speak to, but save me a dance." As he steered Amelia away, she inwardly cringed.

"Ah, sorry if I was—"

"Don't apologize," he said through a smile. "She is . . . an unlikable individual. And if you see me dancing with her later, I beg you to come save me." The light humor in his voice eased the tightness in her chest.

"You're not friends with her?"

"No. I've done business with her brother, but that's the extent of our relationship. She's here because she wants to show off her jewelry and be seen. She doesn't care about our community." It was clear he did care.

Amelia wondered what was wrong with herself. Why

she didn't feel more of a spark for him. The setting tonight was perfectly romantic. Afro-Cuban jazz played in the background, the band he'd hired nothing less than spectacular. The music—along with the servers walking around wearing fedoras and the birds-of-paradise centerpieces—gave the auction a vintage, glamorous Old Havana feel.

"There's something I need to tell you," he continued, pulling her closer to the dance floor, expertly maneuvering through the throng of people. "I had you checked out before asking you on a date."

Gathering her thoughts, she took a sip of her champagne before responding, "You mean like investigated?"

He nodded. "Yes. I don't date much and I'm careful when I do."

Whoa, he must be wealthier than she'd realized, something that made her incredibly uncomfortable. "Okay." She wasn't even certain how to respond.

He rubbed a hand over the back of his neck, seemingly uncomfortable as well, which was at odds with the polished man. "I wanted to be up front with you. I should probably apologize, but I'm not sorry. I've gotten burned in the past by women who wanted only one thing from me."

The ghost of a smile touched her lips. It was refreshing that he was being so honest, but also a little unnerving. "I Googled you," she admitted. Definitely not the same thing as having her investigated, though.

He smiled, the charming man perfectly back in place. His hair was a honey brown with just a few faint hints of gray peeking through. "And?"

"And you seem pretty decent."

He laughed at that. "You do wonders for my ego."

Shrugging, she took another sip of her champagne. "So, what did you find out about me that I probably wouldn't have shared on a first date?" She couldn't help wondering what he'd discovered in his investigation. Probably that she'd changed her last name. Maybe he'd figured out why, maybe not. She wasn't going to offer up the information, not unless they got to know each other better. It was too hard to talk about. Having her name linked to her mother, a prostitute, wasn't something she'd wanted for the rest of her life.

"You're the owner of two successful restaurants, something I already knew anyway."

"How do you know they're successful?"

Now he shrugged, all casual innocence. "About a year ago I looked into buying commercial property near La Cocina de Amelia. I checked out the surrounding businesses to see how profitable they were."

Smart. "Did you buy the property?"

A brief nod. "I did. I wish I'd gone into one of your restaurants back then, though. Maybe we would have met sooner." His eyes darkened at that, undeniable heat simmering there.

She felt her cheeks warm up just a bit at the boldness in his gaze. She still wasn't sure she felt anything for him and loathed herself for it. Loathed that after a decade she still had lingering feelings for a man she knew she'd never see again. It was her own fault, but it didn't lessen the emotions one iota. Glancing away, she nearly dropped her glass when she spotted Nathan freaking Ortiz moving around the edge of the dance floor, headed her way.

Nathan. Ortiz.

Had she lost her ever-loving mind? She gave herself a hard mental shake and looked away. When she found her gaze drawn directly back to the man again, she realized that no, she hadn't lost her mind.

Taller than her—but who wasn't?—muscular, yet lean, he filled out his tuxedo with absolute perfection. He had the sleek lines of a graceful predator. Though he wasn't looking at her, there was no doubt in her mind that he'd seen her and was making his way over here. He was moving with far too much purpose. What was he doing here? Was he living in Miami again? The last she knew he'd joined the Marine Corps, but that had been twelve years ago.

She guessed he could be on social media, but she only had accounts for her business, not herself, so she didn't know. She'd been tempted a time or two to look him up but had never followed through. She figured he'd gotten married and had kids by now—not something she needed to see or know about. She didn't begrudge him any happiness, but the thought of him settling down with someone had just been too depressing. Actually seeing pictures of him on social media with a smiling, happy family? No, thanks. It wasn't as if they had any common friends, so she'd never heard an inkling about him over the years. That alone had made it so much easier to bury her curiosity. Or at least ignore it.

Just watching him move was like watching— Gah, she couldn't even think of a good analogy, but a low-grade heat started building inside her, her nipples tightening almost painfully in awareness. The man was even sexier than she remembered, but there was nothing boyish about him anymore. He'd been eighteen the last time she saw him, so he'd be almost thirty now. He had a bit of scruff on his face, not a full-on beard, but oh sweet Lord, he was gorgeous. She absolutely hated that her body just seemed to flare to life at the mere sight of him. Like a switch flipping, she didn't even feel like herself right now. She wanted to crawl out of her skin to escape this surreal sensation of watching the man whom she'd never gotten over make his way toward her and her date.

Amelia tore her gaze from Nathan as he disappeared behind a cluster of people and focused on Iker, who was still smiling at her. Guilt suffused her, but thank God he couldn't read her mind. She wanted to ask him to dance, to drag him out onto the gleaming wooden floor and get away from Nathan. If that made her a coward, she didn't care. When Iker plucked a new champagne glass for her from one of the passing servers, she didn't protest.

"I'd like you to meet an associate of mine," Iker murmured, slipping his arm around her waist in the same way he'd done with Naomi, only this time his grip was tighter, less casual. Definitely a male-territorial thing, if she had to guess.

When she turned in his arm, looking up to meet his associate, she shouldn't have been surprised to see Nathan. But the shock of seeing him up close was a punch to her senses. Blood rushed to her face and she inwardly cursed her reaction.

"Amelia, this is Miguel Ortiz."

Miguel? Nathan's eyes were the same dark espresso she remembered. She didn't know what to make of the name Miguel but didn't comment on that. If he was using another name, she figured he didn't want to admit they knew each other. So she didn't acknowledge that she knew him, instead smiling politely as she held out a hand.

He took it, shook her hand almost stiffly, formally. It was weird touching him again after so long. Just feeling his skin against her brought up far too many memories. Ones that should stay buried. The man had always been so talented with his fingers and mouth. So, *so* talented. Something she shouldn't be thinking about.

"A pleasure to meet you." His words were raspy, but it was clear he didn't plan to acknowledge her either. Okay, so he was definitely using an alias.

She'd be lying if she said she wasn't curious why. No matter what, she certainly wasn't going to call him out in front of anyone else. She swallowed hard, forcing her throat to work. "You too." Two words—she was a freaking rock star. She swallowed again, this time subtly. "Are you in antiquities too?" she asked, looking between the two men, thankful that she seemed to have herself under control.

Nathan looked at Iker, something dark in his gaze. "Something like that."

She wasn't sure what passed between them, but Iker seemed annoyed. He was still all charm, but something had shifted.

"Would it offend you if I asked your date for a dance?" Nathan asked, his gaze perfectly placid and polite. But there was something in his eyes she couldn't get a handle on.

"I don't speak for Amelia." Iker's voice was butter smooth.

Now Nathan turned that laserlike focus on her again. "Will you dance with me?"

A soft Cuban beat filled the air as the lights dimmed a fraction. "Uh . . ." She glanced at Iker. She didn't want to be rude and they'd both already danced with other people earlier in the evening. Still, it felt as if it might be impolite to say yes, but she really wanted to talk to Nathan—or Miguel—and ask why he was using another name and why he was in Miami. For a brief moment she wondered if he was in some sort of criminal business, but almost immediately she discarded that idea. The Nathan she'd known had seen the world in black and white; he'd been so damn honorable about everything. Since she wasn't going to find out by guessing, she let her curiosity win. "Do you mind?"

Iker's expression was soft as he shook his head. "No, but save the next one for me." Surprising her, he kissed her forehead in a sweet gesture.

Before she could react or think, Nathan took her hand and she found herself in his arms. She was glad she'd worn heels so she was better matched for him, heightwise. He was six feet tall, the same as Iker. But Nathan's presence was somehow bigger, more intense. Of course that was probably just to her, not to the entire room.

As one of his big hands landed on her hip, more of those stupid memories pushed themselves up, including the one of her at his school's prom. It had been so damn cliché, but they'd lost their virginity to each other after the prom. It was a sweet memory, one she'd always cherished. Despite the surreal quality of the situation, she wanted to lean into him, to soak up all of him. It had been so long since she saw him, since she ended things with him in the worst way possible, and it was difficult to believe he was here. She still felt guilty about the way she'd cut him out of her life so abruptly.

"The beard's new," she murmured as they swayed with what could have been a practiced rhythm. It seemed that years of separation didn't affect that. Their movements might as well have been choreographed.

To her surprise, the hint of a smile played across those full lips. "How long have you been with Iker Mercado?"

"I don't answer your questions, *Miguel*, until you tell me why you're calling yourself—"

The grip on her hip tightened, a clear indication for silence, before he gently spun her in time with the steady beat. She was incredibly grateful for the simple three-step dance pattern. Unlike some of the complicated dances from earlier in the evening, this one she could do without thinking. Which was good, because way too many questions invaded her mind. He was obviously being secretive for a reason, and she wanted to know why. Her mind circled back to the criminal angle, but she couldn't make that work in her head. It just didn't fit. Still, twelve years had passed. People changed.

They were silent as they danced, and though she figured she should probably wonder or care if Iker was watching them, she had eyes only for Nathan. But as she looked into his dark eyes, it was a reminder of all she'd lost. She was the one who'd ended things with him because of her own cowardice and deep-seated issues. She'd been so ashamed back then, so immersed in her own pain at what she'd lost that she'd brutally cut him out of her life. It was one of her biggest regrets.

Pain she thought she'd locked up bubbled to the surface, clawing at her insides. If she thought too hard or long about everything that had gone down between them, she'd slip into a funk and not be able to get out of it for a day or so. She couldn't do that now.

Still moving in time with the music, she looked at his chest instead of at his face. It made it easier to breathe.

"Are you going to say anything to him?" Nathan finally murmured.

She figured she understood what he meant. Would she tell Iker that his name was Nathan? She didn't even have to think about it. No matter what, she could never betray him. It didn't matter how many years had passed. He was the boy—now man—she'd lost her virginity to. The first person she'd ever loved. Hell, the first person who'd ever loved her, because her mother certainly hadn't. "No, but you *will* give me answers."

"Not here," he said simply. Since he hadn't said no, she understood he meant to tell her later. Which just piqued her curiosity even more. "You look beautiful," he continued, his grip possessive.

Slight irritation popped inside her at the way he held her. "Thank you. You look good too."

His lips quirked up almost playfully. "Just good?"

Seeing him almost smile did something strange to her insides. She should be pushing him for more answers but found herself giving him a half smile. "Would 'handsome' make your ego feel better? Or maybe . . . 'pretty'?" She snickered at the dark look he gave her. When they were together he'd gotten grief from plenty of the boys in her neighborhood for being "a pretty boy." Until he'd kicked the ass of more than one of them.

"Are you and Mercado serious?" Nathan's gaze grew even darker, all traces of amusement fading.

She shouldn't tell him a damn thing. He wasn't even using his real name. Still, she couldn't seem to stop the truth from coming out. "It's our first date."

Though it was marginal, his grip on her relaxed. "Good." There was a wealth of meaning in that one word.

"When do you plan on answering my questions?" Because she had plenty.

"Meet up with me after the auction." He wasn't even bothering to ask her, just ordering.

It pissed her off. Despite her curiosity, she pursed her lips and met his gaze dead-on. "If I'd ever had a mother who cared about me, I'm sure she would have told me not to meet up with strangers. And you, *Miguel*, are a stranger." A stranger who'd seen every inch of her naked.

His jaw tightened in annoyance. "I'll answer your questions, I swear."

There was no real way she was just walking away after missing him and wondering about him for twelve damn years. She couldn't even pretend not to be rabidly curious. "Can you remember my phone number if I tell it to you?"

He nodded, so she quickly rattled off her number. It was slight, but she felt him relax a fraction. As the song ended she stepped away from him, surprised at the feeling of loss as his arms fell from her. She quickly turned, making her way back to her date.

Iker was talking to two men, but he frowned over her head, likely at Nathan, as she made her way to him. She pasted on a smile for Iker when he met her gaze, though, hoping it looked real.

Unfortunately all her thoughts were on the man she'd left on the dance floor and the answers she'd soon be getting from him.

Chapter 3

Spook: jargon for the word "spy" or someone involved in espionage. It is a synonym for "apparition."

A melia shut the bathroom stall door behind her and locked it before sitting on the already closed toilet lid. She'd tried to mingle and make small talk with Iker and his associates, but after a while it had become impossible. Feeling too edgy, she'd stopped drinking champagne and had switched to water.

Seeing Nathan had brought up too many memories, most unwanted. Though it was almost harder to stomach the good ones, because they just reminded her of all she'd lost. Of what could have been. She should have just been honest with him back then. Of course her older self had a lot more maturity and years under her belt, so it was easy to say that.

As she tried to steady her breathing, she stared at the shiny tile floor. An image of blood covering another bathroom floor flashed in her mind. She shuddered and blinked, trying to banish the image. It was no use, though. Seeing Nathan—or whatever he was calling himself—had opened up a wound inside her. One she'd kept patched up since she was seventeen.

For a moment that was all she could see. Dark crimson pooling on the floor and coating her legs as she collapsed, curled up in agony. That floor had been dingy, the bathroom a lot smaller. And the pain . . .

She jerked her head up at the sound of heels moving over tile. Someone else was here.

The interruption pulled her back to reality. She would not have a breakdown at this event. Nope, she'd save that until she got home. Nathan had said he'd contact her, but she wasn't sure she even believed him. Maybe he'd just said he would answer her questions so she wouldn't tell Iker his real name. Not that he should ever fear that. She felt a loyalty to Nathan, whether he was a criminal or not.

On unsteady legs she stood but gained strength as she took a few more breaths. Time to shelve all those thoughts and get back to her date. She wasn't going to stay, though. She'd make up an excuse about work soon, whatever it took. Because she couldn't be in the same place as Nathan and *not* remember. It didn't matter that she'd had counseling to get her through what she now knew had been a depression; seeing him was a stark reminder of too many things.

When she opened the stall door, some of the tension fled her when she saw Maria Cervantes standing at a huge, gold-framed mirror on one of the walls, applying lip gloss. "Maria," she said, pleased it wasn't a stranger.

Maria smiled warmly, the petite dark-haired woman meeting her gaze in the mirror. "Hey, I've been hoping to get you alone tonight."

"I'm surprised your husband let you out of his sight," she teased, already feeling more like herself, as she moved to one of the sinks. Maria's husband, Cade, was huge, probably six feet five, and looked more than a little intimidating. With jet-black hair, a skull trim that made him look fierce, and a plethora of tattoos, the man didn't look like the society types Maria had been linked to in the past. Amelia wasn't even sure what Maria's husband did for a living, but the way he looked at Maria was enough for Amelia to know he was completely head-over-heels for her friend.

Maria snorted and turned from the mirror. "He's probably hovering somewhere nearby. So, Iker Mercado? He's quite a catch, according to gossip." She leaned against one of the sinks as Amelia dried her hands.

Now it was her turn to snort. "It's our first date and honestly probably our last. He's very nice, but . . . I don't know. I just don't feel that spark, I guess." She didn't want to talk about herself, though. "Did you know that Danita quit a couple weeks ago?"

Maria didn't move from her position against the sink, but her gaze hardened just a fraction, before she smiled placidly. Considering that Amelia's mother had been a prostitute, she'd learned at an early age to gauge moods and expressions of people, namely her mother's clients. It was the only way she'd survived her childhood—and it was one of the reasons she'd succeeded in business. She wasn't ever going to end up like her mother.

"I know." Maria's tone was neutral.

Ah, okay, then. "Do you know why?"

"I was hoping you might." There was a subtle bite

to Maria's words—an unexpected one—that got Amelia's back up.

How the heck would she know why the woman had quit? Months ago Amelia had started working with Maria, helping get some of the women from Maria's community center placed in two of Amelia's restaurants. After how hard it had been for her to make something of herself, she tried to help women in similar situations. It was why she'd reached out to Maria. "I hired her because of your recommendation and because I saw something in her, but . . ."

Amelia shook her head as frustration and a healthy dose of hurt welled up inside her. "She just sent me a lame note, which sadly is more than some employees bother doing when they quit. I didn't expect it, not when we'd become friends. And, Maria, she's the fifth person you've sent my way to quit like this." Twelve women had actually come through her restaurant, but seven had given her face-to-face resignations and two weeks' notice. It was the service industry and for a lot of them, it was a temporary job. She understood and accepted that, but she didn't like it when employees just quit with no notice.

Clearing her throat, she continued. "Not that I'm blaming you or plan to stop hiring women you recommend. It's just . . . I don't know. Danita and I had become friends. She blindsided me." She felt lame letting her hurt show but decided to go for honesty. There was no reason to hold back.

Maria's expression softened at her words and she pushed up from her leaning position. "There's something we need to talk about. It's important."

Amelia blinked at the abrupt change. "Okay."

Maria shook her head. "Not here. Tonight, though. Can you meet me at Bayside? I want privacy for this and we can use my office." When Amelia hesitated, Maria continued. "It's about Danita."

Alarm slid through her veins. "Is something wrong?"

Maria paused. "Maybe, I just can't talk about it here."

"Okay, we'll meet. You want to talk after the auction? Or I was planning to leave early," she said sheepishly. Which earned her the ghost of a smile from Maria.

"We were too. Cade hates these things. Can you meet me there in an hour?"

"Sure." The request was a little odd, but Amelia trusted Maria. The woman had been through heartbreak last year, losing her mom in a terrorist attack that killed hundreds of people. Yet Maria was so strong about everything and had never wavered in her work for the community center. It was hard not to like and trust her. "Fair warning, I'm going to make up a work excuse, so don't blow my cover."

Maria's lips quirked up. "Your secret is safe with me."

"I'll text you when I leave. Okay?"

"Perfect."

As Maria headed for the door, Amelia pulled her lip gloss from her simple black clutch. She heard Maria murmuring a hello to someone else, and then the door shut softly behind her. The click of heels sounded before Collette Mercado, Iker's daughter, stepped into view.

Collette's perfect eyebrows arched. "Amelia, I wondered where you'd gotten off to. Heard you got Naomi

Baronet in a pissy mood." She laughed darkly before Amelia could respond. "That woman is such a lazy bitch," she murmured, moving to the big mirror next to Amelia. Her perfume was subtle, with notes of lavender.

Amelia felt a little strange around Collette, mainly because Amelia was only three years older than her. It wasn't just that, though; there was an edge to Collette. She was always direct, sometimes to the point of being brusque. It was so at odds with the tall, beautiful woman's outer appearance. Her honey brown hair was the same shade as her father's, but she must have gotten her dewy olive skin from her mother.

"She's just jealous of you, don't worry. She's been after my father for years. Just for his money, though. So thank you for annoying her." Collette pulled out a tube of gloss as well and smiled at her in the mirror.

Some of Amelia's tension eased. Half smiling, she put her lip gloss back in her clutch, closing it with a snap. "I'm glad I could help."

"We should do lunch soon," Collette said, not looking at her now as she regarded herself in the mirror. "Regardless of whether you and my father work out. I want to talk to you about the restaurant industry."

"Oh, uh, okay." Amelia didn't know if she planned to see Iker again, and it felt a little strange to meet up with his daughter if she ended things with Collette's father.

"I'll call you. We'll set it up." Then she was gone as quickly as she'd come.

Amelia knew that Collette worked with her father sometimes. Not that she needed to, if gossip was to be believed. But maybe she was looking to buy a restaurant as an investment—because Amelia couldn't imagine the tall, striking woman who got her hair blown out once a week actually working in a restaurant, getting her hands dirty.

Not that any of that concerned Amelia. Right now all she cared about was making an excuse to leave and getting out of here. She wanted to meet with Maria, but the truth was, her stomach was tied in knots at the prospect of talking to and seeing Nathan again.

"Damn, that was easy," Cade said to Nathan, turning the volume down on the laptop as Maria exited the bathroom.

Even though she wasn't an NSA agent, they'd wired her for this op. Just as Nathan had been wired earlier when he was dancing with Amelia. But he'd turned off the recorder, something Cade was still confused over. His friend thought there'd been interference or a malfunction.

Nathan looked over at Cade, who was sitting in the passenger seat of the NSA-owned SUV. Though Cade had turned down the volume, they could hear the muted movements of Maria as she made her way out of the convention center to meet them. Normally they'd have a command center van as their base of operations, but tonight had simply been about information-gathering and making contact with Iker Mercado again. The man was suspected of illegal antiquities dealings, but he'd led a very clean life. At least on paper. He'd never been nailed down by any government agency, but if someone was involved in the smuggling of humans, he could be involved. Or know who was doing it.

Nathan had made contact with him twice over the past two weeks, but he'd known nothing about Amelia being involved with him. He'd read over the files multiple times, but she hadn't been one of Nathan's targets during this op and her last name was Rios, so he hadn't realized it was his Amelia. Now he wished he'd been more diligent. Being blindsided tonight was his own damn fault. And it was a rookie fucking mistake. Not good for his first op back on duty.

Reaching over to the laptop, he muted the connection completely, not wanting Maria to overhear anything. "My cover is potentially blown. I know Amelia," he blurted before his teammate could ask what he was doing. He needed to be straight with Cade. "And there wasn't a malfunction with my listening device. I turned it off when I was dancing with her."

Cade's eyes widened, but he was silent for a moment as he watched Nathan. "How do you know her?"

He'd lost his virginity to her and had been so fucking in love with her that he wasn't sure he'd actually ever moved on. He'd dated other women, but being in the military and then working undercover for the NSA hadn't been conducive to relationships. At least that was what he'd always told himself. Deep down, he'd always carried a torch for Amelia. Life had dealt her a shitty hand, but she'd never let it get her down, had always been so damn stoic about things. But he sure as shit wasn't telling his friend and teammate that. "My grandmother lived next door to her mom. We knew each other in high school." A simple explanation for something exponentially more complicated.

Cade's brow furrowed. "How'd she react to your name?"

"She didn't, and she won't tell Mercado." Of that he was almost sure. Almost. He wasn't going to risk his life on that assumption, though. He had to bring his boss in on this and he really needed to talk to Amelia directly. Once he got his shit together. Seeing her tonight, on the arm of one of their suspects no less, had made something dark inside him snap. For the last twelve years he'd made it a point not to look her up. She was the one who'd ended things, and it hadn't been pretty. He'd fucking begged her to talk to him, to explain why she was cutting him out of her life. But she'd been so remote, as if they were strangers. Then her mom had been evicted from her rental not long after Amelia broke up with him, and he had no idea where they'd ended up after he went into the Corps. And when he was in the Marines, it had been easy to forget about everything else other than staying alive and keeping his buddies alive in war zones.

Not that he hadn't thought about tracking her down, seeing where she'd ended up. If he had found her online, he wouldn't have trusted himself not to try to see her again. Or worse, he'd hated the thought of her ending up married to someone, having someone else's kids. Not knowing had seemed like a hell of a better deal. Then three months ago he'd almost died in an op. He hadn't wanted to die without facing his past. Without facing *her*.

So he'd opened a fake social media account and had

slowly started going through Facebook profiles in Miami and Florida—not that he'd found her. Yeah, he could have used company resources and located her a lot sooner, but he hadn't wanted to for multiple reasons. The main one: the longer it took for him to find her, the longer he was still in the dark about her life. Despite his near-death experience, he still hadn't wanted to find out that she was happily married and he was just a footnote in her life. Pathetic? Yeah, but he didn't care.

"Hmm," was all Cade said. "So, why'd you turn off the recorder?"

"I wanted privacy." He'd have to call Burkhart tonight, tell him everything. Mostly everything. Burkhart might pull him from the op, but he was going to plead his case. It wouldn't make sense to pull him when he'd established contact with Mercado already. And if Amelia didn't blow his cover, there was no need to step back from this. He wanted to keep her away from Mercado anyway. That possessive need he felt for her was still there, even after so many years. It was as if it had just locked back into place after seeing her. Which pissed him off. He'd spent years keeping all that shit under wraps, but seeing her again brought it all back to the surface.

"You've got to tell Burkhart," Cade said, mirroring Nathan's thoughts.

He nodded once. "As soon as Maria meets with Amelia, I will." Because he and Cade were going to be with Maria at Bayside. They'd stay out of sight, but the conversation between the two women would be recorded and he and Cade would be in the next room. His gut told him that Amelia wasn't involved with the

missing women—at least not the Amelia he'd known—
but they had to be sure whether she knew anything
relevant or not.

The back door opened and Maria slid in. "I feel like
a super-spy tonight," she said breathlessly. "Did you
guys get our conversation?" Amelia had been one of
Cade's future targets, but since Maria had a relationship with her, and Amelia had been at the auction,
they'd decided to reach out to her tonight. They'd be
able to gauge her reaction later one way or another.

Maria's office had been wired to include video and
audio capability. They'd planned to get Amelia down
there later in the week, but now turned out to be a better
time. She couldn't have been prepared for Maria to ask
her to her office tonight, so she'd be off her game. Not
to mention that seeing Nathan after so long would have
messed with her—he'd witnessed that clearly in her
eyes. Nathan could admit that he'd been shaken seeing
Amelia too. It was much better to have this meeting
when her guard was down. And Cade had been right—
getting her to meet with Maria had been easy. Hopefully
it was because she was concerned about Danita.

Cade nodded at Maria and shot Nathan an unreadable look as he started the SUV. Thankfully Cade
didn't say anything about what Nathan had done.
Instead he turned back to his new wife. "You did great,
sweetheart."

"Thanks. I don't think she's involved, though. Honestly Amelia is awesome. I saw her expression. She's
concerned about Danita and unless I'm wrong, she's
kinda peeved about the other women quitting on her."

"She or her restaurants are connected to some of the

women," Cade said as Nathan steered out of the parking lot. They'd opted not to use valet tonight so they could make an easy getaway and because they didn't want any nosy drivers having access to their vehicle.

"Yeah, well, so is Bayside, and I'm not involved." Maria sounded almost indignant. "I just don't think she's tangled up in whatever's going on."

"We'll find out soon," Cade said noncommittally.

"So, what's the deal with you two?" she continued as Nathan drove.

Frowning, he looked at her in the rearview mirror. "What do you mean?" She wouldn't have been able to hear them talking, and unless Cade communicated to her telepathically, she shouldn't know anything.

"The way you and Amelia were dancing . . . *caliente*." She wiggled her eyebrows suggestively, laughing lightly. "I mean, it was subtle, but there seemed to be a vibe going on."

He just shrugged. Maria might be Cade's wife and yeah, she'd been read into this op because of the unique situation, but he wasn't divulging any more until he talked to Burkhart. Still, it bothered him that Maria noticed the attraction between him and Amelia. If she'd seen it, others had too. Including Mercado.

He'd been taken so off guard, still felt raw at being so close to her. Shock had punched through him when she didn't call him out on his use of an alias. And damn, had she looked good. Better than he remembered, which should be impossible. He'd wanted to pull her into his arms and devour her. Her arms had been bare in the long dress she'd worn. They were lean, muscular, maybe from her job. From the file he knew that she owned two restaurants and worked long hours. She was still curvy with a small waist, but there was a leanness to her now that hadn't been there before. Her blue eyes were still the same. They reminded him of the Caribbean, so bright and beautiful he could drown in them.

Tightening his jaw, he shoved those thoughts out of his head. He had a job to do. At least fifty women had gone missing and were likely being sold into slavery. He wasn't going to rest until they were found and the operation running them was smashed to pieces.

He couldn't imagine that Amelia was involved in any of it, but if she was, history or not, he'd do his job and she'd pay for her crimes.

Sid watched from the front seat of his SUV as his target strode across the nearly empty parking lot, her purse held against her side tightly. She was walking straight toward him and had no idea. He'd parked in a neighboring parking lot so that his vehicle was only yards away from her little car. They were separated by only a line of palm trees so he'd be able to move in from the shadows, knock her out, and carry her to his SUV with no chance of being seen by anyone at the restaurant if they happened to come out.

She was a looker at eighteen years old, the type of woman who'd only get hotter as she got older. Her long, dark hair was pulled up, the tail streaming down her back like a waterfall. Too bad he couldn't touch the merchandise, because he wouldn't mind tangling with that one.

His boss had ordered him to take the girl tonight.

It had to be tonight for some reason and he wasn't certain why, but he didn't ask questions. Not when the money was so good.

He had to be careful with her, though. He was under strict instructions to never hurt their products. So he'd have to take her carefully. She couldn't be more than a hundred and fifteen pounds, so even if she put up a fight, overpowering her wouldn't be a struggle.

Not with his training. He might have been kicked out of the Army, but they'd trained him well beforehand.

Moving quietly, he opened his driver's-side door and gently let it move back into place, not letting it click completely shut. The dome light didn't come on, because he'd disabled it. He didn't want her to see him until it was too late. Doing another visual sweep of the lot, he checked to make sure none of her coworkers at the seafood restaurant had followed her out, but he'd already done a head count as other employees left throughout the evening. According to the information he had on her, she was closing tonight, so there would be a cook or two inside still closing up and a manager, but she was the last waitress out.

It was shitty that no one walked her to her vehicle, but good for him. His information on his targets had never been wrong. He didn't like that all the facets of their operation were kept insulated, but he got paid well, so he kept his concerns to himself. Money made it easy to do a lot of things.

His friends thought he was a bounty hunter, so it was easy to explain away his odd hours. In a way, he did hunt people down for a bounty, so the title was fitting.

Smiling to himself, he watched as she let out a curse

and started to bend down in front of her back tire. He'd punctured it a couple of hours ago and later he'd have one of his contacts tow the vehicle for him, but it gave him the perfect opening to subdue her without a struggle. Taser in hand, he stepped closer to the line of trees, thankful for the darkness to cover his movements.

He was close enough to her that he could hear her creative, colorful curses. Heart pounding at the thrill of bagging his prey, he had started to step out from behind one of the trees when a loud male voice stopped him.

"Hey!"

Sid froze for just a second, looking behind him. The other parking lot was completely empty.

"What happened to your car?" the male voice asked.

Sid turned and realized the man hadn't been talking to him. From the file he had on the restaurant employees, he knew the man was one of the fry cooks. He wasn't wearing work clothes, but jeans, a T-shirt, and a light windbreaker. He must have come from the rear of the restaurant, which was why Sid hadn't seen the guy. Still, he inwardly cursed. He could have been seen. Taking out someone else wouldn't have been an issue, but he wouldn't leave any witnesses. It was easier for everyone if his jobs stayed clean.

"I must have run over a nail or something," the girl said, irritation in her voice.

"I'll give you a ride home. You can call a tow truck in the morning."

Sid blended back into the shadows as they continued talking, his heart rate jacked up. That had been close. Too close.

This girl wasn't like their normal quarry from what

he understood. Normally they found women and lied to them about a job opportunity. With this woman, they were just taking her. It felt like an unnecessary risk, but the boss wanted her for a reason. If he had to guess, it was because a client had requested a woman with a certain look or ethnicity and this girl fit the bill. *Gonna be disappointed tonight*, Sid thought as he slid back into his SUV. He didn't start it, though, waiting until the girl and fry cook were long gone.

He'd follow her home. Maybe he'd just take her from there instead. It was only eleven; he had plenty of time to still kidnap her. Because he couldn't afford to screw up. The last guy who'd failed had ended up with a bullet right between the eyes.

Chapter 4

Cover: facade, vocation, purpose, activity, false
identity maintained by an undercover operative.

A melia couldn't stop the edginess that had settled
in her bones since getting in her Jeep. Too many
old conversations and memories kept playing in her
mind. Now that she was away from the noisy auction,
she had too much time alone. Too much time to wallow
in her thoughts.

She'd made an excuse about a work emergency and
needing to take care of it herself. Iker had been under-
standing, even offering to come with her—which had
made her feel even guiltier. She rarely lied and wasn't
one to hang on to guilt for nonsensical things she had
no control over, but she actually felt bad about lying
to him. She really wanted to finish that conversation
with Maria, though. Especially since her friend seemed
to know more about Danita.

The way Danita had just up and quit had been odd.
Amelia had even tried calling her, but her cell phone
had been disconnected. She'd e-mailed too, but with
no response. Not exactly strange, since she hadn't put

in her two weeks' notice; maybe she'd been too embarrassed to talk to Amelia after that.

As Amelia turned down a street that would get her to the center faster, she noticed the same car that had been on her tail since a couple of blocks away from the auction following her once again. It was possible the driver had followed her the entire way and she just hadn't noticed. She was so used to paying attention to her surroundings, but she'd been distracted as she left the auction.

Not caring if she was being paranoid, she made a sharp right turn, barely slowing down as she did it. Her tires squealed before she righted the wheel.

The car followed, gaining speed.

A low-grade panic hummed through her veins. She knew the streets of Miami like the back of her hand, but she was in a dicey area. She needed help, but the only people she saw on the streets now were homeless, hookers, or dealers. Freaking great.

She gunned the engine. The nearest police station was fifteen minutes away and she didn't want to head to Bayside. She couldn't lead whoever was behind her there.

There was a red light ahead. *Damn it.*

Her heart in her throat, she flicked her gaze to the rearview mirror again. The vehicle was almost on her now. Her fingers tightened around the wheel. Suddenly the brights flooded her mirror, making her instinctively flinch away. She twisted the mirror to the side so the glare wouldn't blind her.

Her Jeep jerked forward as the driver rammed into her. Her seat belt locked hard against her chest, making her gasp. Jeeps were made sturdy, so she didn't feel a huge impact. She snapped her hand back to the wheel, holding it steady as she pressed on the gas. Red light or no, she had to run it.

The driver gained more speed in a burst, slamming into her again, propelling her through the light. She held tight as her Jeep swerved to the right. Unable to keep it steady, she braced herself as she careened into an IHOP parking lot. Narrowly missing a Pontiac that had to be forty years old pulling out of the entrance, she hit the brakes to slow but didn't stop.

Heart racing, she continued through the brightly lit, packed parking lot, ignoring the two guys who shot her the bird for nearly clipping them. As she passed them, she twisted her rearview mirror back into place. The car wasn't there. No one was following her. The two guys were now making obscene gestures to her, but she ignored them and steered to the second entrance to the twenty-four/seven pancake place.

As she pulled up to the entrance, she saw no one coming from either direction, so she tore out into the four-lane road, making a left. She wasn't stopping at this place, not at this time of night. It might be more dangerous here. Her palms were damp as she drove, but she kept an eye on the rearview mirror, taking the most efficient route to the community center.

She was almost positive no one had tailed her. And there was no sense in heading to the police station now. Whoever had been following her wasn't anymore and she had literally no information on what the driver or car looked like. She didn't have a make, model, or even color. It had been a dark color, maybe black or blue, but she couldn't say for sure. She couldn't say *anything* for certain. She knew how the legal system worked and she sure as hell wasn't wasting her time down at one of the police stations where she'd have to wait to talk to someone and then fill out paperwork that wouldn't amount to anything tonight.

No, thank you.

She'd drop by when it was convenient for her and make a report for insurance, but that was it.

When she made it to the community center, she was thankful to see Maria's vehicle in the side parking lot through one of the gates. She started to call Maria, but the gate automatically opened for her. That was when she saw the headlights of Maria's car flash twice.

She must have a remote control to the security system. Whatever it was, Amelia was glad she didn't have to wait to be let in. As soon as she steered through, the gate started to close.

Relief speared through her as it did. She parked next to Maria and walked to the back of her Jeep as Maria got out of hers.

"You made good time," her friend said, walking toward her.

"Yeah." Surprising, considering her detour. She winced when she walked around the back and got her first look at the damage to her bumper. Her shoulders and neck were stiff, but she figured she'd be fine in the morning. Sleep and a glass of red wine sounded perfect, but first she needed to hear what was going on.

Maria's eyes widened. "What happened?"

"Someone rammed into me on the way here. Twice." Instinctively she looked over her shoulder, glancing around the community center parking lot. There weren't any other vehicles around and the security fences were high enough that they'd hear someone trying to scale them. Still, she wanted to get inside. After the night she'd had, her nerves were completely shot.

Maria let out a quiet gasp. "Did you call the police?"

Amelia shook her head. "Not going to waste my time. I'll make a report tomorrow for insurance, but seriously, it'll be a big hassle tonight going down to the station." Not that she didn't respect the cops; she definitely did. She was friends with some uniforms and a couple of detectives who came into her restaurants with regularity, but it didn't negate the fact that calling them or going to the station—on a busy Friday night—would be pointless without any information to give them.

Maria's expression was worried. "Are you sure you're okay? We can call someone now. Do you think maybe you need X-rays or something?"

Amelia was touched by the concern in her friend's voice. "I'm okay, but thank you. . . . Where's Cade?" she asked suddenly. No way would Maria's hulking, slightly overprotective husband have let her come down here alone at night.

Maria actually blushed. "Uh, I told him to wait inside. I know he's kind of intimidating and I also know that my request to meet me here so late at night is pretty weird, so I didn't want you to feel ambushed."

A smile teased her lips. "So he's probably watching us from one of doors right now?"

"Oh yeah. Look, I'm sorry for being so cryptic before. I just wanted privacy and the space to show you . . . something." Maria motioned that they should head toward the nearest set of double doors.

Amelia fell in step with her. "And showing me 'something' isn't cryptic at all."

Maria's lips pulled up at the corners, but the smile didn't reach her eyes. "A couple weeks ago Leah and I noticed that some women we've helped here have sort of just gone missing. Not legally, but moved and cut all contact with everyone." One of the doors opened as they reached it, with Cade standing on the other side next to the silver button that worked this set of doors.

He nodded politely at Amelia and murmured a greeting. She did the same and stepped inside with Maria.

"Cade, someone hit Amelia's Jeep," Maria said immediately.

His entire body went rigid. "Are you hurt?"

Feeling her face flush, Amelia shook her head. She didn't want to make a big deal of this. "No, it's fine," she muttered, shooting Maria an annoyed look.

Her friend just pursed her lips. "It's not fine. That's scary."

"Did you get a good look at the driver, the vehicle, the—"

Amelia shook her head again, cutting off Cade. "I don't even know if it was a man or woman driving. The driver blinded me with the brights the first time they hit me. The second time they hit me I drove through an IHOP and hurried out a side exit. They didn't follow through the parking lot and I'm guessing it was impossible for them to turn around and figure out which way I'd gone. I wasn't followed, so if you're worried about a security issue here, don't. I wouldn't have come here if someone had been following me. I'd have just gone straight to the police station. And"—she held up a hand when it was clear Cade was going to pepper her with more questions—"I'm not calling the police right now, so leave it alone. I'll make a report tomorrow."

He blinked once, maybe at her forceful tone. Then he simply nodded stiffly. He wasn't happy about it, though, that much was clear. Well, too bad. She'd been taking care of herself a long time.

Cade stayed behind them, and even though he was intimidating as Maria had said, it was a relief to have a huge guy like that at their backs. Despite what Amelia had said, she was still out of sorts because of what had happened.

"So, all the women you mentioned have done what Danita did?" she asked, wanting to get the focus back on why she'd come down here. When Maria nodded, she continued. "Did you know she turned off her phone too?"

Maria nodded again. "Yeah." Now her voice was resigned.

The click of their heels echoed along the dimly lit hallway. Luckily they didn't have to go far to Maria's office. The light was already on inside, showing a comfortable, welcoming space. Hand-drawn pictures, sketches, and even oil paintings from various kids Maria had helped over the years covered her walls. A leather chair was behind her desk, and two worn but comfortable-looking seats were in front of it.

"I'll let you guys talk," Cade murmured, before disappearing down another hall in the direction of the gym.

"He doesn't have to leave," Amelia said. Yeah, he

was a big guy, but it wasn't as if she was scared of him. Especially not after he'd been all concerned about her "fender bender."

"Oh, I know, I just wanted to talk to you in private." Maria slipped off her high heels as she entered the room. Her dress was an eggplant color, the deep purple stunning against her bronzed skin.

Amelia was tempted to take off her heels as well, but she knew once they came off, they weren't going back on.

Maria moved to her desk and flipped open a blue binder. "You can sit," she said, not looking up as she thumbed through some of the pages.

Amelia did, wondering what the heck was going on.

Less than thirty seconds later, Maria sat in the chair next to her and handed Amelia the binder. "There's a lot of information in there, but if you start on this page, it's the list of women who have gone missing in the last year."

Amelia's eyes widened as she scanned the names. "There's got to be at least forty names—"

"Fifty. So far."

"You're telling me these women are all *missing*?" Nausea swirled in her stomach.

"Yeah."

Amelia's temper spiked, sharp and fast. "And you haven't called the cops yet?" She practically shouted it, then forced herself to rein herself in. She needed to hear all the facts first.

Reaching out, Maria flipped one of the pages. "Keep reading. The women all left jobs or school or both. All of them turned in notice at work, some more abruptly than others. They've all stated that they found work elsewhere. All of them had their phones turned off within days of leaving for their 'new job.' The main thing they have in common with each other is that they're virtually alone in the world. Yes, they've got friends, but no family, no significant others, and no real estate ownership. Nothing to tie them to one place. They're all over eighteen, but none of them are over twenty-eight. It's a pretty tight age range."

That sick feeling intensified as Amelia continued flipping through the pages. Sure enough, she recognized twelve of them. She flipped back to the first page and twisted the binder so Maria could see it. "These women," she said, indicating seven of them, "all told me they found new jobs. They were all part-time anyway, so it wasn't out of the ordinary. Though . . . three of them never picked up their last check." Which wasn't all that strange. Waitresses made well below minimum wage because their money came from tips. Their checks were nominal. Still, now it made Amelia wonder if there was something more going on.

She pinned Maria with her gaze. "We need to go to the cops. As in tomorrow morning." She would go now, but she wanted to set up a meeting with a detective friend of hers so they got someone who would listen. Not just some random person. "They've got resources we don't. They could look at, I don't know, like, credit card records or something. Maybe—"

"The ones who had credit cards haven't used them since they've gone missing, and all of them have closed their bank accounts. They've also deleted their social media accounts—the ones who had them anyway."

As Amelia digested what her friend had just laid out, a few things became crystal clear. "You're already working with the police." Otherwise how would she know all this stuff? Finding out about social media accounts was one thing, but knowing about freaking bank account information was something else entirely.

"Sort of." Maria shifted almost nervously in her seat. She paused, as if waiting for something, then continued. "Cade is in law enforcement."

Amelia blinked once, but she wasn't exactly surprised. The man moved with a military sort of bearing. "What branch?"

Another very slight pause as she tucked a loose strand of hair behind her ear. "FBI."

Maria was lying. Amelia saw it in her gaze. She didn't think the law enforcement part was a lie, but she didn't buy the FBI part. Maria's cheeks tinged just a shade darker as she'd said "FBI." That, combined with the nervous hair thing . . . Amelia forced her expression to remain concerned, which wasn't hard, considering that she was. She was also slightly terrified now.

Maria had given her all this information freely, then told her that her husband was FBI—and was lying. Amelia was alone in the community center and no one knew where she was other than the two people here. Why was Maria lying to her? What if he wasn't law enforcement? He looked like a scary biker, not a federal agent. Oh God, what if they were somehow involved in this? It wouldn't make sense for Maria to show her all this, but maybe she'd just wanted to see Amelia's reaction, to see if she suspected something . . . Amelia needed to get some space so she could think, but for now she made herself respond. "That's good, then," she said, glad her voice sounded normal. "What do you want me to do? I'll do it. If Danita is missing we need to find her."

Maria seemed to relax at her words. "Cade will want to interview you, go over everything you know about the missing twelve women. It won't be tonight, but as soon as possible."

"I'll make time in my schedule," she said quickly, then wanted to wince. She didn't want to sound too eager, but the truth was, she was eager to get the hell out of here and call her detective friend. "Tomorrow, if you'd like?"

Maria nodded. "I think that will work. He would have been in here, but I thought it might be less overwhelming if it was just the two of us."

Amelia nodded, as if grateful. "I appreciate it." She let out a short laugh, but she didn't buy any of this. The FBI had let one of their agents bring his wife in to talk to Amelia? No freaking way. Something more was going on here, she knew. Hoping she didn't seem too eager, she set the binder on the edge of the desk and stood. "I'm exhausted and you're right, this is overwhelming. Unless you have anything else to show me, I want to get home and start making a list of things I remember about each woman's time of employment. Friends, stuff like that. That would help, right?" God, she just wanted to get out of here.

Maria smiled, looking relieved. "That would be great. Cade will probably contact you in the morning. Do you work tomorrow?"

"Yeah, I'm scheduled to stop by both restaurants in the morning, but I can shift stuff around."

"Great, I'll walk you to your car."

Amelia nodded, glad she knew how to keep cool when inside she was scared. She had a shitty mother to thank for that. That survival skill was one of the only good things she'd gotten from her childhood.

"Did something about her seem off to you?" Cade asked as he and Nathan watched Maria and Amelia on the laptop.

The recording of Maria's office was crystal clear. The NSA's Miami home base had patched them in to the feed. It didn't matter that they were only a few doors down from Maria; they were on standby in case she needed them. Now it was clear she didn't.

Cade's wife had played tonight perfectly. Well, almost. She'd paused before saying who Cade worked for. "It was slight, but when Maria said you worked for the FBI, Amelia stopped breathing. For just a second. Could mean nothing."

"No, I saw it too. She might not believe Maria."

"She didn't ask to see your ID or anything either." Amelia was a hard woman to read; she'd always been like that, but she'd been ready to get away from Maria and the center. "How did she seem about her Jeep being rammed?" Nathan hadn't been able to get that out of his head. The thought of someone going after Amelia made him see red. He'd wanted to see the damage for himself but hadn't been willing to risk being seen by her or anyone else.

Cade lifted a shoulder. "Annoyed, but not concerned. Could be a case of simple road rage."

"Maybe." Nathan didn't believe in random, though. According to Cade someone had run into her twice. "I want to see if we can get a hit from any traffic cams, maybe of the actual attack or her attacker's license plate. She said she was near an IHOP?"

Cade nodded. "I'll ask Karen to do a search for us. And whether it was random or not, Amelia seemed pretty disgusted at the thought of women going missing."

Nathan nodded, relieved in that knowledge. She might not believe Cade was who he said he was, but it seemed unlikely she was involved with the missing women. Her financials certainly wouldn't suggest it, but her reaction had been real, plain and simple. "When you talk to her in the morning, I'm going with you."

Cade shot him a sideways glance.

"After I talk to Burkhart," he muttered, pulling his cell out. Pushing up from his seat in the break room the volunteers used, he dialed his boss.

Burkhart answered on the first ring. "I want you to go with Cade to the meeting with Ms. Rios tomorrow," he said by way of greeting. "She showed a raw reaction to what Maria told her, but she's still spooked about something."

"We both caught that too. I don't think she believed Maria when she said Cade works for the FBI . . . Listen. I know Amelia." He quickly launched into the explanation of how his grandmother had lived next door to Amelia's poor excuse for a mother. How they'd been friends but hadn't gone to the same high school. There was no paper trail linking them anywhere, no pictures that he knew of. Except a couple of prom pictures and some photographs they'd taken at the beach together that he'd saved. He'd never been able to get rid of those last few. It was a tether to his past, something he knew. He wasn't sorry for it either. Of course he didn't tell Burkhart the personal details or about his real relationship with Amelia. He made it sound like a casual high school dating thing.

When he was done with the basics, Burkhart was silent for a long moment.

"Why didn't you tell me before now?"

"I didn't know. I . . . fuck, boss, I scanned her file, but I didn't delve into it, since Cade was the one who was going to make contact with her. Her last name's different now, so I didn't make a connection. Not that it's an excuse. I screwed up and I take full responsibility for it."

"Why do you think she didn't call you out and use your real name with Mercado?" Burkhart asked, ignoring Nathan's apology.

"We have a history together and she's . . . loyal to her friends. I promised to give her answers, promised to call her and explain what was going on."

"She could have already blown your cover."

No way in hell. He reined in his automatic, emotional response. If he showed emotion, Burkhart would pull him tonight without a second thought. "That's true. I don't think she did, though."

Another silence stretched between them, seemed to go on forever. Finally Burkhart spoke again, his voice clipped. "You'll go to the meet tomorrow . . . Damn it, she's making a phone call."

"What?" She'd literally just left the center.

"Amelia Rios is calling someone right now. Keep your line open." Burkhart ended the call abruptly.

Ice filled Nathan's veins as he turned back to Cade, who'd already packed up the laptop and their equipment. Nathan could hear Maria's heels echoing off the hallway in the distance as she made her way to where they were. He tuned it out as he tried rationalize why Amelia would be calling anyone this late at night—technically morning now. She didn't have a boyfriend, and by her own admission this had been her first date with Mercado. It wasn't normal to call people after midnight without a serious purpose.

He might have told Burkhart there was no way Amelia would have sold him out to Mercado, but what if after meeting with Maria she'd changed her mind? What if she was involved in all this after all?

She could blow his cover, a cover the NSA had spent years building. Not only that, but she could tip off whoever had taken the women that someone was looking into them. If the kidnappers got spooked, they might decide it was easier to kill the women they'd taken and close up shop. Since the NSA didn't know what their end game was, it was impossible to narrow down the many possibilities of what *could* happen.

The one thing he did know, if Amelia was involved with taking and hurting women, he'd bring her in himself.

Chapter 5

Classified information: information held back from
universal circulation for reasons of national security.

As the gate to Bayside closed behind Amelia, she
pulled her phone from her clutch. Certain no one
was following her as she steered out onto the street, she
felt her hand still trembling slightly as she dialed Detective Joel Sinclair. The shaking was from the culmination
of the night's events: from seeing Nathan, to being randomly rammed on the road, and now not knowing what
was going on with a woman she considered a friend. It
was all too much to handle. She turned on her Jeep's
Bluetooth system so she'd be hands-free as the phone
started to ring.

When she realized it was close to one in the morning, she cringed. Crap, Sinclair was probably asleep—
or with someone. The handsome detective would
never want for female company, she was sure. Feeling
guilty, she started to end the call when he picked up.

"Amelia?" His voice was raspy, but not groggy.
"What's up? You okay?"

"Yeah, listen, I'm sorry—I just realized the time. I shouldn't have called. We can talk in a few hours—"

"Nah, I'm up. Seriously I'm on a stakeout, bored out of my mind, sitting in an unmarked right now drinking stale coffee."

She laughed lightly. "You're such a liar."

"But a handsome one."

Her lips curved up. He'd been just as cocky the first time she met him years ago. He and some other detectives came into Plátanos Maduros a couple of times a week and she'd formed a friendship with him. "That's true. And so humble."

He snorted. "So, why are you calling this early?" Now it was all business.

She was thankful because she didn't think she had the energy for more small talk. Feeling paranoid, she glanced in the rearview mirror. "I . . . God, I don't even know where to start."

"Try the beginning."

She sighed, not sure where that was. So she decided to start with the auction tonight—leaving out any mention of Nathan/Miguel—and how Maria asked her to meet her at Bayside. Sinclair was familiar with Bayside, as many of the local police were. As she drove, she told him about their meeting in Maria's office, all the paperwork Maria had shown her, and her claim that Cade was part of the FBI.

When she was done, he let out a low whistle. "That's a whole lot of information."

"I know." Amelia took another random turn, not wanting to go directly home just yet. She wanted to be certain she wasn't being followed.

"And you say twelve of these women worked for you?"

"Yeah. Can you look into them? I want to see if what Maria is telling me is the truth and I also want to know if her husband is who he says."

"You think they might be lying?"

"I don't know. I can't imagine why they would. Unless they wanted to see how much I knew about the missing women because . . ." She left the thought hanging in space, not wanting to voice any more when Sinclair could draw his own conclusion.

He was silent for a moment and she could hear him scribbling on paper. They'd been friends long enough that she knew he was writing down everything she'd told him, probably using bullet points. He had an interesting shorthand.

Finally he spoke. "This is tricky, since these women are of legal age and haven't actually been reported missing by anyone—at least according to Maria. You know the full names of your twelve offhand?"

Amelia quickly rattled them off, also listing other information she remembered about the women off the top of her head. "I'll get you more information later today once I get a chance to look at my employee records."

"This is good for now, but yeah, get me everything you have. I've got a serious caseload at the moment, but I'll make time for this. Give me a day to enter this information into various databases and I'll see what pops up."

Relief slid through her. "Thank you for this. And I'm sorry for calling you so late."

"No worries, I'm glad you came to me." There was

no trace of his sleep in his voice now. The workaholic detective was firmly in place.

"Listen, something else happened on my way to meet Maria. I thought it was possibly random, but now I don't know. I mean, it might be, but—"

"Amelia, just spit it out."

She relayed the "incident," as she'd started to think about it, for the third time that night. Thankfully Sinclair agreed to make a report for her—that she'd simply have to read and sign—and see if he could tag the license plate of the driver who'd attacked her using a traffic cam. Now she felt stupid for not thinking about that before. There were so many traffic cams that of course the police would be able to find something. Or at least look, especially since she'd run a red light. The cameras automatically took pictures of people who ran red lights. She hadn't been thinking earlier, though, just reacting.

"Is there anyone you can think of who'd want to target you?"

"Not really." She didn't have any enemies that she knew of.

"No competitors?"

She let out a short laugh even though it was a fair question, considering how tough the restaurant business could be. "Not where my restaurants are located. My only 'competition' is corporate-style places. They're not struggling for business and I'm not crossing into any small business owners' territory, so . . . no." She racked her brain, trying to think of who could have tried to run her off the road like that.

"You fire anyone lately?"

"Uh, yeah. I let go a couple guys go recently. Both about a month ago."

"Names?"

"Neal Gray and Rodger Turner. The first for harassing my female staff and Turner because he was lazy. Neal was pretty lazy too, so it's hard to see either of them motivated enough to come after me. Especially a month later."

"Hmm," was all he said as he paused, likely writing this down as well. "You got a security system at your place?"

"Yes."

"Good. What about a Taser?"

"I've got pepper spray, but I also have a small pistol—and a concealed weapons permit," she quickly added. Not only was she a single woman in a big city, but she owned two restaurants, which meant a lot of late-night deposits. She had to be careful when she was working, and sadly, this was one of the survival things she'd picked up from her mother. Her mom had held down a regular job as a waitress during the day, but at night she'd sold her body—and kept a gun for protection. It had saved her mom's life more than once. And Amelia hadn't always lived in the nice neighborhood she did now. When she'd been working crazy hours trying to save enough money to start her own place, she lived in the cheapest places she could find, which meant sketchy neighborhoods. She'd never been oblivious about the type of protection she might need.

"Okay. Do you know how to use it?"

A fair question. "I go to the range every two weeks."

"Good. Until I know more, don't meet with Maria or her husband alone. I'll look into them asap, see what I can find."

"I owe you."

"Yeah, you do. You can buy me dinner next time I stop by one of your places."

"Deal. You can bring a date. I'll cover both of you."

He laughed lightly. "You wound my ego, Rios. I thought you wanted me for yourself."

Maybe if there had never been a Nathan Ortiz in her life, she could have let herself open up to someone else. Strangely enough, she wished she had a way to contact him right about now, tell him about what had happened. She immediately chastised herself at the thought. She hadn't seen Nathan in over a decade; she shouldn't be thinking this way. "With our schedules we'd never see each other. It's a recipe for disaster."

"Yeah, yeah, one day I'll convince you to go out with me." His tone was light, teasing. "Text me when you get home, let me know you're inside safe."

"I will. And thanks." After they hung up, a weight she hadn't realized had been sitting on her chest lifted. Instead of heading straight home, she drove around for an extra ten minutes to make sure she wasn't being followed.

As she reached the turnoff to her cul-de-sac street, even more of that tension lifted. Tonight had been freaking crazy on too many levels, the main one seeing Nathan Ortiz. The car incident and strange meeting with Maria should probably rank higher on her "holy shit" list, but Nathan was at the top.

Even now she could picture him clearly in her mind.

Tall, dark, and handsome. He certainly fit the bill. He'd always hated being considered a pretty boy, and now he was simply striking to look at. Like a beautiful fallen angel. Even his beard, something she'd never thought of as hot before, looked good on him. She was going to need to take a cold shower just thinking about him. Thinking about how delicious he'd looked in that tux.

Mentally shaking herself, she pushed all thoughts out of her mind as her house came into view. She and Nathan were done, had been a long time ago. All she wanted right now was wine and a few hours of sleep so she could think clearly. Because as soon as she woke up, she was scouring all her records for any bits of information she could find on the women who were allegedly—and probably if Maria's information was correct—missing.

"You sure this is the best approach?" Cade asked from the driver's seat. Maria had headed home after the meeting at Bayside, but Cade and Nathan weren't done for the night. Not even close.

Nathan nodded, looking at the map on his laptop. The red dot that indicated Amelia's phone wasn't heading to her address. "Yeah . . . Elliott," he said, talking to the analyst on the other end of the phone. They had him on speaker as they drove to Amelia's place. "Is what I'm seeing right?"

"Yeah, looks like she's just driving around in circles, but she's slowly making her way to her home. I can see it in her driving patterns." Nathan could hear Elliott typing away on his keyboard. Tall and a little lanky, the analyst with a pattern of short zigzag braids on his head was very good at his job.

If Nathan couldn't work with Karen on a job, Elliott was his second choice and was just as skilled. Since Karen was in Maryland now and Elliott in Miami, it made more sense for Elliott to be the one on this small op. Though Karen was doing a lot of behind-the-scenes stuff as usual.

"We're heading straight there—just wanted to check. Listen . . . " He cleared his throat, trying to figure out how to broach the subject without sounding as if he cared for personal reasons. When Burkhart had called Nathan back after listening to Amelia's conversation—after what felt like a fucking eternity—his boss informed them that Amelia had called a local detective. Burkhart was now convinced she wasn't involved with kidnapping the women, but unfortunately she'd brought someone else into this whole thing. Which meant low-level damage control. So now Burkhart had called in a favor and was on his way to the detective's house along with a captain in the Miami PD.

While Burkhart was handling that, Nathan and Cade needed to pull Amelia into the loop and stop that flow of information before she told anyone else. If the wrong people got wind that a government agency was sniffing around for intel about the missing women, shit could go wrong fast. He'd seen it too many times.

"What did the conversation between Amelia and that detective sound like?" he continued. Out of the corner of his eye, he saw Cade glance at him. He ignored his friend, stayed focused on the laptop. The dot that indicated Amelia's phone was moving along at thirty-five miles per hour not far from where he was. He wished he was with her right now. Knowing some-one had rammed her earlier—twice—tied him in knots. It didn't matter that he'd never gotten the answers he wanted from her, not even after putting his pride aside and basically begging her to talk to him; the thought of someone trying to hurt her shred-ded him.

"Friendly enough. Possibly flirty, but they sounded like they're friends more than anything. She was defi-nitely concerned about the whole situation."

"Thanks." Even though it made him feel stalker-ish, he was going to listen to the recording later. For the op, he told himself, unable to believe the lie for a second. After years of compartmentalizing his thoughts of her, now he felt consumed to know everything about her. And not for work reasons.

"This is it," Cade murmured, turning down a dead-end street. "How do you want to do this?"

This wasn't part of their original op. Hell, even talking to Amelia tonight hadn't been part of their plan, so right now they were making decisions on the fly. "Stop a few houses down from her place. I'll get out, wait for her at her house while you park a street over." He'd wait on the porch, not break in. Though he could if he wanted. B & E skills were something he'd gained long before joining the NSA. Amelia had been his teacher.

But he didn't want to piss her off any more than this early-morning visit was sure to do. He remembered what a temper Amelia had and figured when she found out he'd been at Bayside at the same time she was there *and* was part of an operation that originally suspected

her involvement in kidnapping and possible sex trafficking, she'd be pissed. He slid his earpiece in. "I'll keep
my recorder on the whole time," he continued when
Cade didn't respond.

Satisfied, his partner nodded.

The street was upper middle class, the houses
mostly two-story, with actual space between the yards.
From the financials he'd read on Amelia, she did well
for herself, though it had taken years to get where she
was and to afford her home. She'd always sworn she'd
make something of herself, vowing to never end up
like her mother.

It made him so fucking happy she'd done just that.
No matter how things had ended between them, that
she'd pretty much ripped his heart out, he couldn't help
being proud of her. The restaurant industry had one of
the highest failure rates, so her success was even more
impressive.

Shelving those thoughts, he slid from the vehicle,
quiet as a ghost, as soon as Cade stopped the SUV. They
couldn't account for everything, like nosy neighbors,
but at this early hour, most people were locked in tight
for the evening. Especially in a neighborhood like this.

Moving down the sidewalk quickly, he stuck to the
shadows. He'd changed out of his tux and was wearing
black cargo pants and a black long-sleeved T-shirt. He
was armed, as he usually was, but his weapon was
holstered and tucked away.

"Looks like she's almost here," Cade said through
his earpiece. "Should be turning down her street in
less than a minute. I'm pulling out now. There's a park
two blocks over I'm going to wait at."

"Sounds good," Nathan said quietly. He didn't need backup for Amelia and the truth was, he wanted time alone with her. Even if it wasn't technically private, considering that Elliott and Cade would be able to hear their conversation. God, he just wanted to see her again. Seeing her and holding her after so long was a combination of heaven and torture.

When he reached her house, he strode up the stone walkway to her front door. A white slatted enclosure wrapped around the porch. There were two rocking chairs on it with a small table in between.

"She's turning now." Cade's voice was quiet.

"I see her," Nathan said as the flash of headlights illuminated her street. He backed against one of the walls of the porch, using a giant potted plant as part of his cover. When they talked he was going to tell her that she needed sensor-activated lights. Anyone could just wait in the dark here, lurking and ready to attack. Kind of like him, except he wouldn't be attacking her. Even the thought made him ill.

The purr of her engine was soft as she pulled into the driveway. From his angle against the far wall, he couldn't see her, but he heard the garage door opening. Once he heard her pull forward, he stepped out from his hiding spot and strode back down the walkway, stopping at the back of her vehicle. He immediately noted the damage to her Jeep and planned to ask her who she thought could have done this. Whoever it was, they weren't going to get away with it.

He knew just showing up like this would likely scare her, so he knocked on the back window of the Jeep—which would probably scare her too, but there was no way around it. There was movement in the front of her vehicle, but it was too dark to see much. He backed up, giving her enough space to see him in the moonlight—and hoped she didn't close the garage door on him. "Amelia, it's Nathan," he called out, knowing she'd hear him.

The driver's-side door remained closed.

He stepped forward again. "Amelia."

"What the hell are you doing here?" she demanded, stepping out silently from the opposite side of the vehicle in that hip-hugging black dress that showcased every delicious line and curve.

The sight of her made his mouth water. The raw reaction to simply seeing her annoyed him. She moved like a ghost, as quiet as any trained operative he'd worked with. He noticed she'd taken her shoes off too. A throwback skill to when she was a kid and wanted to be invisible at her home. The thought made his stomach twist.

"You keep your dome light turned off?" he asked. It should have turned on when she slid from the passenger-side door.

She blinked in surprise. "You show up at my house unannounced—when you shouldn't even have my address—at one o'clock in the morning, and that's what you want to ask me?"

He lifted his shoulders casually, keeping his game face on. This was his first job since his injury. He'd overlooked her in the files and didn't have room for another mistake. He'd had the best training in the world, first in the Corps, then with the NSA. He couldn't afford to be sloppy. Ever. It was fucking weak.

For now he ignored her question, wanting to get

her inside and out of view of neighbors or anyone else. They hadn't done enough recon of her place to know if Mercado was watching her. That was doubtful, but just in case, Nathan wanted to cover all his bases and keep her safe. "We need to talk."

She crossed her arms over her chest, temper flaring in her eyes. The moonlight gave him enough visibility to see her, but her eyes looked dark, not the vivid blue he knew them to be. "You've got my number," she said, her voice testy.

"I work with Maria's husband." He glanced over his shoulder, scanning the quiet street. "Can we talk inside where it's private?"

She let out a sound of frustration—as if she wanted to strangle him—but nodded and turned away from him. He followed her into the garage, stopping when she grabbed her small purse and shoes from the vehicle. Without looking at him, she pressed the button to close the garage, then let herself into what turned out to be a mudroom. An insistent beeping started and she moved directly to the keypad on the nearest wall.

She looked at him over her shoulder and raised an eyebrow. "Turn around."

Doing as she ordered, he shut and locked the door that connected to the garage while she disabled her alarm system. She still didn't speak to him as she opened another connecting door. This one entered into her sleek, modern kitchen.

She flipped on a light, dropping her shoes haphazardly as she made her way to a clearly custom-made wine rack. The crosshatched rack was above a granite countertop where a laptop and a stack of papers sat.

Below the countertop was a small refrigerator for chilled wines. She plucked a bottle of red from the higher rack and took down a wide-mouthed glass.

"You want a glass?" she asked without turning around.

"I'm good."

She snorted. "Sit while I open this. I can't think with you hovering."

Sighing, he took a seat at one of the ladder-back chairs at the center island. He wanted to talk to her but guessed that she needed to get her bearings. He could see it in the way her hands slightly trembled as she popped the cork—and he hated that he'd made her feel this way. Still, he knew on a certain level, she trusted him at least somewhat.

Otherwise she wouldn't have let him in the house and wouldn't have turned her back to him. "Amelia, I'm sorry to just show up like this."

Glass in hand, she turned to face him but didn't cross over to where he sat. Just watched him warily. "Talk. Now."

He scrubbed a hand over the back of his neck and was surprised when her gaze tracked the movement with just a bit of undeniable . . . lust. It sent a jolt of awareness through him. He'd never stopped wanting her. Years and miles of separation hadn't seemed to make a difference. The woman had gotten under his skin and he'd never been able to get over her. From the moment they met, everything about her had been real. No pretenses and no games. Maybe that was why he'd been so drawn to her.

"What I'm about to tell you is classified. Maria's

husband and I are working on a covert op right now. Everything Maria showed you is true; women in Miami are going missing and we're trying to find out why they're being taken and by whom. We need to stop this operation."

"Maria works for the government too?" Amelia's voice held more than a hint of sarcasm.

"No. We just thought it might be easier for her to talk to you."

"Why talk to me at all? From what she showed me, at least fifty women are missing and I don't know the majority of them. What could she possibly . . ." She set her wineglass on the counter as her brow furrowed. "You guys think I'm involved?"

He shook his head. "No. We know about your call to Detective Sinclair—"

She shoved away from the counter and crossed over to the island, her movements jerky. The granite countertop separated them, but it did nothing to hide her sparking temper. "You're listening to my freaking phone calls?"

He nodded once. He'd be as honest with her as he could. After she'd made that phone call to Sinclair, Burkhart gave Nathan operational latitude with Amelia. He could tell her as much or as little as he thought necessary so she'd keep quiet about this and . . . fuck, he didn't even want to think about the other reason. Burkhart had made it clear he'd use Amelia to get to Mercado if she was open to it. Nathan didn't want her involved at all, though. "Yes. Iker Mercado is at the top of our suspect list right now, and when you showed up as his date, you moved up on our list too."

Her mouth opened the slightest fraction, her expression one of complete incredulity. "Wait, I was on the list to begin with? As someone who could actually kidnap women for . . . whatever purposes?"

"You were a person of interest because of your connection to some of them—though I didn't realize it was you until I saw you at the auction. You changed your last name." He could guess why too.

"So now you're convinced I'm not involved?" Apparently she was going to ignore his statement about her last name.

"Yes."

She seemed to relax at his words before she asked, "You're with the FBI?"

He pulled out a badge and ID and slid them over the counter to her. The credentials themselves were real, but his information wasn't. He couldn't tell her that he worked for the NSA. Not yet. Maybe never. So the FBI it was.

She looked hard at them, then shrugged. "These could be fake."

"They could be," he agreed.

Amelia watched him for a long moment, her vivid eyes searching for something. Finally she sighed. "What do you want from me, Nathan? Are you worried I'll blow your cover with Iker? I don't even plan on seeing him after tonight—last night." She shook her head, looking suddenly exhausted as she turned back to the other counter and picked up her wine.

"Will you sit next to me?" he asked softly, wanting her close. He hated this mistrust between them.

Surprise flickered in her eyes, but she nodded and

rounded the counter. Her dress barely rustled as she sat next to him and turned the chair toward him. Watching him with eyes that missed nothing, she was silent, waiting for him to continue.

"My team and I need to know everything you know about Mercado." Because fuck what Burkhart had told Nathan, he didn't want to bring her deeper into this. Not if he didn't need to.

"It's not much. He's in antiquities and a really respected businessman. He owns a ton of property in Miami; he's got a grown daughter; he never remarried after his wife died . . . uh, I don't know. We've literally been on *one* date, last night. The majority of what I found out about him is from Google. If you're really with the FBI, you're going to know more than me. Why do you think he's involved in kidnapping women?"

Now was the tricky part. "Do you remember hearing about a man named Paul Hill last year?" She'd have had to be completely cut off from the media not to.

It took less than a second for the name to register. Her lips twisted in clear disgust. "Yeah, I remember the news reports. That whole thing is revolting. They're still arresting people involved, right?"

He nodded, pushing back the rage that surfaced whenever he thought of that scum. Dead scum, thankfully. Hill had sold women and children to the highest bidder as if they were property, had run a huge international sex slave ring with a base here in Miami. The city was still recovering from a terrorist bombing that was a direct effect of his crimes. "Yeah. Some of the people involved—buyers—fled the country, but various branches of law enforcement are slowly hunting them down." He hoped they got them all, but he knew in the end, there were still sick bastards out there living their lives, hurting innocent people.

"What does that have to do with Iker or the missing women?"

"Maybe nothing. But my team is determined not to let another person take Hill's place."

"You think Iker is involved in the slave trade?" Her face pale, she idly traced the stem of her wineglass.

"We don't know, but he's involved in more than just antiquities. He's never been convicted, but he's been brought in for questioning multiple times for suspected smuggling."

"Of people?"

He shook his head. "No, but he's been linked to smuggling in antiquities taken during various wars in addition to rhino and ivory smuggling." It was big money and very illegal. Not to mention fucking cruel. "We've only got rumors at this point, but if someone is involved in taking women in Miami, chances are high Mercado is involved or knows about it. Which is why I want you to stay away from him."

Amelia didn't respond, just took a long sip of her wine as she seemed to digest what he'd told her. As she did, Cade's voice came over his earpiece. "I'm at the front door. Burkhart wants me to talk to her."

Damn it, he wanted more time with Amelia alone and he had a bad feeling he knew exactly what Burkhart wanted Cade to tell Amelia. "Cade's at the front door," he said to her.

She looked at him in surprise. "How—"

He turned to the side so she could see his small earpiece.

"Other people are listening to this conversation?" Her voice went icy now.

He nodded, hating everything about this situation.

Her jaw clenched once, but she slid off the chair. "I'll let him in, then."

He moved quick, sidestepping her so he could check to see that it was Cade. Overprotective? Yeah, he didn't care. When he saw his teammate through the peephole, he opened the door.

Dressed much the same as Nathan, Cade stepped inside and nodded at Amelia, looking almost apologetic. "I'm sorry we—"

"Can you just tell me what you came here to say?" Her question could have been construed as rude, but Nathan heard the exhaustion in her voice, could see it on her face. This was definitely the Amelia he remembered, getting right to the point.

Cade let out a sigh of relief, clearly glad not to have to make any small talk. "Our team has run multiple diagnostics of Mercado's personal security. We can't infiltrate his online system because—why isn't important. We need someone inside his house and close enough to his computer to clone all his information. We could try breaching the place, but if you get yourself invited there as his date, it will be clean and easy to get all the information we need and you won't have to do a damn thing."

Surprise flickered in Amelia's gaze, but Nathan turned away from her, pinning a glare on Cade. "No fucking way."

Cade's expression remained neutral. "Boss said if she's willing, we're bringing her in. It's a onetime thing and she'll be compensated. And," he said, turning to her, "you'll have to sign some nondisclosure papers, regardless."

Nathan started to protest again, but Amelia spoke first. "You really think he's behind kidnapping women?"

"It's a statistically high probability he's involved in illegal activities," Cade said. "If not kidnapping women, he's still a criminal."

"If he is taking women, why do you think he's taking them?"

"We don't know. But they're young, attractive women who could be viewed by the predators of the world as easy prey. No one has missed them until recently."

Nathan tried to rein in his temper but was finding it difficult. "Damn it, Cade—"

Cade glanced at Nathan, his eyes hard. He didn't have to say a damn thing for Nathan to understand what he was silently communicating. If this was anyone else, Nathan wouldn't balk at bringing her in. Amelia had already proven she wouldn't blow his cover; she'd gone straight to the cops when she learned about the kidnapped women, and she had the perfect in with Mercado. She could be a good asset.

"What would I have to do?" Amelia asked, interrupting their silent conversation.

Cade focused on her again. "Get inside his house under the pretense of a date. We'll clone your phone and we'll be listening the whole time. You won't need to do anything other than get within fifty feet of his computer. From there our guys will do what they do. If something goes wrong we won't hang you out to dry. We'll breach the house in a full assault. . . . You'll just have to stay alive until we can get to you." His words were blunt, but true.

She needed to know what she was getting into. It was why Cade was laying everything out for her. Didn't mean Nathan had to like it.

"You don't have to do this," Nathan said. "You're not trained."

She glared at him. "I don't need training to go on a date. And Iker has a reputation for being selective about the women he dates—and for treating them well. I've never heard anyone say anything bad about him in those regards. Does the FBI have different information?" She looked at Nathan as she asked the question.

Though it pained him to admit it, he shook his head. "No. But if he's involved in the sex slave trade, who's to say he wouldn't hurt you?"

"We'll be listening the whole time and have a backup team waiting nearby. Only minutes away," Cade said.

"I'll be part of that team," Nathan interjected. He didn't care what Burkhart or anyone said; if she went inside Mercado's house, Nathan would be as close as he could get.

"I'll be compensated?" Now she looked at Cade.

"Yes."

"How well?"

He blinked, as if he hadn't expected the question. But Nathan had. Amelia had no problem bartering. When they were teenagers she'd dragged him to countless flea markets and thrift stores, always looking for deals. "I'll have to confirm anything with my boss, but what did you have in mind?"

"After I talk to Detective Sinclair and confirm that you're both who you say you are, I'll help you—if you pay off the rest of my loan for Plátanos Maduros." It was the second restaurant she'd opened up recently, Nathan knew. She owned the building on her first. "And your boss will give a donation to the charity of my choice. Since you clearly have files on me, you should know who I donate to. You'll double my yearly donation." Her voice brooked no argument.

Cade looked as stunned as Nathan had ever seen him, but he covered it quickly. "I'll be back in a few minutes." Moving economically, he hurried out her front door.

Amelia turned to Nathan and tapped her ear as soon as Cade closed the front door behind him. "Can you . . . ?" She trailed off, silently asking him to turn off his earpiece.

Not caring about protocol, he did. The NSA had gotten what they wanted from her at this point. "It's just you and me now."

"I would have done it anyway, in case you're wondering," she said softly. "I just want you to know that."

"I know."

Her eyebrows lifted a fraction. "How?"

"Because you care about Danita. I heard it in your voice when you were talking to Maria."

For a moment she looked torn between anger and another, indefinable emotion. Then she sighed and stepped closer to him. For just a moment, that high wall between them seemed to crumble. God, he wanted to pull her into her arms, to shake her and tell her not to fucking do this. They'd get to Mercado another way. There was always another way. He just wanted Amelia safe.

"Do you think we could have lunch or dinner without listening ears? I still have more questions," she said softly.

Completely taken off guard, he nodded. He didn't have to think about his answer. Maybe that made him a masochist, but he didn't care. "Yes."

She reached out as if to touch him, but the door opened and her arm dropped. They both turned to the door.

Cade looked pleased and that sinking feeling in Nathan's gut intensified. "Your terms are acceptable. Now we just need to go over our game plan."

"We'll go over the plan, but I don't do anything until I've talked to Sinclair and I've got a written contract with outlined terms I agree to. And my attorney will have to approve."

Nathan hated the thought of sending Amelia into a potential viper's nest. No matter what, he'd be on the other end of her comm when she was in Mercado's house.

And if God forbid something did go wrong, he'd do anything to get her out. It didn't matter that she'd broken his heart by walking away from him as if he had meant nothing. She still owned a part of it, and he could never let anything bad happen to her.

Chapter 6

Operational latitude: the broad scope of flexibility
that an agent has on a mission when making mission
decisions.

Wesley Burkhart opened the second row door of
the SUV he was in, then slid over so Captain Jarvis Nieto of the Miami PD could get in. Despite the
ridiculous early-morning hour, the man looked alert—
and annoyed with him.

"You don't know how to ask for a small favor, do
you?" Nieto shut the door behind him with force
before strapping himself in. His movements were precise, probably bred into him from his Navy days. He
was only five years younger than Wesley and in good
shape.

Wesley's driver immediately pulled away from the
curb without a word.

"Is your wife annoyed?"

Nieto just snorted. "No. She's a cop's wife."

Which meant she was accustomed to her husband
leaving in the middle of the night. Wesley nodded
once. "Good. Did you talk to Detective Sinclair?"

"Yeah. Told him not to talk to anyone, including Amelia, before I got there."

Considering they now had Sinclair under surveillance, however temporarily, Wesley already knew about their recent conversation. But he wanted to see how up front Nieto was with him. He'd worked with the captain before, after the Westwood bombing last year, and he genuinely liked the man. From what Wesley had found out about him, and through his own interaction with Nieto, he cared deeply about his city, and while he could play politics, he put his job and people first, not his own personal gain. "Thank you."

"Don't thank me. Tell me why you pulled me out of bed at one thirty in the morning."

Wesley handed him a manila folder. Nieto would get to read the file on the missing women, but he couldn't keep a hard copy. It was why Wesley hadn't been willing to risk sending Nieto anything electronically. Wesley didn't suspect a leak anywhere, but he was keeping this whole thing locked down tight. The more people who knew about it, the bigger chance the wrong people found out. "Read the highlights. My team is working on this, but we're not checking in with any other agencies." Which, yeah, was fucked up, but Wesley didn't care. At all. He wasn't going to waste time with red tape or procedure when his guys could get the job done. "If you and Sinclair help us wrap this up, you'll get all the credit for bringing down whoever the ringleader is."

"Hmm," was all Nieto said as he flipped to the next page. Then, "Stop and pick up coffee and muffins. There's a place a block from Sinclair's home. We'll drive right by it. He'll be easier to deal with if we feed him."

Wesley nodded at his driver, who'd merely glanced at him in the rearview for confirmation.

By the time Nieto had read most of the file, they'd made it to Sinclair's condo complex, coffee in hand. They buzzed him at the gate and were let in immediately.

"What do you want from us?" Nieto asked, handing the file back to Wesley while his driver looked for guest parking.

"For now, I need Sinclair to confirm to Amelia that my guys are FBI." And it was possible that sooner or later this deception would get back to the FBI, but if they played this right it wouldn't. "I need this shit quiet and can't afford any other agencies to get wind we're here. Mercado could have sources we don't know about. He's managed to avoid arrest for a reason."

"Maybe the reason is that he's clean." Nieto's voice was dry.

"You believe he is?"

"No. He's definitely into smuggling. But the slave trade?" Nieto shrugged. "Nothing should surprise me anymore, but I never would have pegged him for being that dirty."

"He's not our only suspect. We've got a wide net, but Mercado is in the top five. I want to either eliminate him or bring him down." And they had the perfect way to do it. If Amelia Rios could get into Mercado's house, it would be simple for his team to hack the info they needed.

Nieto's frown deepened. "I don't like asking my man to lie."

"Even to save lives?" That was something Wesley didn't have a problem with.

Nieto's jaw clenched as he looked away and out the window. The complex was brightly lit, with palm trees lining the sidewalk they'd just pulled up to. Wesley didn't think Nieto was seeing anything, though.

Finally Nieto turned back to him. "I'll tell Sinclair that he's going to get a call from Amelia Rios and that he'll confirm what she's been told. I'm going to tell him your guys are FBI, so I'm the only one knowingly lying, not him. And I'm going to go meet him now, *alone*, and order him not to dig deeper into your guys. It'll piss him off, but he'll follow orders for the time being. He could recognize you and I don't want him to put it together that you're NSA."

Wesley was silent for a moment. Most civilians wouldn't know who he was unless they searched his name or paid attention to the news. A cop would have a greater chance of actually recognizing his face, especially after the Westwood bombing. He'd tried to stay out of the media, but some things were unavoidable. "Okay. Don't lie to me, Nieto. I'll find out."

The captain just gave him a hard stare before getting out of the vehicle.

Wesley allowed himself to relax as Nieto headed up to Sinclair's place. After working with the captain on the terrorist attack in Miami, he had a good feel for the man. He was going to trust his gut that Nieto would help them out with this and be discreet. With so many innocent women's lives on the line, Wesley was almost certain Nieto would come through for him because in spite of the dregs of humanity he'd dealt with as a cop over the years, he still cared about the innocent and he loved his city.

Amelia smoothed a nervous hand down her body-hugging black-and-teal dress as she stepped out of the walk-in fridge. It was a little dressier than she normally wore to her restaurants, but she wasn't staying on today to help out and supervise.

No, she'd apparently lost her mind, because she'd agreed to help the FBI starting today. Nathan, Cade, and a couple of computer geeks had met at her house early this morning—thankfully giving her a few hours to sleep, then meet with her attorney to go over the contract for her fee, and to contact Sinclair. Phase one, as they'd called the first step in their operation, seemed like a risk to her, but she'd find out soon enough. As soon as Nathan picked her up.

Nathan Ortiz. It didn't matter that she'd touched him, held him, been so damn tempted to kiss him; it still felt surreal that he was back in her life—however temporarily—and working for the government. Well, the government part didn't exactly surprise her. He'd always been such a straight arrow—unlike her. She'd figured he'd go into some sort of law enforcement if he didn't stay in the Corps. She wanted to ask him why he'd gotten out of the Marines and so many other things.

He hadn't been at his grandmother's funeral, though his parents had been. They hadn't known who Amelia was and she'd kept it that way. She'd simply told part of the truth; that she'd been an old neighbor of Benita's. For some reason Benita and her daughter,

Nathan's mom, had a falling-out and while he'd been allowed to visit his *abuela*, his parents never had. Nathan had wanted to introduce her to his parents so many times, but Amelia had always said no. She'd never felt good enough back then. His parents had been respected members of the community and her mom had been a prostitute. It had been too shameful, too embarrassing to even contemplate meeting them. What if they'd found out about her mom and then forbade Nathan to see her?

And now it was too late to ever meet them. She'd read in the paper that they'd died a couple of years ago in a head-on collision with a drunk driver. She'd thought about going to the funeral, but it had been in Tallahassee, where they'd moved to almost as soon as Nathan had joined the Corps. Though the real reason she hadn't gone was that she was too afraid to see Nathan. If he'd brought someone with him, a wife . . . just no. She'd liked living in her bubble of not knowing much about what he'd done since she broke things off. Now that bubble was popped, and she wanted to know everything.

"Eat," Manuel, one of her full-time cooks, said, handing her a small plate with two *empanadas de verde con queso* on it.

Blinking, she took the plate and wondered how long she'd been staring off into space like a complete maniac. The doors to the fridge and walk-in freezer were in the hallway off the main hub of the kitchen, but her surroundings crashed into her, the steady hum of the early-afternoon servers and cooks loud enough that she shouldn't have been able to zone out. "Thank you."

"You look like you need some comfort food." In his

fifties, Manuel and his wife had been working with Amelia for years. "Everything okay?"

"Yeah, just . . . nervous about a date." Better to be honest about everything that she could right now. It wasn't as if she was worried Mercado was watching her movements, but according to Nathan and Cade, she needed to act as if he was at all times. There was no room for error.

Manuel's eyebrows rose. "Same man from last night?"

"Uh, no."

His bushy eyebrows rose even higher, a seemingly impossible feat. "Two men, two different nights? It's about time you started dating," he said before she could respond, approval clear in his voice. "You're young—you need to enjoy yourself more."

"Manuel, get your ass up here!" his wife shouted, making Amelia smile as he moved into action, practically jumping.

Feeling more relaxed, she took a bite of the *empanada* and had to bite back a groan as the melted cheese and spices hit her tongue. She'd been too nervous to eat breakfast, but this should help her find her balance before Nathan arrived. Comfort food was always a smart choice.

Instead of doing her normal rounds with the customers, she headed back to her office, mainly to hide. Before she'd even sat, Tessa, one of her weekend hostesses, popped her head in.

"Hey, boss, there's a man here to see you. Says he's picking you up for a date." Her grin turned mischievous. "If you don't want him, I'll take him."

Amelia was surprised by the sharp stab of possession that punched through her. Especially since Tessa was in freaking college and clearly teasing. But when it came to Nathan, logic didn't come into play. The man had her twisted up, same as when she'd been a teenager. "Thanks, I'll be up there in a sec."

Tessa's smile remained in place as she nodded. "Sure thing."

Standing, Amelia picked up her purse and took a deep breath. She could do this. This whole "phase one" was simple. Or at least Cade and Nathan seemed convinced it was.

The walk through the kitchen and then through the dining room area took longer than she'd wanted. She stopped to talk to two servers having a crisis, then to greet a few regular customers. By the time she made it to the hostess stand, she found Tessa and another server—who should be working—standing behind the hostess stand staring at . . . Nathan's ass.

Sweet Lord. There was a lobby area right when customers entered and he was leaning against the frame, his broad back to them, looking down at something. Probably his phone.

"Shouldn't you two ladies be doing something?" Amelia whispered as she came to stand behind them.

They jumped, cheeks pink with embarrassment, when they turned to face her. They were both taller than her, even in her heels, so she put her hands on her hips as she looked at them. She gave them her best "boss stare," which wasn't very intimidating at all.

Tessa cleared her throat. "We were just—"

"I know what you were doing and I don't blame

you, but get back to work," she said in a mock whisper, sidestepping the stand. The second she did, it was as if Nathan sensed her.

Or maybe he'd known she was there all along.

When he turned and pinned her with that dark gaze, her entire body flared to life, her nerve endings sizzling with raw awareness. She wondered if it was sad that a single look from Nathan got her hotter than pretty much all foreplay with anyone else. At least he seemed just as affected as she felt.

For a moment anyway. His gaze swept over her quickly, but with an undeniable hunger, before a charming smile slid onto his face. She thought it looked a little fake but didn't care. Maybe this was part of his role as Miguel Ortiz—a criminal looking to do business with Mercado. Nathan hadn't actually gone into many details about who Miguel was supposed to be. Just that he was a businessman visiting and hoping to buy up some real estate. As his date this afternoon, she would be clueless about his shady dealings.

"You look beautiful," he murmured, reaching out and clasping his hand around her hip. His fingers flexed, digging slightly into her. The move was so bold and a little unexpected as he pulled her close. Taking her even more off guard, he leaned down and brushed his lips lightly over hers. It was a cliché, but sparks went off between them. A simple touch of lips shouldn't affect her so much, but that deeply buried need for him took on a life of its own, desperate to taste more of him. She wanted to melt into him, to part her lips and allow him entrance.

Her fingers barely skimmed over his hard chest, the

material of his suit jacket soft. She couldn't seem to do any more, though. It was as if her brain had forgotten how to function.

She stood there, rooted to the spot, until he murmured, "Relax, this is all part of our cover today."

His words were like ice water right in the face. He'd just kissed her as part of their cover. Okay, she wasn't stupid, he'd probably felt something, but he hadn't done it because he'd wanted to, he'd done it for his cover. That brief brush over her lips and she didn't want to relax, she wanted to take all his clothes off. Peel that charcoal gray suit off him and kiss every inch of his ripped, naked body.

Instead of indulging in that insanity and getting arrested for public indecency—and tearing open old wounds—she took a small step back and smiled as she slid her arm around his waist. "I'm ready if you are." Or she'd thought she was. This morning everything had seemed so easy, and though she wasn't having second thoughts, it was overwhelming.

His arm around her was possessive as they stepped out the front door into sunshine. It was still spring, so the weather was perfect. Low humidity, sunny, but cool enough that she might need a light sweater at lunch.

"You okay?" he asked quietly as they strode across the packed parking lot.

"Yeah, but now we've given my staff gossip for a while." She leaned into him, feeling more like herself as they walked together. Maybe it was pathetic, but she wanted to take advantage of their time together, since she didn't think it would last. She wouldn't have to act as if she enjoyed this. Even if it was a combination of heaven and hell. She'd walked away from him and held back something he'd had a right to know. It had taken years for her to come to terms with everything, but it had been too late to be honest with him about what she'd lost—what they'd lost. She could come clean now, but . . . God, she broke out in a sweat even thinking about it. It wasn't as if she could just blurt it out right before lunch. Not when they were both supposed to be focused.

"You've never brought a man you're dating to work?"

"Uh, no." And she wasn't going to expand on that any time soon. Especially not if anyone was listening. "Is it just the two of us right now?" she asked as they reached a silver Lexus. She'd tried to look for an earpiece and hadn't seen anything on him but needed to know.

His mouth curved up a fraction as he opened the passenger door. "Just us."

She slid onto the smooth leather seat and had just strapped herself in when Nathan joined her.

"No earpiece, I swear," he reiterated as he started the engine. Maybe he knew she needed to be reassured. "This part of the op has to remain as if it's just the two of us. If Mercado suspects anything is off, it could put you in danger. We figured you'd act more natural without a team listening in."

"Yeah." And she was relieved.

"You having second thoughts?" He pulled sunglasses from the middle console and put them on.

She didn't like not being able to see his eyes. "No.

I just . . . I think I feel a little bad, which is stupid. If Mercado is a criminal, then screw him, but if he's not, I feel bad using him this way. And I've been thinking about your plan and I'm not sure it'll work. If he sees us having lunch, won't that make him more likely to just cut his losses and walk away from me?"

Nathan snorted, the sound so amused it made her smile. "Not a man like Mercado. He's selective about who he dates, and according to you, he pursued you pretty hard." When she nodded, he continued. "He's going to see you out with me—a man he's already feeling competitive of—and be pissed. Men are simple creatures, Amelia."

She shook her head. "Is that right?"

"Yep. He's going to ask you out again. He'll want you even more when he sees you out with me. It's a caveman mentality. And it wouldn't work with everyone, but my team of analysts thinks it will with Mercado."

"That's . . . kind of sad." She wondered if it would work on Nathan.

He lifted his shoulders. "Told you, we're simple."

That was bullshit, but it still made her smile, which she figured was his point. "Okay, why does he feel competitive of you?" Because neither Nathan nor Cade had explained what Miguel Ortiz allegedly did for a living.

Another shrug, this one more forced.

"You're not going to tell me?"

"I can't."

"Oh." That made sense, she supposed. His cover ID would be classified, or maybe there was another reason. Whatever it was, she wasn't going to push. At least not about that. She knew when to pick her battles and she had a lot more questions, most of them personal. "So, where are you living now?"

"Uh . . ."

"Seriously? You can't even tell me that. Fine, can you tell me why you left the Corps?" Because it had been a dream of his to enlist and serve his country. She'd thought he would stay in for decades.

The tightness in his shoulders loosened as he paused at a stop sign. "Simply, the right job came along."

"Do you do a lot of stuff like this, helping missing women?"

He paused, as if contemplating his answer. "Sort of. It's usually a little bigger scale than this."

"I'm sure the women will appreciate your help." Amelia fought off a shiver as she imagined the reasons the young women were being taken.

"Yeah . . . So, how is it that you're single?" The question sounded casual enough, but there was a tightness to his body once again.

Since "because I never got over you" was a pathetic answer, she said, "Work keeps me busy. Most men don't want to compete with my job." Which was actually true. Since she was eighteen she'd been a complete workaholic. Dating and relationships had barely registered on her radar. She'd been determined to be successful, and her personal life had become a casualty.

He made a sort of grunting sound that could have been in commiseration. As if he understood what she meant. Unlike him, she wasn't going to ask if he was single . . . Was she? Apparently she had no self-control, because the words just tumbled from her mouth. "Are you with anyone?"

"No." The immediate answer soothed something jagged clawing at her insides. Something she hadn't been aware of.

A tense silence filled the air as they neared their destination. There were so many damn things she wanted to say to him. Mainly she wanted to tell him the truth about why she'd ended things. She'd been so young and afraid before. Afraid that he'd hate her or never look at her the same, but now . . . Well, *right now* certainly wasn't the time, but she would tell him soon. And there were other things she wanted to say as well. "I went to Benita's funeral," she said quietly.

His hand jerked ever so slightly against the wheel. "You did?"

"Yeah. A lot of her friends showed up. She lived in that neighborhood forever." Amelia smiled as she thought about sweet Benita, who'd baked for pretty much everyone in her small neighborhood at one time or another. Whether for birthdays or baby showers, she'd always shown up with baked goods in hand.

"I hated that I couldn't be there." There was a dose of self-loathing in his voice.

"Your parents told everyone you were overseas, and Benita would have understood. You know that. I shouldn't have said anything. I'm sorry." What the hell was wrong with her? They both needed to be ready for their upcoming "show," not drowning in memories.

"No, it's nice to talk about her. She left me her house."

He pushed his sunglasses onto his head and shot her a quick glance as they pulled into the hotel's entrance.

There was a line for valet and she found herself thankful they had to wait. She wanted to soak up all the extra time they had together when they weren't playing a part, when it was just the two of them. "I'm not surprised. Did you sell it?"

"No, I rent it out. It's a nice monthly income and . . ." He shrugged as he glanced at her. "I don't think I could ever sell her place. It holds too many memories." His eyes were full of heat and longing.

They'd shared their first kiss on his grandmother's back porch. And a lot more in the bedroom he used when he'd stayed there. "Did you ever think about us over the years?" The words came out barely above a whisper. Her heart pounded against her chest, blood rushing in her ears, as she waited for him to answer. She shouldn't have asked, because she wasn't sure she could take the answer. Hell, she didn't deserve one. Not after the way she'd ended things between them.

"All the fucking time, Amelia." The words were guttural, raw, and so honest they sliced right through any barriers she'd managed to put between them. For just a moment she leaned forward. Maybe to kiss him, she wasn't sure.

But a short horn blast from behind them made her jump. Nathan cursed under his breath and turned away from her as he pulled under the valet parking overhang. His jaw was tight as he put the car in park, his frustration clear.

Maybe it was just as well. *Liar,* her inner voice shouted. Amelia desperately wanted to kiss him again.

And not a chaste brush of lips, but the real deal. Walking away from him had shredded her, but she'd wanted to feel pain. She'd felt so guilty all the time that she'd felt as if she deserved the pain. Now that she'd come to terms that what happened wasn't her fault, she needed to tell Nathan everything. Later, though.

She put those thoughts on hold—though she was definitely coming back to them later—and forced a smile she didn't feel as one of the valet employees opened her door.

It was showtime.

Chapter 7

Operational objectives: small steps or phases of an operation that lead to the success of the goal.

Nathan kept his hand at the small of Amelia's back as a hostess led them to the outdoor patio seating. He'd chosen this hotel's restaurant specifically. Mercado owned the hotel and was often here on Saturdays. Not something Amelia would know, though.

Mercado would likely guess Nathan, aka Miguel, had known, though. He'd see it as a subtle challenge. Which was exactly the point. Nathan might hate the idea of Amelia going to Mercado's house for the op, and the truth was if he could convince her not to, he would. But if they could bring Mercado down, using Amelia as an in was the way to do it fast and easy. Because right now they had no fucking clue where the women had disappeared to.

It wasn't as if his team wasn't looking either. The missing women had simply vanished, fallen off the grid in a way that his team knew they'd been taken, and unfortunately he figured some were gone forever. Either dead or wishing they were. His gut twisted at the thought, and part of what he was feeling must have shown on his face, because the hostess jerked back when she looked at him and hurriedly set their menus down on the table before skittering off on impractical high heels.

"Is that fierce look how you attract the ladies?" Amelia asked in an amused voice as she sat. The tabletop was glass, so he got a great view of when she crossed her smooth, bronze legs.

"There's only one woman I want." She probably thought he was acting, but it was the truth. He pulled his chair closer to her, not because it was part of the op, but because he wanted to be close to her. Fuck, he wanted to be *inside* her. He wished he could hate her for the way she'd walked out of his life as if he meant nothing. Hell, even indifference would be better than this gut-clenching hunger he experienced every time he was near her. But deep down he knew there was a reason she'd ended things between them. She'd been too damn stubborn—that being the understatement of the century—to tell him what it was. It hadn't mattered how much he'd asked—begged—her to tell him then, she'd flat-out refused. God, she'd been so cold too, nothing like the warm, fiery Amelia he'd known. Then her mom had fucking disappeared with her and he'd had no way to track her. In the end he figured it had been a good thing. At least then. He'd gone off to the Corps, and without social media or a way to talk to her, it had been easier for him to deal with the complete severing of their relationship.

He was going to find out soon enough, though. He wasn't an eighteen-year-old boy anymore and he wanted some answers. Or at least closure. God, he'd never been able to get rid of the idea that she'd cheated on him. Maybe the guilt had been too much. He wouldn't have thought it possible she'd ever do that, but it was the only thing he could think of. It was probably why he hadn't pushed harder. He hadn't wanted to know if she'd betrayed him like that.

"Is that right?" she asked seductively, scooting close until their knees almost touched.

His entire body tightened at the sexy drop in her voice. He flashed to an image of her riding him, her long dark hair falling around her full breasts like ropes. She'd always used that sexy tone when turned on. And like Pavlov's freaking dog, his body responded to it.

"Did you wear that dress to drive me insane?" he murmured just as a server approached their table.

She didn't answer, but her cheeks reddened, making his dick wake up. He'd managed to keep his hard-on at bay, but Amelia in that dress was too much for his self-control. Of course it wasn't the dress, but her. Petite with full breasts and toned, bronzed legs, she was a walking wet dream. The fact that he'd seen her naked didn't help him any either. Her hips were a little curvier than when they'd been together, but her upper body was stronger, leaner.

"What can I start you two off with this afternoon?" the server asked.

"Two glasses of champagne, and we need a few minutes," he said without looking up, his eyes only for Amelia. He'd never ordered for a woman before, but this was all part of his cover. Miguel Ortiz was a domineering man who took control of all situations, including his dates.

"Uh, right away, sir." The man disappeared as quickly as he'd arrived.

Amelia's lips twitched slightly, as if she was fighting a smile. "Let's get back to your other question. Yes, I wore this dress just for you. You like it?"

God, he wished he knew if this was part of her act or if she was being real. "All I can think about is peeling it slowly from your body." His words were low, guttural, and there was enough space between their table and the others that no one could hear them. He wasn't lying either. He hoped she knew it too.

Her cheeks flushed again and she had started to respond when her gaze flicked over his shoulder and slightly widened. She shifted in her chair, as if nervous, and he didn't think she was acting. Mercado must be here. Good.

A small dose of adrenaline surged through Nathan. If Mercado was involved in taking so many women, Nathan would take pleasure in bringing him down. Fucking with him in his own restaurant was icing on the cake. They just had to find proof because the man certainly wouldn't confess.

Nathan half turned, acknowledging Mercado's presence as he approached.

The man made a straight line for their table too, no pretenses. Dressed in a casual suit with no tie, he smiled easily as he came to stand under the umbrella of their table. "Miguel, Amelia." His smile tightened ever so slightly when his gaze landed on Nathan. "I hope my people are treating you well."

"You own this restaurant?" Amelia asked, her question seemingly sincere.

When Mercado looked at her his expression lost that icy hardness, something Nathan found interesting. Mercado seemed to be genuinely interested in her. He nodded once. "I own this hotel and the adjoining two."

"Oh, uh . . . it's lovely here." Once again her cheeks flushed, as if she was embarrassed. She was doing well.

If Nathan hadn't known she was lying, he'd believe her. Of course he didn't think the embarrassment was fake. He knew she felt bad about bringing a date to one of Mercado's places, since she'd just gone on one with the man last night. He thought she might not be totally convinced Mercado was guilty. Even if he wasn't, Nathan didn't want her going out with the man in the future. Something inside him had shifted at seeing Amelia again. He loved his job, loved serving his country, but he didn't want to be alone forever. And he could never just settle. It wasn't in his DNA. He was like his *abuela* in that way. Her husband had died when she was twenty-nine, leaving her with one daughter. She'd never remarried and, according to her, she'd never had the desire to.

Nathan gave Mercado a pleasant smile and slid into his role as Miguel, discussing the restaurant and his intention to buy a new boat that afternoon. He was just a little arrogant, but not over-the-top. By the time Mercado left their table, Nathan was glad to be rid of him. From Amelia's barely perceptible sigh of relief, she was glad to be alone with Nathan too.

He could tell Amelia wasn't sure about their plan, but he had no doubt that after seeing her out with "Miguel," Mercado would be asking her out again soon. Then they just needed to get her inside his house.

Lunch had been good, but Amelia was itching to get out of this place. She hadn't seen Mercado again, and she was glad for it. Nathan had seemed to slip into his role so easily, but it felt strange to her. Well, the flirting and teasing with Nathan had come easily, which in itself was disconcerting. They'd flirted throughout the meal and while she knew it was just part of their show, it had hit way too close to home.

She'd liked it, had allowed herself to imagine what it would be like to let Nathan kiss her again, what his hands stroking over her breasts and between her legs would—okay, she was shutting that thought down right now.

"I need to use the restroom before we leave," she murmured, standing.

Nathan stood with her and made a move as if he'd come with her, but the server had arrived with their check. Which was just as well; she didn't need a freaking escort to the bathroom. And she wanted space from him. Being around him made her feel too many things, some welcome, some not. She hated the way her body simply flared to life around him, hated not being in control when she knew he didn't return the sentiment. Sure, he was attracted to her, but she needed more than that.

On her way out of the restroom, she was surprised to find Mercado waiting for her. He leaned casually against the sparkly tiled wall that provided an extra enclosure for the restroom doors.

He straightened when he saw her, his expression unreadable. "I'm sorry to ambush you, but I wanted to speak to you in private."

She didn't have to feign surprise to see him. "Iker, I didn't realize this was your place or I never would have come on a date here."

His lips curved up slightly. "I know. Under other circumstances I would advise you to stay away from Miguel. He's a dangerous man, Amelia." Worry crept into his gaze as he continued. "But I know it would sound false coming from me now. So I'll just say watch your step with him. And I would like to take you out again. Tonight, if you're free."

Wow, Nathan had been right about the male ego. She decided to ignore the first part of what he said. "I'm working tonight, but I'm free tomorrow."

His smile was one of pure male satisfaction. Yep, this was definitely about Nathan/Miguel as much as it was about her. Men were such strange creatures. If she saw a guy she was dating out with someone else, she'd just move on—because she didn't share. After setting a time for Mercado to pick her up, they stepped out of the enclosure to find Nathan striding their way.

He looked annoyed to see them together and she wasn't sure if that was real or acting. Iker didn't say anything, just headed in another direction as Nathan approached.

"You ready?" he murmured, wrapping an arm around her.

"Oh yeah." Phase one of their mission had been accomplished. She'd managed to snag another date with Mercado. Now she just needed to get inside his house. From there, Nathan's people would do all the work via her cell phone connection. They'd also be on standby so she didn't get kidnapped too. That she knew Nathan would be part of the team listening in on her was the only reason she was willing to go through with everything.

Sid drove by his next target's ranch-style home, a basic copy of the rest of the homes in the quiet neighborhood. No outside lights were on and no visible lights in the front of the house.

All the yards along the street were neatly mowed with garbage and recycle bins set at the curb for tomorrow's pickup. Including hers. And her car was parked under the carport. Since it was close to midnight, it was a good time to make a move if he was going to take her now. He'd already gotten grief for not snagging her last night.

She was young, barely college-age. He'd followed her home last night and had driven by here a few times today while she was at work to see if there was any movement at her house. She'd seemed friendly with that guy the other night and she could have given him a key if they were fucking. Sid needed to cover all bases. He'd thought about moving on her last night, but there had been another car in the driveway. Maybe that guy had stayed over.

Today there hadn't been any movement at her home from what he could tell, and just her car under the carport. Since this looked like the kind of neighborhood to have nosy neighbors with too much time on their hands, he'd switched vehicles during his drive-by checks.

According to his file she went to the University of Miami and didn't have a roommate or parents. They'd died and left her this house. No security system listed. Still, he wanted more intel and his boss was getting not exactly sloppy, but anxious for him to take this girl. That was never a good sign. They had such a good operation going. It wouldn't be smart to get impatient and start taking too many girls in a row. But she must fit a profile someone wanted. Like the others taken, she had no family. Though she did have friends.

But so had some of the other targets, and that was easily dealt with by shutting down their online accounts. Still, something about this kidnapping felt wrong to him, just too damn impatient. They'd been so smart, flying under the radar, running this operation right under everyone's noses. It was brilliant. What the hell was he going to do, though? He couldn't question the boss. Not when he was pulling in such good money. Besides, he knew his life would be worth nothing if he tried to back out. He'd just become a target himself. No way would he allow that to happen.

He rolled his neck once as he pulled up to a stop sign. Girls went missing every day. This bitch would be no different.

Turning left, he headed down a block before he turned around. He'd have to be fast. Hell, he'd done it before. Usually with a longer lead time to watch the girls' movements, but this would work. If someone got in his way, it was just their bad luck.

When he pulled back down her street, he parked in front of her next-door neighbor's house. He already had the materials he needed to take her, so after pulling on gloves and taking another quick scan of the street, he slipped from his SUV. The air had a fresh scent to it.

This was a good time of night to take someone, especially in a neighborhood like this, where old people went to bed early.

That familiar urgency hummed through him, an insistent buzz as he made his way to her house. He walked past her driveway, continuing to look for any signs of life. In the distance he heard the rumble of an engine as a car drove past her quiet little street and a dog barking, but nothing else.

Where her and her neighbor's front yard connected, he turned, moving straight for the privacy fence guarding her backyard. He tested the latch once, smiled when he found there was no lock. If there had been, he'd have just scaled the fence, but this made his life easier. One less step to take.

Heart pounding, he slipped through the fence, letting it quietly close behind him. He moved quickly along the stucco wall, hoping she didn't have security sensors. When he reached the end of the house, the wide double lights didn't flick on. He allowed himself a sigh of relief before he peered around the corner. He eyed the small open porch with patio furniture. Nothing out of the ordinary and only one dim light visible through a small square window.

If he had to guess, he'd say it was coming from the kitchen. People often left on a light in their house when they went to bed at night, either in the kitchen or living room. The size of the window indicated a kitchen. Using the shadows as cover, he moved along the back of the house until he reached the patio.

The back door had a pitiful lock, one he picked in less than sixty seconds. All his muscles pulled tight as he slowly opened the back door. It creaked slightly, making him pause.

No movement inside.

He pushed it open farther, just enough so he could slip inside. He found himself in a mudroom that opened right into the kitchen. He'd been right. A pale yellow glow shone over a double sink.

Sid pulled out his Taser, ready to wrap this job up now. All he had to do was subdue her and then he'd restrain her arms and legs and gag her. After that he'd pull his SUV into the driveway and dump her in the back. Simple.

His rubber-soled boots were silent as he moved through the house, checking the living room first to make sure she hadn't fallen asleep on the couch.

When he reached the hallway, two bedroom doors were closed, but the one at the end was cracked open. A very thin stream of light peeked out the crack. Maybe she had a night-light.

Blood rushed in his ears as he bypassed the other rooms and made a beeline for the last one. No sense in checking the other two when his gut told him exactly where she was.

This door didn't creak when he pushed it open with

his boot. He smiled to himself when he saw her lying there on the queen-size bed, dark hair pillowed around her beautiful face. She was peacefully sleeping.

Not for long, he thought perversely.

He got a hard-on seeing her like that, hated that he couldn't do anything about it. He paused a moment, just watching her, savoring this time. In a few seconds he'd see the fear in her eyes as he woke her up. It wouldn't last long because he couldn't afford to let her make any noise, but for those precious moments, there would be confusion and then terror in her eyes. He craved seeing it from his victims. It was his one guilty pleasure.

After he dropped her off to his boss, he'd find some action in no time. If he couldn't find a willing woman at a bar, he'd just hire someone.

Chapter 8

Hooking: to set up a target using a specific
lure (bait).

Nathan automatically stood as Amelia stepped into her living room, all the muscles in his body pulling taut. "What the hell are you wearing?" he practically shouted, earning a pissed-off look from her and surprise from Elliott, Cade, and Maria—who was simply there for moral support.

"A little black dress. Pretty standard for a date." Her words were edgy, stress cracking through her calm facade.

Which made him feel like a dick, even as he suppressed that primal, possessive instinct to keep her safe, to call off phase two of this op. It had been a day and a half since their "lunch date," since that fucker Mercado had asked Amelia out. The time had passed too quickly from then to now. He'd been working, running down leads, and she'd been working and living her life as normal. Things had to be as normal as possible in case anyone was watching her. So far the NSA hadn't found that to be so, but they weren't taking any chances. He'd resisted the urge to call her, to check in. It would have been stupid and weak.

"You look perfect," Maria said, shooting a quick frown at Nathan before looking at Amelia again. "A perfect blend of sexy and classy."

The dress was slim-fitting and had a high collar with black lace, but it was short enough to show off a lot of leg. Too much leg, in his opinion. He didn't want anyone else seeing all that smooth skin. Didn't matter that he had no claim on her, that he should just get the fuck over her; he couldn't help imagining peeling the dress slowly off her body—so he knew Mercado would be thinking the same thing.

When she turned toward Elliott, answering something the analyst asked, Nathan saw that the back of the dress had a wide circular cutout in the center, revealing most of her back and dipping low enough that it sloped too close to that luscious ass for his comfort. Annoyance surfaced, but he reined in his own bullshit.

Mercado would be picking her up for their date and she needed to be calm and sure of herself, not questioning anything about tonight. Ever since their date, though, and those light kisses, Nathan had been all twisted up inside. He couldn't even lie to himself and say he'd been acting or role-playing.

Because those kisses had stirred up too much inside him. He'd made a decision today that he wasn't letting her push him out of his life again. Not before he got some damn answers, some closure at least. But he wanted more than that; he wanted a place in her life. Didn't matter that she had no idea who he really worked for or that he had no idea why she'd ended things between them; if they could get past those hurdles, he wanted to see if what they'd once had was still real.

They were virtual strangers after so many years apart, but seeing her again had woken up way too many emotions inside him. He couldn't just walk away. Hell, three months ago when he thought he might die in that bombed-out Metro Station, he'd vowed to look her up again. Then he'd chickened out and kept putting it on the back burner because he was too afraid to know if she'd settled down with someone. To have her thrown back in his life again, on the job no less, felt like fucking fate. His attraction to her certainly hadn't changed. If anything, it was even more incendiary.

He'd wait to push until after she got an invite to Mercado's and the team had the intel they needed. Once her part in this was done, he was taking the gloves off and getting some damn answers.

"You're sure he or his security guys won't be able to tell something is different with my phone?" she asked Elliott. Amelia perched on the edge of one of her couches where Elliott was closing down one of his laptops.

"Not even if they take your phone apart or scan you. I'm simply using your phone's wireless to hack into his system. Because of the security he has in place at his residence, I can't route in to it any other way." Elliott's voice was steady, his words matter-of-fact.

It seemed to have a soothing effect on Amelia. She smoothed a hand down the skirt of her dress and nodded once, as if to herself. "Okay."

"You can do this." Nathan crossed over to her,

hoping he sounded reassuring. If Mercado was involved in taking these women, Amelia needed to be ready for tonight. He was certain she had been until he'd opened his mouth.

"Thanks." She stood from the couch and he was aware of Cade, Elliott, and Maria quietly heading to her kitchen.

Nathan was thankful for the little bit of privacy.

She wrapped her arms around herself. "What if I don't get an invite to his house?"

"If you don't, then you don't. We'll get inside another way. There is always another way." Mercado had tight security and they'd looked into using a cleaning service or something similar to infiltrate, but as of now that was out. He was very conscious of who was in his home. Smart, but damn annoying.

She pushed out a breath. "Okay. I needed to hear that. And there are worse things than going on a date to a nice restaurant, right?" Her expression grew slightly pinched. She didn't seem scared, just nervous.

He hated that she'd potentially be in harm's way, hated it bone deep. He didn't care about protocol or keeping his distance. He pulled her into his arms, tugging her close. To his relief, she didn't protest, just slid into his embrace, wrapping her arms around his waist as she laid her cheek against his chest. He loved the feel of her against him, the perfect way she fit. And he loved the subtle show of trust she was giving him. He set his chin on top of her head. "If you want to back out, you can. There's still time." He wished she would.

"No." She didn't even pause as she stepped back to look at him. Her response wasn't exactly a surprise. The

Amelia from his teenage years had a stubborn streak a mile wide. When she decided on something, she didn't often back down. "This is the smart choice. He asked me out before this operation even started and I have no connection to any government agency. He won't suspect me. And I need to do this. For Danita. If she's still alive . . ." She trailed off, her jaw going tight for a moment.

Yep, that was the Amelia he knew. Seeing her so determined to take part in this warmed him from the inside out. Not caring that his teammates were in the other room, he leaned down and crushed his mouth to hers. Some primitive part of him needed to leave his mark on her before she went out with another man. Fake date or no, he didn't care. Even though it made him feel vulnerable, this would show her that this wasn't part of his cover. His feelings for her were real.

She let out a small squeak of surprise but didn't pull back for even a second. She melted into him, arching so that her breasts rubbed against his chest while her tongue danced with his.

He wanted to find the nearest flat surface, hike her dress up around her hips, and bury himself inside her. His body practically trembled for her. He started to slide his fingers through her hair but stopped, using control he didn't know he had. Mercado would be here in an hour; she couldn't look as if she'd just been with another man. Breathing hard, he stared down at her, pleased that she looked just as affected as he felt. She also looked surprised by the kiss. Her lips were slightly swollen, but Nathan knew it would fade by the time her date got here. Even thinking that she was going out with someone else left a sour taste in his mouth.

"I need to go," he rasped out. He hated leaving her, but on the off chance Mercado showed up early, the man couldn't get a whiff that anything was out of the ordinary. That meant the team had to clear out, including him.

Swallowing hard, she nodded. "Okay. When . . . when will I see you again?" She whispered the words.

The need in her voice punched through his senses. After their date yesterday he'd dropped her off at one of her restaurants and then hadn't seen her again until just an hour ago. He was working different angles on the op, and on the off chance Mercado had been watching her at work, Nathan couldn't just hang around her. Things had to appear normal. "We'll be tracking you tonight through your phone and I'll check in once you've made it home safely. I'm part of the surveillance team, so I'll be nearby at all times." He wasn't letting anything happen to her.

"I know. I just mean, when will I see you again? Not for this op." Her words were still low, as if she didn't want the others to hear.

"I'll call you." When her face fell, he continued. "Tomorrow." Hell, he didn't know if he could make that happen, not with everything they were doing, but he'd try. "And remember—if you can't get an invite to his house, don't push it. Let it come naturally."

"Okay, I will." She seemed more at ease now and for that he was grateful. She nodded toward the kitchen. "I'll walk you out."

He didn't want to leave, but it was time. Dax, a new member of this op, was parked in her garage in a white SUV. They'd parked there and entered through her kitchen so her neighbors wouldn't get a peek at any of them. Sure, someone might ask about the SUV, but Amelia was going to say she'd been test-driving one if it ever came up. An easy lie that she could back up with an alibi his team had created at a local dealership. So far it didn't appear as if Mercado was following Amelia's movements, but if for some reason he got nosy and started questioning her neighbors, they were covering all their bases. Because Amelia's safety came first on this op.

In the kitchen just Cade was waiting. Maria and Elliott must have already got in the SUV.

He nodded once at Amelia. "You're ready for this." A statement, full of authority.

"You know it." Her voice was strong now.

Thank God. Nathan squeezed her shoulder once. "We've got your back." He needed to remind her just one more time, more for himself than for her.

She smiled, the relief in her eyes the last thing he saw before he and Cade exited as quietly as they'd come. Now they just had to wait to see how her date went. If she got the invite, it would be time for the next stage. If Mercado invited her over to his place tonight, they were ready for that too. Though Nathan hated the idea of her going over there after a date. He hated the idea of her going there at all.

Shaking himself, he put all that away. It was game time. Amelia was depending on his team to have her back. That meant he had to be completely focused.

* * *

Amelia glanced at her phone for the tenth time in as many minutes. Mercado would be here soon, so she needed to stop fidgeting. It was hard, though, when all she could think about was this stupid date. Well, that and the way Nathan had kissed her.

And how she'd kissed him back. It had felt too natural being in his arms again, flicking her tongue against his. Her body was primed for him, her nipples hard against her bra cups. Not the best timing, she chastised herself. And not the best idea. Once she confessed everything to him, things would be different between them. He probably wouldn't even want to be in her life again, let alone kiss her.

Her cell rang in her hand, making her heart rate kick up ten notches. She cursed herself for the jumpy reaction. When she saw the number for Plátanos Maduros, her stomach rumbled. She'd been too nervous to eat much, and right now she could definitely go for some comfort food. Her second restaurant was known for the various ways they cooked plantains, hence the name. She wanted more of those *empanadas*. "Hello?"

"Hey, Amelia, it's Sylvia." One of her managers, and her tone was stressed.

The busy sound of the restaurant filled the background, so Amelia knew she was likely using the phone behind the bar or near the hostess stand. And Sylvia didn't call unless it was necessary. "Is everything okay?"

"Yeah. . . ." She sighed. "I know you're going on a date tonight, but I just wanted to let you know that Tessa didn't show up this afternoon. I've been trying to get a hold of her the past couple hours, but she's not picking up. Her phone rings but no answer."

Amelia's doorbell rang, making her cringe. Talk about timing. She headed for the living room, her heels softly clicking against the wooden floor as she crossed the foyer. Nerves danced in her stomach. "Have any of the girls said anything?" she asked as she opened the door to find Mercado standing there.

Dressed in casual slacks and a blue button-down shirt, he looked handsome and put together as usual. She was just thankful Nathan and his team were listening; it eased the knot inside her.

"I'm sorry," she whispered, stepping back and motioning him inside as Sylvia continued.

"Yeah, no one knows anything."

"Did you talk to Jonas?" She shut the door behind Mercado, not sure if he'd want a drink before they left or not. The only good thing about getting a work call was that she didn't have time to be stressed about Mercado anymore.

"No, why would I?"

Jonas was one of her guys who worked in the back. "I caught them making out in the parking lot a few days ago. I think they might be an item so check with him. Can you cover for her tonight?"

"Yeah, we'll pick up the slack, no problem. I just wanted to let you know. She probably just flaked or fell asleep. I know she picked up an extra class this semester and it's been stressing her out."

Tessa wasn't the type to flake out, but . . . she was in college and young. Amelia would give her a break. "Thanks. I'll try to call her tomorrow. Text me with any more issues, but I'm turning my phone to silent after this."

"Okay, and sorry for bothering you tonight."

As soon as they disconnected, Amelia smiled apologetically at Mercado. "I'm so sorry. I got a work call right as you arrived, but the phone is off for the evening, so I'm all yours."

His smile was charming and just a little heated. "I like the sound of that." That was heat in his voice too. "Is everything okay at work?"

"Oh yeah, just employee stuff. When you hire teenagers or college-age kids, you have to expect certain things." She gave a light laugh, thankful it didn't sound forced. If she treated this as a normal date, she'd be fine. "Did you want a drink before we leave?"

He shook his head. "No, but I have a small change of plans."

She picked up her purse on the foyer table and slid her phone into it. If Mercado planned to kidnap someone, she didn't fit the bill of the type of women being taken. She had roots and people had seen her out with him before. No, she wouldn't be a target. "Oh?"

"If it's all right, I'd like to cook for you tonight. I don't want to seem presumptuous or for you to assume I'm inviting you to my home for anything else other than dinner, but I did promise I'd cook last time we went out. I'm not as good as you no doubt are, but . . ." He smiled that easy smile again, lifting his shoulders. "My daughter tells me I'm decent."

Holy hell. She'd gotten an invite to his house without even having to try. Blood rushed in her ears for a moment, but she found her voice and nodded. "That sounds great. I'm ready. Just let me set the alarm." She set it to away mode and as the beeping countdown started, she opened the front door for them.

After she locked up, she turned to find him waiting on the doorstep, his arm slightly bent for her, so she linked hers through his. A twinge of guilt threaded through her, but she squashed it immediately. It wasn't as if she and Nathan were in a relationship or *anything* and this date wasn't real.

As they strode down her walkway to his waiting car, she realized someone was holding the back door open for them. She almost jerked in surprise but caught herself. Of course he would have a driver. She'd met him at the auction, so she hadn't known, but she shouldn't be surprised. If she had to guess, this guy was his security more than a driver. Nerves started to dance along her spine. Not because her inner voice told her that something was off, but because she knew he was a suspect in mass kidnappings and likely slave trade. Her gut told her differently, but . . . she'd been wrong before.

"I have a confession to make," she said once they were in the backseat. The leather was smooth against her legs. She was so damn thankful Nathan was listening in right now. It made this easier to do—made her feel less vulnerable.

His lips quirked slightly. "Oh?"

"When I told you I Googled you, I read an article about your home on one of those architectural sites. I think it was a reference to the previous owner?" She phrased it as a question even though she knew the answer. Cade and Nathan had told her she needed to sprinkle lies and truths to make things believable and turn things in the direction she wanted them to go. She hoped he picked up her thread of conversation.

He nodded, relaxing against the seat and turning his body toward her so she had his full attention. She still couldn't see him as a kidnapper. "It's one of the reasons I bought it. I like the privacy of Star Island, but the customizations made it move-in ready for me."

Star Island was a private, very exclusive neighborhood in Miami Beach. "If you'll indulge me with a tour before you cook, I'd be in heaven." It would be the perfect way for her to get access to all the rooms, or at least close enough to the one that Nathan's team needed. They'd shown her a floor plan so she knew where she needed to be. And if he gave her a tour when they first arrived, it wouldn't seem weird if she had her purse with her. If he gave her one after dinner, it might seem odd if she picked up her purse and carried it around.

"I'll indulge anything you want." His voice dropped an octave as he tucked a strand of loose hair behind her ear, his thumb grazing her cheek, lingering a little longer than necessary.

She froze for a moment, wondering if he planned to kiss her, and had to fight back a sigh of relief when he let his hand drop. She definitely wasn't cut out for this undercover business. It was too nerve-racking.

She hoped that Elliott got whatever it was he needed from Iker's computer, because she didn't want to have to go through another date again.

"She's doing great." Elliott gave a nod of approval as his fingers flew over the keyboard. "And, as we suspected, Mercado has a guy scoping out your 'home' right now. Check it out." He pulled up another screen showing images of video feeds from the place the NSA had set up as Miguel Ortiz's Miami home base.

Mercado had already done one search after Nathan had reached out to him, which made sense, considering "Miguel" wanted to do business with him—but that was before Nathan had made a move on Amelia. Now it appeared the man had decided to do another check. Mercado had already run the financials of Nathan's alias, along with reaching out to people Miguel had worked with in the past. He came up exactly as he was supposed to. A businessman interested in real estate and smuggling on the side. All hidden well enough under respectable businesses. Similar to Mercado.

"Not gonna find anything," he muttered, listening to the conversation between Mercado and Amelia. The guy was too smooth. And there had been a pause in their conversation, as if that bastard had kissed Amelia.

The thought made Nathan want to grind his teeth. He was glad they didn't have video right now. He didn't need to see her out with someone else who wanted her as badly as Nathan did. Well, not as badly. No one else could want her that much. As Elliott worked, Nathan pulled out his cell phone and called Burkhart.

His boss was working on multiple things right now, but this op was a priority. He answered on the first ring. "How's your girl doing?"

She wasn't his girl, even if he wanted her to be. And he knew Wesley didn't mean it that way. Hell, he shouldn't even be thinking in those terms. "Solid. Got an invite to the house tonight, so we're moving forward.

The target wants to cook for her." He kept his voice devoid of too much emotion. He'd promised Burkhart that his history with Amelia wouldn't interfere with anything, and he had to keep that promise.

"That's great. You, Cade, and Dax are on standby as the backup team if anything goes wrong. I'll send three more guys your way, but if things sound like they're getting hot, use operational latitude."

"Affirmative." Some of his tension eased as they disconnected. He hoped they wouldn't need the backup, but he was glad to have it.

"Since we know their destination I'm going to take an alternative route to the neighborhood," Dax said, glancing at them in the rearview mirror. "Don't want anyone to spot us."

Under normal circumstances it would have been difficult to infiltrate the gated neighborhood, but Maria had called in a favor—or her father had. One of his clients had an empty house in Star Island. It was on the market, but the real estate industry was bad now, especially for a house selling in the millions. So it was sitting empty and Nathan's team was using it as a base.

It was close enough to where Amelia would be that Nathan wasn't completely out of his mind. Still, seconds counted in matters of life and death, and if God forbid something went wrong . . . he'd do everything in his power to save her.

Chapter 9

Dry clean: actions operatives take to determine if
they are under surveillance or bugged.

Standing on a plain rectangular desk, Tessa reached
up, skimming her fingers over the lower edge of
the window where the two panes met. Even standing
on the desk, the window was too high. She could feel
the outline of a lock, tried to move it, but it wouldn't
budge. Next she tried to grasp the bottom lip of the
lower half of the window, but of course it didn't move
either. Not when it was locked.

She couldn't stay here—wherever here was. All she
remembered was the horror of waking up to a gloved
hand over her mouth and the face of a man who looked
positively gleeful. Maybe a little insane. She'd started to
scream when a jolt of pain had shot through her. After
that she couldn't remember anything.

She'd woken up in this room that looked a little bit
like a hospital room. But it wasn't. She'd tried the door
and found it locked. She'd banged on it and shouted
for help until someone told her to be quiet for her own

safety. A female voice from nearby had said it with urgency; with *fear*.

Tessa had listened.

All she knew at this point was that she'd been taken from her home in the middle of the night and was someone's prisoner. Her pajamas were still on and it was dark outside, so she didn't think that much time had passed. And she didn't think she'd been sexually assaulted. Didn't mean it wasn't going to happen. She might just be a freshman in college, but she was a criminal justice major and knew what kind of horrors were out there. Not firsthand, but she wasn't completely naive. Besides, she watched the freaking news.

A shudder skittered through her, but she brushed it off. She needed to find a way out. Or a weapon. Since the window exit wasn't working out, she got off the table and slid onto the tiled floor. It was cold beneath her bare feet.

The door handle rattled. Fear detonated inside her, making her freeze up. A moment later a man wearing scrubs walked in pushing a small rolling cart. He was only a couple of inches taller than her, maybe five feet eight. He had dark hair and a clean-shaven face and his expression was neutral. He propped the door open and for a moment she fantasized about ramming into him, using the cart to knock him down so she could make a break for it.

Those thoughts died when another man—the man who'd taken her—stepped into the doorway behind the one in scrubs. Though his expression didn't change, his eyes had a wild quality to them.

She belatedly noticed he had a gun in a holster on his hip.

Before a deeper fear could take root, the shorter man spoke. "You will take these twice a day, once in the morning and once in the evening. You'll take them with your food." He held up a capped bottle and rattled it slightly. Then he motioned to the small refrigerator she'd seen earlier, but hadn't opened. "There is water and multivitamin juice inside. I will bring you food in the morning and you will get exercise and time outside if you behave."

Behave? Like what, this was prison? Fear slid through her, the iciness making her muscles turn rigid.

"The television also works," he said, nodding at it. "If you break it, you won't get another one, so don't be foolish. If you want books or magazines, let me know. And don't ask any questions right now. You came in later than expected and I'm tired. If you insist on harassing me with questions or pleas for freedom, I'll lock him in here with you." He jerked a thumb over his shoulder at the man who'd kidnapped her, his eyes completely devoid of emotion. "Be smart, get some sleep, and we will discuss your new home in the morning."

Tessa wondered what was worse, the lack of emotion or the hint of crazy she saw in the man with the gun. In the end, she didn't care. She just wanted to be left alone so she could break down without an audience. Tears threatened, but she ruthlessly shoved them back. So she nodded and took the bottle from the man. He picked up the covered tray and set it on the desk before quietly exiting with the other man.

The door shut and was locked from the outside, the

*snick*ing sound making her nauseated. At least she was alone. But she had no idea what was going on, who these people were, or why they'd taken her. About a dozen horrific scenarios raced through her mind, all the horror movies she loved so much coming back to haunt her in vivid detail.

Terrified but exhausted, she dimmed the lights and made her way to the twin bed in the corner of the sterile room. She doubted she'd be able to sleep but got under the white sheet anyway and curled on her side. Though she tried to hold them back, she let her tears fall, hot and wet, against the pillow. She wondered what the hell those pills were. Maybe something to make her more compliant. God, she couldn't even think about that right now. All she knew was that she wouldn't simply go along with whatever they wanted.

Amelia tried not to fidget with her purse or act as if she couldn't wait to get home while Mercado's driver steered down her street. Mercado had given her a tour of his house—and it was amazing—before dinner. And dinner had been lovely, Mercado the perfect host. It was so hard to imagine that he was involved in kidnapping and selling women. She knew monsters could have all sorts of faces, but her gut didn't tell her to run from him. Her survival instincts were strong too. They'd been honed at a young age. God, she'd been . . . six when one of her mother's clients tried to touch her. From that moment on, she'd quickly learned to read people and situations. So it bothered her that she didn't get a bad vibe from Mercado.

She wished she'd had a way to communicate with

Nathan to find out if his team had managed to hack into Mercado's computer system. Elliott hadn't known how long it would take to use her cell phone as a gateway, so she had no idea if her being in Mercado's house had even helped the operation.

When they pulled into her driveway, Mercado got out, not waiting for his driver—who wasn't making a move to get out anyway. Instead Mercado held out a hand for Amelia as she slid from the vehicle. The fear she'd felt before dinner was gone, but nerves still skittered through her. She just wanted to get inside and be alone—and, okay, contact Nathan. Not just because she wanted to see how the operation had gone either; she wanted to hear his voice. That kiss he'd given her earlier made her heart rate kick up just thinking about it. And she didn't want Mercado to try to kiss her.

"I had a very nice time tonight." Mercado's voice brought her back to the present, forcing thoughts of Nathan to the back burner.

"I did too." She turned to face him as they reached her front door. She'd forgotten to leave her porch light on, but there was enough illumination from the moon and streetlights for her to see. She started to reach into her purse for her keys when Mercado stepped a fraction closer, completely invading her personal space.

Oh, crap. Did he plan a good night kiss? He seemed so traditional that maybe—he cupped her cheek gently, his thumb stroking over her skin. She didn't want anyone touching her but Nathan.

Maybe something of her reaction showed, because he let his hand drop, his expression contemplative.

"Why did you agree to go out with me again when you're dating Miguel?"

She was surprised by the question but lifted her shoulders. "He and I have been on exactly one date. I wouldn't call that *dating*." In case Nathan needed her to get into Mercado's house again, she wanted to keep things open with him.

He was silent for a long moment, his gaze falling to her mouth before he met her eyes again. "I would like to see you again."

She must have been decent company for him to ask her out again. Unless maybe he suspected something? That tightness was back in her belly, but she smiled and nodded. "I would too. This week I'm pretty busy with work, but I can make time."

"Good." There was a sensual note in his voice as he stepped closer again, leaning down this time.

She had to order herself not to stiffen up as his mouth teased over hers. The kiss was barely a kiss, just a brief brushing of lips, but guilt still bloomed inside her. Which was absolutely ridiculous. She'd done nothing wrong.

Before he'd made it to his car, she'd unlocked her front door and stepped inside. By the time she locked it, she realized the beeping of her alarm hadn't gone off. She knew she'd set it.

Panic bloomed inside her for all of a second until Nathan stepped from the shadows of her living room. She pushed out a short sigh and clicked on the small lamp on her foyer table. She hadn't expected him to be waiting for her, but she couldn't deny the burst of pleasure at seeing him. Pleasure and relief. Tonight had gone well, but Nathan's presence smoothed out the edges of her nerves. She wasn't afraid when he was around. "What are you doing here?" she asked quietly.

"That fucker kissed you." His words were a growl and not even close to an answer. Her heart rate kicked up as he moved toward her with the lethal grace of a predator. His clothes were as dark as his expression.

But the look on his face . . . Before she could ask again what he was doing there, he had her backed up against the front door, his hands caging her in on either side. Gasping, she slid her hands slid over his chest, a shiver rippling through her at the feel of taut muscles.

His erection was unmistakable.

"It was barely a kiss and just part of the . . ." She struggled for the right word. She wasn't an operative or even close, but she managed to finish with "job."

"Don't care," he rasped out before he slanted his mouth over hers. His tongue slipped past her lips, completely demanding.

There was so much she needed to tell him, should probably tell him before things went any further, but when he shoved her dress up to her waist without warning, she stopped thinking.

The move was so primal, so Nathan. He'd always been like that, desperate to have her whenever they'd managed to sneak time alone together. Looking back, she'd wondered if it was teenage hormones, but as he ground his hips against her, his thick length pushing against her abdomen, she knew it was the chemistry between them.

Groaning into his kiss, she grasped his shoulders

and lifted herself up so that she wrapped her legs around his waist. With her dress bunched up and so few barriers between them, it wouldn't take much for him to be inside her.

Her inner walls tightened at the mere thought. Nathan Ortiz. She'd never thought she'd see him again, had been too much of a coward to even attempt to look him up.

Yet here he was, back in her life, kissing her like a man who'd been deprived of sex for a thousand years. And though he hadn't said the actual words, she knew he wanted to wipe away Mercado's kiss.

Her nipples tightened against the built-in cups of her dress as she arched against him. The friction primed her even more, the dampness between her legs growing by the second.

One of his hands moved to her hip while the other cupped her face. As his tongue danced against hers, she could feel the energy humming through him. If she let him, he'd consume her.

Suddenly he tore away from her mouth. His body and hand on her hip kept her pinned against the door. The way he looked at her had her entire body lit up with heat and hunger. There was no way he could be stopping now. Because this simply couldn't end with a kiss. She needed him too badly.

"I still fucking jerk off to thoughts of you." He said it so savagely, almost accusingly. As if he didn't want to think of her when he touched himself. She didn't blame him, not after the way she'd so coldly ended things. The statement took her so off guard, both because of the savageness and the admission.

Hell, she couldn't believe he was standing in her foyer kissing her at all. She knew this had nothing to do with his mission. Maybe he wanted to get her out of his system? The thought should hurt her more, and though it stung, she still couldn't blame him. God knew she'd never gotten him out of her system.

There was no rhyme or reason for it either. She'd had sex since him and knew he must have, but no one had ever made her feel the way he did. For a long time she'd wondered if it was because he'd been her first, but now she knew that had nothing to do with it. She wasn't sure how to respond, couldn't find her voice anyway.

When he slightly moved back, taking all that warmth away from her as he separated their bodies, she started to protest until she realized what he was doing. Hand still on her hip, he went down to his knees as her heeled shoes clicked against the wooden foyer floor. If he wasn't still holding her hip, she wasn't certain her legs would keep her up.

With her dress shoved up, she felt exposed but not vulnerable with him. Never that. At least not in the sexual sense. Nathan would never hurt her, not physically. It wasn't in his DNA. If she wanted to stop this, he'd stop.

She didn't want to. It didn't matter that there were still issues between them; she needed him.

Keeping his gaze pinned to hers, he slowly tugged her panties off. His eyes seemed somehow darker tonight. He never looked away as he tossed them to the side and lifted one of her legs, spreading her wider for him. She propped her heeled shoe on his shoulder.

Everything about this moment was so intimate.

Maybe too intimate. While she could never be physically vulnerable with him, emotionally was a whole other beast. Once they crossed this line—and they were definitely having sex tonight—it would rip her open if and when he walked out of her life. She couldn't know for sure that he would, but Nathan was a black-and-white kind of guy. Or he had been. He'd never seen the world in shades of gray. Things were either right or wrong for him. She didn't know how he'd react when she told him why she'd ended things.

Still looking at her, he trailed a finger up her inner calf, then thigh. She was already shaking with the need for more when he oh so slowly slid his thick finger along her wet folds.

He shuddered, his eyes going heavy-lidded for a moment. "This is for me." A simple statement. No smugness, but a pure male satisfaction.

She nodded, mainly because she couldn't force her vocal cords to work.

"I didn't like you out with him," he murmured, slipping a finger inside her.

That much was definitely clear. Her lower back arched. "I know," she whispered, amazed she had the ability to talk as he pushed into her wetness. The feel of him inside her, even just his finger, had her nipples getting even harder. She wanted to strip her dress off and feel his body against hers, on top of her, as he took her. She'd always loved the feeling of being completely and utterly possessed by him. And she wanted it again. So much that it scared her.

"I don't care if it was for part of the op." Again with that possessiveness.

It shouldn't turn her on. She'd never liked that whole macho thing, but with Nathan it was different.

Letting out a rough, raspy sound, he tore his gaze from hers and leaned forward, flicking his tongue over her clit without warning. The sudden, intimate kiss had her reacting, not thinking. She didn't want to think anyway, not right now.

She rolled her hips against his face as she slid her fingers through his short, dark hair. When he moaned against her clit with such gratification, her inner walls started convulsing faster and faster around his finger. It wasn't going to take her long to come.

Pleasure slid through her as he continued to stroke and caress those sensitive nerves with his very talented tongue. It was as if he knew the exact pressure to tease her right to the brink of orgasm, but not push her completely over. Maybe he simply remembered the way her body reacted to him.

Until he slid a second finger inside her and sucked her clit hard. The simultaneous actions were too much.

"Nathan!" Her climax was sharp, battering her nerve endings as he continued thrusting his fingers in and out of her.

Her heel slipped, her leg sliding down his back as her orgasm seemed to go on forever. He grabbed her leg, gently moved it off his shoulder as he stood. She reached for the button of his pants, but he moved faster, taking her hands and pinning her wrists above her head on the door.

His expression was fierce as he brushed his lips over hers. "Taste yourself," he murmured darkly, the erotic words making her tremble.

After that orgasm she thought she'd be relaxed, sated, but she realized they were just getting started. It had been like this with them before. He'd just taken the edge off for her.

She arched into him. "I want to taste *you*."

Her words seemed to set something off in him. She doubted he'd let her actually taste him right now, not when his erection was pushing so insistently against her abdomen.

His breathing was ragged as he let one of his hands drop. The other remained firmly in place, holding her wrists pinned against the door. The pale glow from the small table lamp illuminated the planes of his face, made him seem fiercer somehow.

He nipped her bottom lip between his teeth, sucked, before he started feathering kisses along her jaw. The stubble on his face rasped against her cheek, made her shiver as he continued teasing her. When he pressed down on her earlobe with his teeth, she shuddered.

She could hear him doing something with his other hand, couldn't figure out what it was until he leaned back and let her wrists go.

"If you want to stop, tell me now," he said as he ripped open a condom wrapper.

"Stop and I kill you." She reached for his pants, started on the button as he tugged his shirt over his head.

Moving quickly, he was completely naked in moments, his thick length a beautiful sight. Before she had time to enjoy staring her fill of him, he reached around her and tugged the tie at the top of her dress free, stripping her as fast as he'd done himself.

As her dress pooled on the floor, there was no time to be self-conscious—she was pretty much beyond that anyway—as he rolled the condom over his erection.

She reached for him, sliding her hands up his hard chest, savoring the feel of his bare skin under her fingers when he fisted her hips and hoisted her against the door. Instantly she wrapped her legs around him.

Then he was inside her, the sensation of being filled by him pretty damn close to making her orgasm again.

He buried himself to the hilt and let out a groan as he filled her, stretched her. Instead of beginning to thrust, as she'd thought he would, he paused, looked down at her. Too many emotions were in his eyes for her to sift through. Blood rushed in her ears as she watched him.

That same need she'd always seen years ago was still there. She knew it was mirrored in her own eyes. She wished she understood what it was about him that called to her on the most primal level. Right now she didn't care, though; she just wanted him to find as much pleasure as she had.

She rolled her hips once, a silent demand.

On a moan, he pulled back, his grip on her hips tight as he slammed into her. Each thrust was more unsteady than the last, but he refused to take his gaze off her.

She'd never felt more exposed in her life. It was as if he could see inside her. When his eyes got heavy-lidded, she grabbed his face and pulled his lips to hers. She needed to taste him again. His kisses grew even more erratic until he pulled back and buried his face against her neck.

She clutched at his back, digging her fingers into the hard planes as he began to climax.

"Amelia!" Her name on his lips set her off too.

She held on tighter, some primitive part of her wanting to leave marks as another orgasm slid through her on an unexpected wave of bliss. Closing her eyes, she let her head fall back as more pleasure flowed through her.

She wasn't sure how much time passed, but eventually she became aware that she was still holding on to him with a death grip and winced. She loosened her fingers even as she tried to get her breathing under control.

His own breathing was harsh as he lifted his head from her neck. For one long moment she was afraid she would see regret in his gaze, but as his dark one met hers, all she saw was raw hunger.

There would be no sleep or talking tonight. In the morning she needed to come clean with him about everything. Even if he hated her after that, he deserved the truth.

She'd worry about that later. Now she planned to enjoy every second with Nathan as if it were her last.

Chapter 10

Eyes only: data that shouldn't be discussed without explicit permission.

S id slowly steered the small aluminum boat across the private lake. The sun had only been up for an hour, and even though this lake was on private property and there weren't any homes around for miles, he still liked to dispose of any bodies before sunrise.

It was much easier to be invisible in the dark. But he'd gotten a late start and he hadn't been willing to speed on the way here. Hell, he almost always went exactly the speed limit. He couldn't risk getting pulled over with a dead body in his trunk. No way to talk himself out of that. He would have been arrested and would never see the outside of a cell again.

Even if something went down and he wanted to turn on the people he worked with, he'd be dead before anything went to trial. Of that he was sure. Not that he wanted to turn on anyone; he liked the money too much. He'd been eyeing a vacation home down in Walker's Cay. That wouldn't come cheap.

At least the body drop was done. The lake was deep

enough for their needs. One woman dead and now a new one to replace her. Had to keep that money train going. It was so fucking brilliant he couldn't stand it.

A bird squawked in the distance. He looked over his shoulder as the boat glided slowly. His heart rate kicked up at the unexpected noise. There weren't any ripples along the lake other than his boat. He could see to the other side easily. Thick foliage surrounded most of the lake except for one long stretch of sand where whoever owned this spread of land and the lake must have had it cleared off. It was where he docked his unregistered boat.

If the lake had been attached to a chain of lakes, he'd have registered the boat under a bogus name, but there was no point, since no one knew about this place and there wasn't a possibility of someone stumbling on it through an attached canal. The lake wasn't man-made, but just one of the many thousands of Florida lakes that dotted the state. The perfect dumping ground, though he had others. He liked to spread it out. Gators should get most of the women, if not all.

When he neared the dock, he felt a tingling sensation at the back of his neck. As if he was being watched. He'd been feeling that way more and more lately. Just nerves, that was all. Because if someone was watching him, he'd be in fucking prison by now.

He rolled his neck once, trying to ease the growing tension that always came when he dumped a body. It was only natural that the more he risked, the more nervous he'd be.

With a slightly trembling hand, he grasped the wooden dock and turned off the engine. Without the low hum of the engine, the only sounds were the birds and crickets chirping and a faint wind rustling the trees and overgrown grass.

He tugged at his gloves almost self-consciously. It wasn't cool enough to wear them this time of year, but he wasn't taking any chances. Before moving the body he and the doctor had cleaned it and wrapped it in plastic. He wasn't worried about his DNA being found anywhere, but just in case he was going to spray the boat down with bleach.

Moving quickly, he secured the rope to the metal latches on the dock, then jumped onto it. Other than the chains to weight down the body and a spray bottle of bleach, he hadn't brought anything else.

After a quick spray-down of the boat, he headed back down the dock to where he was parked. Feeling foolish, he nonetheless scanned the foliage along the lake once again, looking for any signs of life. He wore a hat and sunglasses and he was far enough away that if someone had been watching him they wouldn't be able to identify him. And hell, he'd be burning all his clothes as soon as he returned to their main base. No matter what, he disposed of everything when he dumped a body.

Still, he couldn't risk that someone had seen what he'd done. The body had been wrapped up, but if the cops got wind of it and decided to search the lake, they'd find more than one damn body. If he didn't know that this area was so damn deserted, he'd spread the dumps out more, but this was simple and he had a smaller chance of getting caught on this property, since he was so familiar with it.

Suddenly a flock of birds burst into the air from the bank, their flapping and squawking making him jerk back a step. Immediately he cursed his jumpiness.

He needed to just get the hell out of here. No one was here; no one had seen him. He'd been doing this for a while now and he had to stop letting his nerves get the best of him.

Even though he wanted something to take off the edge, he got in his truck and took off. He'd crack open a brew as soon as he got home. But first he had to see the doctor in person, let him know the job was done. He hadn't brought any electronics with him for this, never did. Maybe he'd check in on the new girl, Tessa. He hated that he wasn't allowed to touch the girls, but that didn't mean he couldn't mess with her. His boss didn't know, but he liked to fuck with the new girls' heads. Mentally torture them about what was to come. *Small pleasures*, he thought, his mood brightening as his vehicle rumbled down the road.

Amelia moaned in agony but pushed herself up off the dingy floor. Even in her hazy state, some part of her subconscious knew this was a dream, a memory—a freaking nightmare. But she was unable to drag herself out of it. It just replayed as it sometimes did, without warning.

Her fingers slipped in her own blood, but she managed to grab onto the peeling bathroom countertop and pull herself to her feet.

She couldn't stay here. Her mom worked at the diner, then had clients right after. She'd told Amelia she wouldn't be home. Thank God she didn't have to worry about her mom bringing men back here anymore. She just did them in their cars or pay-by-the-hour rooms. God knew there were enough crappy motels in the city.

Not that she cared about any of that right now. She knew what was happening and it was her fault. She'd never wanted this, never wanted a baby. For weeks she'd wished it would just go away. Now . . . she was terrified that was exactly what was happening. The baby was dying and it was all her fault. Guilt speared through her, as sharp as the agony in her stomach. She might not have wanted it, but she didn't want this.

Oh God, this was all her fault. She'd wished it and now it was happening.

She gritted her teeth, thankful that the pain started to abate. Not much, but enough that she could strip off her bloody clothes and call a neighbor for help. She couldn't call Benita. God no. Nathan's abuela was a devout Catholic, but not only that, she'd tell Nathan.

Even through the cramping pain, Amelia knew she would never tell him about this. Never, never, never. He was a year ahead of her and almost done with high school, would be joining the Corps soon. She didn't want him to know about this. Then she'd have to admit she'd wanted it gone, that she'd done this to something they'd created. He'd hate her if he knew the truth.

Naked and on shaky legs, she stumbled down the hallway to find the portable phone. Thank God her mom had a landline. She was too cheap to pay for a cell phone for Amelia, but at least she had a way to call someone.

Something sharp stabbed through her abdomen, and her vision went spotty for a moment, but she found the portable on the kitchen table. Collapsing into a chair, she forced her fingers to work, to make the call.

She hated calling Daniela, but she knew the older girl wouldn't tell anyone about this. She was kind of a slut but kept her mouth shut about everything. The second the slut thought entered her mind, shame filled Amelia. Who the hell was she to judge anyone?

"Hey, chica, what's—"

"I need help. Now," Amelia rasped out.

"Shit, what's wrong?"

"I need . . . a ride to the free health clinic. I'm bleeding and I can't drive. Don't call anyone."

"Shit," she repeated, one of her favorite words. "I'll be right there." Daniela hung up before Amelia could respond.

Which was just as well because she didn't have the energy. She knew Daniela would never call the cops even though Amelia had told her she was bleeding. No one in this neighborhood called them unless absolutely necessary.

Struggling, she pushed up again, grimaced at the blood on the damn chair. She was leaving a trail everywhere. She'd worry about cleaning it up later. First, she needed help. Desperately.

"Amelia." Nathan's voice was urgent.

Oh God, no. He couldn't see her like this. Couldn't know.

"Amelia, wake up."

Her eyes flew open to meet that familiar, worried espresso gaze. Her heart pounded wildly against her chest, and her breathing was erratic. It took a moment for her surroundings to register. She was in her home. The home she'd bought for herself. Not in that shit hole she'd lived in with her mom as a teenager.

Bits of light streamed in from her blinds, so she knew it was morning without looking at the clock. Not that she wanted to tear her gaze from Nathan's anyway. She swallowed. "I'm okay."

He was propped up on a bent elbow, looking down at her, his expression worried. "You were having a nightmare."

Her throat seized. Now would be a good time for her to be honest with him. Really perfect, actually. But . . . she was selfish. She just wanted a few more hours with him before she confessed everything. "Yeah." Why bother denying it?

"You want to talk about it?" He cupped her cheek, stroked her cheek with his thumb.

Closing her eyes, she leaned into his hold, wanting to savor every second of it. "Not really." At least not yet. Soon, though, she swore to herself. She should have told him years ago, but she'd been so broken then, so full of loathing and shame. She'd hated herself so deeply, hadn't been able to even look at herself in the mirror back then.

It was why she'd ended things with him so coldly, so abruptly. He'd been a reminder, and being around him had simply piled on the guilt. She'd known that if she told him the truth he would hate her, blame her. After all, she'd blamed herself; how could he not? God, it had taken her a long time to come to terms with the fact that what had happened wasn't actually her fault. Now she was just terrified that he'd hate her for not telling him the truth.

He shifted next to her and pulled her close so that she sprawled over his chest. She liked the feel of being completely naked against him. Sex was the last thing on her mind right now, but the skin-to-skin contact grounded her.

When she went to throw her leg across him, cuddling closer, she realized she'd be feeling the effects of their sex for the rest of the day. "Am I the only one who's sore?" she murmured. Damn it, she wasn't ready to come clean yet, knew the moment she did this intimacy would be shattered. She simply couldn't do that yet.

His breath was warm against the top of her head as he wrapped his arm tighter around her. "I was rough last night."

She hummed in contentment. "And early this morning."

His chest rumbled with light laughter as one of his hands slid down to graze her butt. He stroked over it before cupping her. He didn't make a move for anything more, though, as if he understood she didn't want anything else right now. "I can't get enough of you."

"It's weird to be here with you after so long." They hadn't talked last night or this morning. Not real talking anyway. Just lots and lots of sex. Making up for lost time. At least that was how it had felt to her.

"I know. I thought about looking you up a few months ago."

She stiffened slightly. "Yeah?"

"Yeah. I was in an . . . accident, about three months back. I probably shouldn't admit this, but you were the first person I thought of."

She hated the thought of him being injured. At least he was okay now. "You didn't look me up, though." He'd seemed so damn surprised to see her at the auction and he'd flat-out told her he hadn't known she'd changed her last name. If he'd looked her up, he'd have known all that before.

"No. I started to but kept coming up with one excuse after another not to really follow through."

Her skin turned clammy. This conversation could take a disturbing turn very quickly. Being real with each other and opening up meant she walked a fine line with him until she came clean about why she'd ended things—because she knew he'd point-blank ask her soon enough. She figured he'd held off because he hadn't wanted to stress her out before her date with Mercado. "Why did your mother and grandmother stop talking? You never told me," she said, needing to stall.

He shrugged underneath her. "It wasn't one thing, but a lifetime of arguing for those two. My mom hated being poor—not that anyone actually likes it—and didn't understand why my *abuela* wouldn't move away from her neighborhood. My *abuela*, on the other hand, didn't understand my mom's desperate need to put distance between her and the people she'd grown up with. She thought my mom was denying her roots even when she wasn't. She just . . . wanted more from life, wanted me to have more than she had." He let out a short, harsh laugh. "It's why she gave me such an American name. It was a fucking mess with those two, always arguing and picking at one another. Finally my mom just lost it one day, said I could keep seeing my *abuela*, but she was cutting the toxicity out of her life."

"I'm sorry." Guilt pricked at Amelia for asking. He probably didn't want to talk about that any more than she wanted to talk about her nightmare. They'd been together for over a year when they were teenagers, but she'd never pressed him. Back then they'd just been so wrapped up in each other—and she'd been full of hormones. Now she still apparently had those crazy hormones, but she was a lot more curious about his family.

"It's okay. They never pulled me into it. I hated it, but . . ." He shrugged again and rolled Amelia until she was under him.

She slid her arms up his chest before linking her fingers behind his neck. His erection pressed insistently against her abdomen as he looked down at her. "Why'd you change your last name?"

"Mainly to sever ties with her." She didn't need to spell out who for him. "But I wanted something that was mine. Choosing gave me a sort of power."

His lips quirked up at the corners, his eyes going all heavy-lidded again. Just like that, a wave of heat swept through her. "I like it."

She'd like the sound of Amelia Ortiz a lot more. As soon as the thought entered her mind, she was grateful he couldn't read it. That was the last thing she should be thinking of and it embarrassed her that she'd even thought it. This thing with them was . . . well, she didn't know what it was. It was more than casual, at least for her, but she couldn't and wouldn't expect more from him.

"Are you on the pill?" he asked suddenly, the question taking her off guard.

"No." There hadn't been a need in a long time.

"Get on it."

She blinked in surprise at the heated statement—the way he basically ordered her. It should annoy her, and it sort of did, but that demanding voice still made heat bloom inside her. Who was she kidding? Nathan on top of her was the main reason for the ridiculous heat wave taking over her entire body. "You're very bossy."

"Yep." He nipped her bottom lip with his teeth as he rolled his hips against her.

She let her eyes drift closed again as their tongues started to tangle. The demand for her to go on the pill implied that he wanted more than just right now. At that thought, the fears she'd barely been keeping at bay flared to the surface again, clawing, clawing, clawing. She couldn't be a coward anymore.

She had to tell him. She pulled her head back. "Nathan—"

His phone buzzed across her dresser, making her jump as he simply sighed and cursed under his breath. He grabbed it, his jaw tight as he swiped in his code. His expression grew even darker when he looked at the message. "I hate to do this, but I've gotta go." He was already moving off her as he said it.

Relief slid through her that she'd been given just a little reprieve from full honesty. "You want me to fix you something to eat?" She doubted he had time, but she could whip something up for him. The chef side of her hated to send him off without food.

Blinking, he looked at her, as if truly surprised. "I don't have time, but thanks." He sounded grateful too, which was kind of odd.

"Has no woman ever cooked for you?" She inwardly winced. Why the heck had she asked him that when she so totally didn't want to know? He'd told her that he wasn't seeing anyone, and that was enough for her.

Liar, liar, her inner voice shouted. She wanted to know everything about this man, but she was too damn chicken to ask him. Because the more she learned, the more she got tangled in his web—and the harder it would be if things went south with them. And sweet Lord, how could things ever work out with them? He was going to be angry that she'd basically lied to him. That nasty, self-conscious inner voice that told her she'd never be good enough for someone like Nathan reared its ugly head. She squashed it.

"No. Well, except you and my *abuela.*" His expression turned nostalgic as he tugged on his shirt. "Will you cook for me again sometime? It's been a long time." The question surprised her as much as the serious note to his voice.

Without hesitation, she nodded. "You know I will." A smile teased her lips. "I'm so thankful to Benita for all those lessons she gave me." They had literally changed her life. She'd found something she loved, something she could do well, thanks to a sweet neighbor who hadn't needed to look after a lost, mixed-up teenage girl.

"She'd be happy with all you've accomplished." He slid his boots on now, completely dressed, including a shoulder holster with two guns in it.

She shouldn't find the sight so sexy. Just as quickly as heat bloomed inside her, a pang slid through her chest. She understood that he had to go, but that didn't make it any easier. Especially after last night. She'd hoped they'd have more time together this morning. "I'll walk you down." She slipped on the thin cotton robe draped on her chaise, smiling as he watched her with all the subtlety of a hungry lion. He looked as if he was about to pounce. "Don't look at me like that," she murmured.

"Can't help it." His words were raspy, unsteady.

At least he sounded as affected as she was. "Will I see you tonight?"

"I don't know. I don't. Hell, I don't even know when I'll be able to contact you." He scrubbed a hand over his face as they left her room.

"Something bad's happened?"

"Yeah."

"I'm sorry about whatever it is. I know you can't tell me, but is it about Mercado?"

He lifted a shoulder. "Maybe, maybe not. Don't know enough at this point."

"If he calls me what should I say?" she asked as they reached the bottom of the stairs.

"Call me, Elliott, or Cade. I don't know what the status with him is right now, but I don't want you meeting with Mercado alone. Promise me." His expression was hard as they faced each other in her foyer.

"Okay, I promise." During one of their lulls in sex last night, Nathan had told her that Elliott hadn't gotten past all the encryption of Mercado's system. He was pretty sure he could, but she might have to get inside his house again. Not something she was looking forward to, but if it helped find Danita and all those other missing women, she'd do it. "Hey, how are you even going to leave? Do you need my car?" she asked as she typed the code into the wall panel to disarm her security system.

"No. Cade's picking me up now, gave me the all-clear

in his text. Mercado's not watching your house." He glanced out one of the small stained-glass windows next to her front door. "I see an SUV pulling down the street. Listen, I'll call as soon as—"

"It's fine. Seriously. And . . . I know you have a dangerous job." She wasn't even sure what she was trying to say, knew it would be impossible to completely convey her worry for him. "Be careful today," she whispered. She hated that she knew so little about what he did, that he could be running right into danger this morning and she'd have no idea.

"You too." He gave her a fierce, knee-weakening kiss. But he was out the door before she could think, let alone draw in a full breath.

The knowledge that he could have been injured or killed over the years, especially with the career path he'd taken, gave her chills as she locked the door behind him. If he'd died, she wouldn't have known about it. Not unless it ended up on the news. The thought of a world without Nathan in it was almost too much to bear. She shoved away from the door and for once she couldn't compartmentalize her emotions.

Nathan had slammed right back into her tidy world like a tornado, and now . . . she couldn't imagine him not in it. No matter what, as soon as she saw him next, she was coming clean about everything. If he hated her afterward, well, it would likely destroy her, but she had to do it.

Chapter 11

PADI: stands for the Professional Association of Diving Instructors. It is the world's largest recreational diving membership and diver training organization.

"How are the locals handling our involvement?" Nathan asked Cade as he steered down the long dirt road. After Cade had picked him up from Amelia's, they left straight to this meeting point. He didn't know much about where they were headed other than it was a private lake with a lot of surrounding property. Karen or Elliott was trying to locate the owner, but Nathan wasn't sure what the status was on that end.

"Burkhart didn't say." Cade's expression was grim.

Not that Nathan blamed him. All he knew was that a body had been found, a local detective called, and then they'd been called in by Burkhart. And there was no way they'd have gotten a call unless this was related to their case. Especially since Burkhart had told them to bring their dive gear. Like many police departments that had divers trained for search-and-recovery diving or rescue ops, the NSA also had trained divers who carried out the same duties. Both Cade and he were trained because of Burkhart programs. Wasn't a stretch to figure out what Burkhart wanted them to do here.

As the road curved to the left, flashing blue lights came into view. Three black-and-whites with the lights on and five unmarked SUVs were parked near a row of oak trees. Oh yeah, Burkhart had brought in a full team for this. A spread of land was cleared, as if someone had planned to build a home, but the only man-made structure was a wooden dock on a decent-sized lake. There wasn't much of a beach, just a strip of sand, but from what he could see it looked mostly like overgrown weeds and grass dominating the exterior of the lake.

Nathan already had his door open by the time Cade pulled to a stop next to the line of SUVs. He did a quick scan of everyone. Three uniformed officers, Captain Nieto, Detective Sinclair, a couple of plainclothes men, Burkhart, and ten NSA agents, all of whom he recognized on sight. Field-trained, no analysts in the bunch. He also spotted two young boys wearing swim trunks and long-sleeved rash guards. They were barely teenagers. A soccer-mom type of woman probably in her forties stood behind them, her arms crossed over her chest. Her expression was a mix of fear and irritation.

After he rounded the SUV he fell in step with Cade and headed straight for Dax and the rest of their group. "What's up?" he asked quietly as they reached Dax.

"Local kids like to fish here sometimes. They're not supposed to because it's a privately owned lake, but they're freaking kids. Guess they saw some guy dump something they thought looked like a body. When their mom heard them talking, she called the cops. Sinclair"—Dax nodded in the man's direction, and Nathan recognized him from the file they had on the guy—"was the detective who got the case. We got lucky that he was the one called or we might not have heard about it. One of his guys found a body. Twenty-something female. Thanks to those kids they had a pretty good location of where she'd been dumped."

"Is it one of the missing women?" Because why the hell would they have been called in otherwise?

"Yeah. That's what I meant by lucky. He recognized her face—which thankfully isn't badly decomposed yet—and called his boss. Nieto called Burkhart immediately."

"They scan her fingerprints yet?" Nathan asked.

Dax nodded. "Yep. She's from our list. Taken about eleven months ago, and from what the local ME says, she died recently."

So she was kept alive for eleven months. He wanted to know the cause of death. "Who's taking the body?"

"That's what we're waiting on. Burkhart wants it and Captain Nieto isn't happy."

"We've got better resources." That being an understatement. They had a private lab without the type of backlog the Miami PD would no doubt have. They could learn more about the body in less time compared to the locals. A win-win for everyone. They were in a time crunch here, but Nathan knew bullshit agency politics could hamper any investigation. He just hoped that didn't happen now. There were too many women missing, too many innocent lives at stake. Amelia was in the age range of the women who'd been taken. Something that was hard to forget.

"No shit," Cade muttered next to him.

Burkhart glanced over at them, nodded once. Nathan wasn't sure who he was motioning to but broke away along with Cade and Dax, crossing the twenty yards to where the local cops, Burkhart, and the kids were. As they neared, one of the uniformed officers ushered the two boys and woman away toward a minivan.

"Dax give you the rundown?" Burkhart asked. Instead of a suit he wore cargo pants and a dark green Polo shirt today. His weapon was strapped to his hip and visible. He looked like an operator.

"Most of it," Dax answered before Nathan could. "Didn't get to the part about doing the grid search."

Oh hell. That meant they'd be searching the lake for bodies. These women deserved closure, but searching and recovering the dead was one of the shittiest parts of his job.

"You three have the most experience with search and recovery and the best training," Burkhart said to them. He glanced over as Nieto approached. The man was about the same age as Burkhart and in good shape. Burkhart nodded once at the police captain. "Captain Nieto has three men trained for diving. Combined with our ten—thirteen including you three— we've got a solid group. You guys will each head a four-man team. Nathan, you'll have five. We're going to work this lake in a grid." He nodded once more at Nieto, who picked up where Burkhart left off.

"We've got a nineteen-foot patrol boat on the way, should be here in the next few minutes. Small vessel, good for this kind of operation."

"And we've got three more Zodiacs on the way," Burkhart interjected. "Nineteen-foot as well."

Nathan simply nodded. Those were the perfect-sized vessels for evidence-recovery missions in a location like this. They were easily transported and could be deployed almost anywhere.

"My three guys are all trained in evidence recovery and are all PADI dive master–certified. All we want is to find . . . if there are more bodies. We're willing to help, so use us." Nieto's expression flashed with anger as he glanced over at the still lake.

Good, Nathan couldn't work with novices on something like this. Everyone needed to be able to do the job and keep up. "Let's break up into teams, then," Nathan said. "Do we have a map of the lake?"

When Burkhart nodded, Nathan felt a small measure of relief. He also needed to find out what kind of wildlife they could expect, though he figured gators and potentially water moccasins would be on that list. Some days he hated his job.

Hours later, Nathan pulled his regulator from his mouth and tugged his face mask up before climbing over the edge of the inflatable boat. The sun was about to set, and even though a team had put up floodlights along the shoreline an hour ago, it was time to head back in. They were already working in murky conditions; it'd be pointless and, more to the point, dangerous, to continue now.

"I'm calling it a day," Nathan said to the three guys in the boat. Detective Sinclair was climbing in after him, his expression as grim as everyone else's.

Sinclair simply nodded, slightly breathless as he took off his own face gear. The driver wordlessly headed back to shore where two other boats were already waiting.

"You know how many remains yet?" Sinclair asked. They'd been so busy diving and marking off spots as clear or not, none of them knew except Nathan.

He'd radioed Burkhart for the official count an hour ago and got thirty-five. *Thirty-five* dead women.

Murdered women.

Someone was going to fucking pay. He shoved his rage back, locked it up tight. Now wasn't about that. "Thirty-five," he said quietly.

One of the men cursed, but the others were silent. Today had been long and depressing and he was thankful for the silence. There were color-coded little flags floating all over the lake, weighted down near where bodies had been found or marking areas as clear. Some of the bodies still hadn't been recovered, but they'd be brought up tomorrow.

All he wanted to do was go see Amelia. Just get in a vehicle and drive straight to her place. Hell, he didn't even know if she'd be at work or home, but he needed to see her. To hold her.

Once they reached land, they waded to the shore. There was a team of guys waiting to take care of the boat for them. Nathan was running on fumes and wasn't going to argue. Let someone else take care of it.

"The media need to know about this, get the word

out," Sinclair said quietly as they trudged up the sandbank.

The low hum of voices, rumbling engines of the boats, and some vehicles and crickets in the nearby woods created a cacophony of noise. More locals and more of Burkhart's guys had been brought in over the course of the day. The dive teams had remained the same, but they'd needed others to help organize the remains. And even though he'd hated to stop working for even a few minutes, they'd all needed to eat to keep their energy up. Two men were in the process of breaking down some of the food tables. Right now Nathan wanted to get the hell out of here, but he wasn't done tonight. Not by a long shot.

He just lifted a shoulder. "Not up to me." He didn't have the authority to make those decisions, something the detective knew. Neither did Sinclair. The only thing Nathan really knew about the guy was that he was friendly enough with Amelia, had a solid record with the police department, and was now aware that Burkhart and his team weren't actually with the FBI. It had been pretty damn impossible to hide the fact with Burkhart on-site.

Sinclair muttered something under his breath about bullshit politics before stalking off in another direction.

Nathan wasn't sure if the guy would actually leak anything to the media—and expose his lie about being FBI to Amelia—so he did a quick search for Burkhart. When he saw him standing next to a foldout table with mostly empty food platters, he headed that way.

Talking on his cell phone, Burkhart nodded once as

Nathan approached. It took another twenty seconds before he ended his phone call.

"You guys did good today," Nathan's boss said quietly, moving away from the table as two officers started clearing it off. "We covered a lot of ground."

Nothing about today felt particularly good. "I wish we could keep going."

"You need rest. All of you."

"What's the media situation?" Nathan asked, jumping right into it.

"Nothing yet, but we'll start leaking information soon. I want more positive IDs first."

Even their private lab wasn't big enough for all the remains they'd found. Well, the lab was, but they didn't have enough staff on-site. "What are we doing about jurisdiction of the bodies and the case?"

"The locals are going to get all the credit and we'll let the media know that the Miami PD is working in conjunction with a federal task force. We won't get specific about which agency. And we're going to take half the remains as of now for ID purposes. The locals will take the other half. Nieto's received the authority to set up a special team for this. There won't be a backlog for his guys or ours. And we've already got a head start with the names."

Which would make it easier to identify the women if they were indeed the missing ones from their list. Nathan's gut said they were. "Does Nieto trust his guys not to leak anything until we're ready?"

Burkhart gave one sharp nod. "Yes."

"What about the first body? Any news from the lab?" They had an ID, but they needed more than that.

If they got the right piece of evidence, it could help them pinpoint where the women were being kept. Or at least where the deceased woman had been kept and the cause of death. From there it would be about following down more leads.

"Nothing yet."

Nathan had started to respond when Cade and Dax strode up, both wearing neoprene suits and dive shoes identical to his own.

"What's the 411?" Cade asked, crossing his arms over his chest.

"You three go get some rest. You two start at the crack of dawn tomorrow," he said to Cade and Dax. "Nathan, your alias has a meeting with a potential suspect midmorning. I've sent a file to your encrypted account. Get some damn sleep and coordinate with Elliott in the morning. It's just a meet-and-greet, so you'll be going in alone."

He nodded once. Mercado wasn't their only suspect, so Nathan would be working every angle he could to eliminate or take down their suspects. He wanted to be back at the lake, though, searching for more bodies. He felt almost compelled to do so, hated the thought of those bones wrapped up at the bottom of the lake. Some had been scattered, obviously by gators.

But that wasn't his call and he knew he'd be more use in the field trying to find out who was behind this. The remains weren't going anywhere and if he could help the women still alive, he would do everything in his power.

"I'm going to stop by the lab on the way home," Nathan said. Though he had no intention of going to his NSA-owned condo, Miguel's home base for the duration of the operation in Miami. He'd be heading straight to Amelia's after the lab. He needed to see her, especially after today. But he wasn't ready to go there just yet. He was too edgy. And knowing that she was keeping something from him about why things had gone south so many years ago wouldn't make him the best company until he got his shit together.

"I'll go with you," Cade said, pretty much at the same time Dax murmured the same sentiment.

He shook his head. "Not necessary. Go home to your ladies. Is there an extra vehicle I can use?" he asked Burkhart, not wanting to get into a conversation about his teammates coming. Normally he'd welcome the company, but he needed to regroup.

Once he got an extra set of keys to an SUV, he grabbed his duffel bag from Cade's vehicle and changed into dry clothes. In the half hour it took to drive to the lab, he kept the radio off, not wanting to listen to anything. Nathan had contemplated calling or texting Amelia, but he felt as if he were walking a tightrope right now.

He knew himself well enough that he'd be a dick to her right now. He needed to lash out at someone, and he wouldn't let her become an easy target. She didn't deserve that.

At the security gate of the nondescript building on the outskirts of downtown, he showed his badge and did a retinal and palm scan. He'd have to do it again a couple more times before being allowed into the actual lab. Which meant another twenty freaking minutes.

He'd thought the downtime would help him to regroup, but all he could think about was finding that first tarp-wrapped body. Bones, at this point. At the bottom of a cold, dark lake. He'd seen humanity at its worst before. Nothing should surprise him anymore. And really, someone using women, killing them, and then disposing of them didn't surprise him, because he knew what kind of evil was out there.

But it did piss him off. The way humans so often hurt each other for superficial gain was a horrifying mystery to him.

It was one of the reasons he'd joined the NSA when Burkhart recruited him. Did he always agree with the methods the agency took? No. But he knew without a doubt they were doing a lot more good than harm.

By the time he placed his hand on the final biometric scanner outside the lab doors, about half of his pent-up energy had started to fade.

The doors opened with a quiet whoosh of air. One lab tech was at a computer and another stood next to Dr. Tai Nguyen at a table where the body of Ester Pajari was stretched out.

A pale blue sheet was pulled up over the lower half of her body as Dr. Nguyen and the tech spoke in quiet tones.

"Give me one moment, Agent Ortiz," Nguyen said without looking over at him. Her long black hair was pulled back in a coil at the nape of her neck, as usual.

He remained where he was, not wanting to get in her way. Moments later she strode toward him, her white lab coat buttoned up. In the lab she rarely wore heels, and today—or tonight—was no different. In flats, she was about five feet one. She should have appeared fragile, but she had a commanding presence.

"You have good timing. I was just about to call Burkhart." Her expression was unreadable. No surprise, since she rarely showed emotion while working.

"How bad is it?"

"Not . . . what I expected." She pulled her cell phone out of her pocket and dialed before holding it between them. She pressed the speaker button.

Burkhart answered after two rings. "Tell me you've got something, Tai."

"I'm with Agent Ortiz and have news." She didn't wait for him to respond, just jumped in as she always did. "The victim recently gave birth and, in simple terms, when she died, her body was in excellent condition. She'd been taking prenatal pills and getting the recommended amount of exercise. At least her body's health would indicate so."

Something started to buzz inside Nathan. "What about abuse or trauma?"

"None at all. No signs of sexual or physical abuse. Also no drug use. She was in perfect health."

"How did she die?" Burkhart asked.

"Poison. It would have been a painless death, but definitely poison."

"Any idea where she was being held?" It was a long shot, but Nathan had to ask. And he wanted to know what had happened to the baby, but the doctor wouldn't know that. Fuck, he really hated this case.

She shook her head. "The tarp she was wrapped in is common, can be bought at any local hardware store. And her body was cleaned by a pro. There's no one else's DNA on her or the tarp. There also isn't any on the weights that were holding her underwater.

Whoever dumped her took serious precautions to cover their tracks."

Various thoughts filtered through Nathan's mind, but the first one that popped up was black market babies. "She wasn't being abused. There was no drug use. She was kept alive for eleven months since being held, and she recently gave birth."

"Fuck." Burkhart's voice was savage.

His thoughts exactly. "Black market babies are big money, but I've never heard of someone kidnapping women and holding them in a large-scale capacity for this purpose. Usually they just kidnap babies." Not that they knew that the other women they'd found would have similarities to Ester Pajari. But it was in the realm of possibility and one they had to consider.

"I'm sending more remains your way right now, Tai. Call in whoever you want for backup. I need to know if the rest of the women suffered similar fates. Some of the remains will be sent to the Miami PD's lab. I'll put you in contact with their ME so you can coordinate and compare findings."

As Tai and Burkhart talked, Nathan scrubbed a hand over his face. Black market babies were a nightmare. Kidnapping women, impregnating them—via rape or insemination—then killing them and selling off their babies.

"I want to set up a meet with Alexander Lopez," Nathan said before Tai could hang up with Burkhart. Lopez was a Miami weapons dealer who'd worked with various NSA agents—though he didn't know they were agents. He was a criminal, no doubt, but he had a sort of moral code that made it difficult to dislike the guy. If there was a baby market operation going on in Miami and he knew about it, he wouldn't like it. When something offended Lopez's moral compass, he had no problem passing on the information.

There was a moment of silence. "I'll have Selene set up the meeting. She'll get a meet faster, since they have a relationship."

"I—"

"You'll go with her. Now go get some rack time. There's nothing else you can do tonight and I need you sharp for that meet tomorrow."

"Okay." He didn't plan to get any sleep, though. He was headed straight to Amelia's after this. Nathan wasn't sure if Burkhart would approve, which was why he wasn't asking.

He didn't care what his boss said. Not after a day like today.

He needed to see Amelia. Part of him wanted to hash things out with her, but mainly he just wanted to hold her.

Chapter 12

Rack time: common term used by military personnel, refers to sleeping.

Wesley steered into the driveway of the average-looking two-story home in a quiet Coral Gables neighborhood. Hanging flowerpots were along the porch, and two oversize ones were on either side of the front door.

Lights immediately illuminated the driveway and the porch. Either Matias had sensors or he'd heard him. Probably both. Wesley hated coming by with only pieces of information, but Matias was the one who'd turned them onto this case. It wasn't as if the former spy would tell anyone, so that wasn't an issue. Wesley just hated bringing his old friend shitty news.

When he got out of his SUV, the driveway lights flicked off. Just as quickly, so did the front porch ones. The door opened before he'd made it halfway up the walkway.

Matias, wearing long plaid lounge pants and a blue T-shirt, stood to the side, holding the front door open for him. "Is she dead?" he asked, his voice tight as Wesley stepped into his house.

"Not that I know of." The door shut behind him with a snick.

Matias's expression didn't change as he crossed his arms over his chest. "Should I offer you coffee, or is it not that kind of visit?"

"I could go for some coffee." He didn't need it, but he could tell his friend was wound too tight.

Matias tilted his head to the left, indicating he should follow him down a short hallway. "You look exhausted."

"Been a long day." That was an understatement. There was no way they could keep this from the media much longer. Too many people had been on-site, and while Nieto might trust his guys, there was no way he could control them all. Wesley didn't want to keep it from the media anyway. If he could use them, he would. Right now the media could be a benefit in getting names and pictures out to the public. The women taken hadn't had roots, but they'd have had some ties or daily habits. Maybe someone would remember something. At this point they'd take any lead they could get.

"Hope you don't mind instant." Matias got to work, prepping mugs for both of them as Wesley sat at the center island.

"Don't mind at all. I know I don't need to tell you that what I'm about to say is confidential, but I'm doing it anyway. This conversation is off the record."

Matias just grunted as if to say, "No shit."

"I can't give you all the details, but this morning we

got a call about a potential body dump. The body is one of the missing girls."

Matias paused for just a moment before putting the mugs in his microwave, but didn't comment.

Wesley continued. "We've still got too many angles to cover, but it's been confirmed that the woman wasn't abused sexually or physically, had been taking prenatal vitamins, and had recently given birth. Cause of death was poisoning."

"Can you tell me if she's from the list I gave you?"

He nodded. "Yeah, Ester Panjari."

Matias's expression turned grimmer, if that was possible. "What else are you holding back?"

"After the initial find, we've since discovered thirty-five more remains. We're not done searching in that area, so there could be more." He couldn't tell him where it was, but he could give Matias this much. It was possible the location could leak to the media, but they were going to keep as much information quiet as they could.

"So you don't know that she's not there?"

"No, but my gut says she's not." She hadn't been gone nearly long enough.

The microwave beeped, but they both ignored it. "The woman you pulled up, she'd been on prenatal vitamins?"

Wesley nodded.

Matias sighed. "When will you know more about the rest of the women?"

"It'll be a tedious process, but I've got a team and so does the Miami PD, working around the clock. They can tell a lot from bones. If there are any similarities between

Panjari and the others, we'll know soon enough." Wesley loathed the idea that these women had been taken for any reason, but his gut told him they were close to finding out why. Ortiz had been on the right track, thinking about black market babies. It could be big money if organized. But Wesley wasn't jumping to any conclusions until he had more information.

Matias started to speak when Wesley's phone buzzed in his pocket.

No IDs, blood, or DNA work yet, but it's clear that at least 3 victims have given birth. Dr. Nguyen's text was short and to the point.

And the news was exactly what he'd feared.

As he knocked on Amelia's front door, Nathan knew he should have called or at least texted her before just showing up. He'd already been in contact with one of the team members who was watching Mercado's place. The guy was currently at his home, and it didn't appear that Mercado had anyone watching Amelia. Nathan had still parked in another neighborhood and walked here, but nothing seemed out of the ordinary.

He desperately needed to see her. He wanted to hold her in his arms tonight and simply not think about anything else. Sure, he still had a shitload of questions for her, but he didn't want to talk, didn't want to think about what he'd seen today. Not that he could tell her anything anyway.

Relief slid through him at the beeping sound of her alarm being deactivated. When she opened the door he was surprised to see her wide-awake and wearing an apron over jeans and a T-shirt.

She smiled warmly, her expression immediately shifting to concern as she tugged him inside the foyer, shutting the door behind him. "What's wrong?" she murmured, her soft hand cupping his cheek.

He should hate that she read him so well, but he was grateful she did. Closing his eyes, he leaned into her hold for just a moment. Getting lost in her would be so easy.

"Nathan?" Her other hand landed on his waist as she pressed herself against him.

He opened his eyes, looked down into her bright blue ones. The concern there brought up too many damn emotions. And he didn't want to fucking talk. He just wanted to get rid of the anger buzzing through him. After all he'd seen in the world, it still killed him how people treated each other. "Can't talk about it," he rasped out.

Without thought, he backed her up against the front door. What they'd shared last night—how had it only been last night?—was so fresh and raw in his mind. He wanted that again, the release and the connection. He needed her as he needed air. He wanted to taste her, devour her—

Amelia held a firm hand against his chest. "Whatever you're thinking, we're not doing that now."

He frowned, the lust humming through him wild and demanding. "Why not?"

Ducking out from under his hold, she moved quickly down the hall. He watched the sweet sway of her ass, mesmerized for a moment before his legs listened to his brain. But first, he set her alarm before following her. He simply couldn't take chances with her safety.

When he stepped into the kitchen, she was already at the island, laying out soft tortillas onto a plate. A spicy aroma filled the air, probably from the small pan simmering on the stove top.

"Sit," she ordered without looking at him. "And what do you want to drink? I bought beer earlier in case you came by."

"Thanks. I'll get it," he said, moving to the stainless steel refrigerator. "You always cook this late?" He slid onto a chair across the island from her.

She looked up at him and cocked an eyebrow. "No. This is for you, though I didn't expect you this late. I'd planned to put it in the fridge or freeze it." Before he could respond, she continued. "Is your phone not working?"

He blinked in surprise at the question. She hadn't contacted him, so why was . . . It took all of a second for him to realize she was calling him out for not getting in touch. "Yeah. It's been a long day. I should have called on my way here, though. I'm sorry."

"It's okay. It must be hard not being able to talk about your work." Her voice was filled with such compassion as she dipped the tortillas into the simmering pan, one by one.

"It sucks." He'd never thought about it until now. Before, there had never been anyone to share with anyway. He'd always been able to blow off steam about shit with his teammates. But a woman? He'd never even been with anyone long enough to call it a relationship.

"You want to hear about my day, then?" she asked.

"Yes." God, did he ever. He took a sip of his beer, savored the crisp taste as he listened to her talk and watched her move around the kitchen effortlessly. She was very much at home here.

He realized that she could have had someone she worked for cook something for him. She could have brought it home and he'd have never known. Instead she was making something for him with her own hands. Maybe it shouldn't touch him so much, but the sweetness of the act did.

In another pan she was browning beef and adding all sorts of spices, including something that looked like a green chili sauce. His mouth watered at the scents. When she started pulling out the tortillas and piling them with meat and cheese before rolling them tightly, he realized she was making enchiladas. One of his favorites. She remembered.

"You need any help?" he asked when there was a lull in their conversation.

She laughed lightly. "No. You evidently haven't looked in the mirror, because you look as if a harsh wind could knock you over. Sit and let me do this for you."

Her words warmed him inside. "Is it weird that I think it's hot when you boss me around?"

Her gaze snapped up to his, her blue eyes darkening with unmistakable hunger. He was hungry too and not for food. This whole domestic scene should throw him off balance, but he liked being here with Amelia, in the quiet of her kitchen.

"I can take bossing you around to a whole other level if you'd like," she murmured as she rolled the tortillas tightly. She did so with practiced moves, laying them seam down in a greased glass pan.

Heat flared inside him at the unexpected, sexy

statement. "Yeah?" He'd never given up control in the bedroom before. The thought of doing so was a little intriguing. But only with her. Maybe not even then.

"Oh yeah." Her voice was full-on sex kitten now. His cock ached at the sound. "Mow my lawn, Nathan," she purred in a seductive voice. "Vacuum my floors, dust my house. Make everything shine. Faster, harder, you missed a spot." Her mouth pulled up into a wide, mischievous grin as she sprinkled cheese and sauce over the top of the tortillas. "Is that the kind of bossiness you were thinking about?" she asked as she slid the pan into the oven.

To his surprise a laugh erupted from his chest. It loosened something inside him, something he hadn't even realized was trapped. After the day he'd had, coming to see Amelia had been the best decision.

He still wanted to know what the hell had gone wrong between them, but sitting here with her felt so damn right it scared him. She had the power to rip him apart. He should just walk away, but he was already in too deep and like an addict, he couldn't seem to get enough of her.

"Or I could just order you to strip naked so I can have my wicked way with you." There was no humor in her voice as she washed her hands. When she was done she took off her apron, dropped it to the counter, and rounded the island. He couldn't take his eyes off her.

His dick was at full alert as he watched her move. Everything about her was sensual and seductive. She'd pulled her dark hair back into a ponytail. He wanted to tug it free, shove his hands through her hair as he claimed her mouth.

He briefly entertained the idea of letting her take control, but ... When she was in arm's reach, he grabbed her hips and lifted her up onto the countertop.

She let out a squeak of surprise, her hands splaying over his shoulders even as her legs automatically fell open for him. He stepped between them.

"Take off your top," he commanded in a low voice, wanting to see more of her. He practically vibrated with the need, had to restrain himself from stripping her and taking her. She deserved foreplay.

"You first." Her words were a whisper, and if she'd intended them to come out as an order, she'd failed.

Wordlessly he peeled his shirt off. By the time he was tossing it to the side, she'd pulled hers over her head. Her bra was simple black lace with a tiny pink heart in the middle. The perfect swell of her breasts spilling out of the cups was enough to make him forget the ability to speak for a moment.

It didn't matter that he'd seen her naked countless times years ago or again last night, that he'd tasted every inch of her; he needed her again. Desperately.

Even though he'd ordered himself to give her foreplay, to go down on her until she came against his tongue again, he crushed his mouth to hers, demanding everything from her.

The sweet way she moaned against his lips and the way her legs wrapped around his waist, pulling him tighter, undid him. He could feel her hunger was as strong as his own. That was what killed him. The attraction between them was incendiary, yet somehow twelve years ago she'd walked away from him as if he meant nothing.

The thought made something dark inside him surface. He shoved it down. He'd get his fucking answer, but now he needed to be inside her.

Her greedy hands swept over his chest, stroking softly until she reached the button of his pants. Though he wanted to let her free his erection, to feel her fingers wrap around his cock, he grasped her by the wrists.

She made a protesting sound as he held her wrists behind her back. He tugged them once, groaned when she arched her back. Her breasts pushed up like an offering.

He dipped his head, zeroing in on one of her breasts. Through the material of her bra, he sucked on her nipple, hard.

"Nathan," she moaned, her voice a mix of frustration and need. She squirmed against the counter.

Good, he wanted her hot and begging for more.

He gently bit down on her taut nipple, and her legs tightened around him. Wanting nothing between them, he freed her bra, pulled it away from her body. "Hold on to the counter." Another order, one he was glad she listened to.

There was something insanely hot about caressing her while she wasn't touching him with her hands.

He continued flicking his tongue over her nipples, alternating between her breasts, only pulling back when her breathing increased too much. She made a whimpering sound as he pulled away again, releasing her hands.

This time she slid her fingers through his hair and held his head tight before tugging him back to look at her. "Stop teasing."

He was vaguely aware of a timer going off. *Shit, the food.* But she shook her head. "It automatically shuts off after the timer goes off. Now stop teasing me."

He cupped her breasts, holding them gently in his hands. Slowly and with his gaze pinned to hers, he began teasing her tight nipples by just grazing his thumbs over them. Stimulating her, but not enough. Her lips parted, her breathing increased, and he could see the tiny pulse point on her neck going crazy.

His dick ached with need, but he held himself back. Barely. Keeping his clothes on was the only way he was holding on to what little restraint he had.

She rolled her hips against him. "Payback will suck," she rasped out.

His hips jerked again. Taking mercy on her—and himself—he skimmed his hands down her waist, stopping at the button of her jeans. "Lift up."

She let out a shudder of definite relief as he made quick work of her jeans. The sight of the tiny lacy triangle covering the small thatch of hair on her mound tore another groan from him. "You wear this for me?"

She smoothed her hands over his biceps, squeezed once. "I was hopeful you'd come by."

In his haste he practically ripped them off, but she didn't seem to care. Feeling frenzied, he tugged her off the counter. She wrapped her legs around his waist, but he tightened his fingers on her hips.

She must have read on his face what he wanted, because she just grinned in that wicked way of hers and let her legs drop. Her feet had barely touched the floor before he turned her around to face away from him, pinned her against the granite countertop. Her dark hair fell over her back in a silky waterfall. "Are we going to christen every room in this house?"

He couldn't answer. His balls were pulled up too tight as he finished stripping and ripped open a condom. Though he wanted to feel her delicate fingers sliding it on, he rolled it over his erection.

When she wiggled her ass at him, he lightly bit her shoulder. She shuddered, pushing back into him. "Hurry up."

If he could have forced the muscles to work, he'd have smiled at her impatient tone. Instead he reached between her legs from behind.

She was petite, but the height and angle of the counter worked. She spread her legs for him, giving him complete access to her heat. When he slid a finger along her lips and found her soaked, he nuzzled her shoulder, nipping at her again. She'd always liked when he did that in the past, and it seemed now was no different.

He dipped a finger inside her and savored the way she clenched around him. If he'd had more patience, he'd have teased her longer, but he was barely hanging on. He grasped her hips and thrust deep inside her. She let out a sharp cry as he filled her.

"So tight." The two words tore from him. He stayed buried deep, his breathing as erratic as his heartbeat. "Cup your breasts, tease yourself." He needed her to come.

When she did as he said, he slid his hand down her flat stomach and stroked her clit. Once, twice, he continued teasing as she cried out his name. He loved the sound of it, wasn't sure he'd ever get enough of hearing it.

She shuddered against him, her inner walls tightening faster and faster as he stroked. Finally she dropped her hands to the counter with a slap. Her fingers clenched against the flat surface as if she needed something to hold on to.

He tweaked her clit harder, not surprised as she started climaxing around him. His restraint snapped. Pulling back, he began thrusting inside her, his movements harsher and more unsteady with each pump inside her tight heat. The base of his spine tingled as the need for release grew more intense.

When she reached behind herself and grasped on to his hip with a tight hold, he let go. His thrusts were wild as his climax slammed through him. It felt as if it went on forever, the pleasure careening through him too much and yet not enough.

He buried his face in her neck as he came down from the shot of adrenaline. He wanted to stay like this, inside her, and feel her come around him again. Hearing his name on her lips made him crazy.

He kept his face against her neck, inhaled her sweet, exotic scent. And suddenly the words he'd been holding back burst free. "Why'd you end things, Amelia? What happened between us?" He needed to know and he wasn't waiting any longer to ask her. It clawed at him relentlessly, made him wonder if he'd done something wrong. Or if she'd . . . met someone else and hadn't wanted to tell him.

She stiffened under him, but he held her close, his naked body plastered to hers. He wasn't letting her walk away until she answered. Right now they were both exposed.

"You want to talk about this now?" Her inner walls clenched around his half-hard cock.

No, damn it, he didn't. But they needed to. He could never fucking move on or move forward with her if they didn't talk. Slowly he pulled out of her heat and disposed of the condom. Before he'd shut the cabinet door for the trash can, she'd already tugged on her jeans and was yanking her T-shirt over her head, her hands trembling. Her bra and panties were still on the kitchen floor, but she clearly needed a barrier between them.

His gut tightened in warning. It pissed him off that she was pulling away from him. He grabbed his own pants, watching her intently as she sat on one of the swivel chairs. He lifted an eyebrow. He wasn't going to ask again. Either she told him the truth or she didn't. He couldn't move forward with her until he knew what the hell had gone wrong.

"I got pregnant," she blurted, her cheeks flushing red. Shame flashed in her gaze as she stared at him. It was soon replaced by wariness as she raked an unsteady hand through her hair.

He went rigid, tried to conceal his shock. "By me?" The question simply escaped because of her seeming embarrassment, but he immediately wanted to rein it back in. Deep down he didn't think she'd ever been unfaithful. She wasn't built that way. Neither was he.

"Yes, you! I never cheated on you!" Her eyes sparked with pure rage until he held up his palms in defense.

"I know. I'm sorry. Shit, it just popped out." Even though he was wired, he sat in the chair across from her. A baby? She'd been pregnant with his baby? He wanted to take her hands, but she'd crossed her arms over her chest, her body language clear. "You were pregnant?" He felt as if his whole world had just tilted on its axis. Why hadn't she told him?

She nodded. "Yes. And let me just get all this out before you start asking questions, okay?" When he nodded, she continued. "I had no idea until I was about four months along. I guess some women just carry small and I'm small anyway. And I'm rambling." She scrubbed a nervous hand over her face, looking away from him for a second.

When she turned back her expression was shuttered. "When I found out I was pregnant, I was horrified. I . . . I didn't want a baby and I knew you didn't either."

He automatically started to protest, but she shook her head. It wasn't that he'd wanted a kid that young, but they could have made anything work. They'd been committed to each other and in love. Or so he'd thought.

"Let me finish, please. As soon as I suspected I was pregnant, I went to the free clinic and they confirmed it. Barely a week later, I ended up having a miscarriage. It was bad. There was a lot of blood and . . ." She shuddered and it took all his restraint not to pull her into his arms.

He didn't know much about miscarriages, but he knew enough. And she would have dealt with it alone, because God knew her mother wouldn't have been there for her. His stomach twisted at the thought of her dealing with everything by herself. Why hadn't she told him? He'd have been there for her in a heartbeat.

"Why didn't you tell me?" he rasped out, unable to understand. And why had she broken up with him?

"I thought it was my fault," she whispered.

"What?"

"I didn't want a baby, didn't want to saddle either of us with one. We were so young and you were getting ready to leave. I had a lot of dreams, none of which involved becoming a mom that young. I . . . I just wanted it gone. I *wished* for it." She looked away from him, tears spilling down her cheeks.

He wanted to be angry at what she said, but hell, they'd been young with big dreams. He wasn't sure that he'd have wanted a kid that young either. "You're not God! You didn't make it happen!" Why was he shouting? Shit, the last thing she probably needed was his anger, but hell, she'd gone through all that alone and hadn't come to him? Hadn't trusted him enough? *That* was why she'd walked away? A logical voice in his head told him that it wasn't about him, but damn it.

Her head snapped back around. "I know that now, but I didn't then. I could barely handle the guilt of everything. I shut down, didn't want to talk to anyone, especially you. It took years for me to come to terms with realizing I didn't actually *do* anything to make it happen. Some days I still struggle with that reality, that it wasn't really my fault. And I was depressed, something I also didn't realize at the time. I was seventeen, had no real family support system, and you were leaving for the Corps. The one woman I would have turned to for advice was your *abuela,* and I couldn't stand the thought of her being disappointed in me, so that was out."

"You could have come to me." How did she not know that? He slid off the chair, needing to put distance between them.

Her expression was tormented. "I know that *now*. But it took a long time to get to that point. I hated myself, hating looking in the freaking mirror for a long damn time after that. If I couldn't stand myself, I didn't think you'd want me either. I thought you'd hate me when you knew the truth." By the glint in her gaze, he wondered if she still expected that. For him to hate her.

"It was easier to just walk away. By the time I even thought about telling you, it was almost four years later and I had no idea how to get in contact with you. Benita was gone and your parents would have had no clue who I was. They weren't even living here anyway. Hell, even if I could have found you, I had no idea if you'd want to hear from me anyway. For all I knew you were married with a family—something I didn't want to know anyway. I . . . I'm not trying to make excuses, just tell you how I reacted to everything back then. I was seventeen and blamed myself. Being around you after that was too hard and I had no freaking coping skills. I'm sorry I hurt you by walking away. So damn sorry. If I could go back and change things, I would. I'd change everything." Her voice cracked on the last word.

Nathan struggled to find his voice. All these years. All these years she'd kept this from him. "I thought it was something I did! It was all I could think about for *years*." He wanted to pull back his anger, but it came spilling out. Knowing the truth, he couldn't actually blame her. She'd been seventeen and, from the sound of it, very depressed. That didn't mean he wasn't allowed to feel anything. "Damn it, Amelia!" They could have worked it out if she'd told him. He would have done anything to be with her. A dull ache spread against the base of his skull.

She didn't say anything, just sat there watching him with sad, teary eyes. He didn't know what to say, how to feel or act. There were too many emotions. Anger, resentment, betrayal, and . . . grief. Grief at knowing they'd lost twelve years together over something he gladly would have stood by her side through.

All he knew was that he needed distance before he said something he would regret. The pain and guilt in her eyes were too much. He wanted to shout at her even as that voice in his head told him to pull his head out of his ass, that with her background her reaction to what she'd gone through was completely in the realm of normal and understandable.

But knowing all that didn't change the emotions clawing at him. He'd been screwed up over her for years, wondering what he'd done wrong. The truth was, she hadn't trusted him. Not really. That was what cut the deepest. She'd thought he would abandon her when she needed him most. He felt sick.

"I need to get out of here," he finally rasped out.

Because being in her presence simply wasn't an option anymore. If he'd expected her to argue, he would have been disappointed. Part of him was when she slid off her chair and just nodded. Accepting that he was leaving.

Feeling as if he were on autopilot, he headed for the front door with Amelia walking silently next to him. She turned off the alarm before wrapping her arms protectively around herself once again.

That need to protect and comfort her flared to life,

but he ruthlessly shoved it back down. "Set the alarm after I leave." The words came out like an order, but that was pretty much all he could manage right now.

Without waiting for a response, he left. For just a moment, he waited on the front step and listened. When he heard the door lock and then the faint sound of the alarm beeps, he left, running down her street to burn off the anger inside him.

The muscles in his legs strained as he pushed himself to the limit, but as fast as he ran, he'd never be able to outrun the past.

Chapter 13

OSINT—open-source intelligence: information derived
from publicly available sources.

Hands on her hips, Amelia frowned at the week's
schedule she'd posted on her office door. Tessa
had been slated to come in this morning and it was
half an hour past when she should have been here. It
wasn't uncommon for her front-of-the-house staff to
arrive right on time or a few minutes late—that was
just the nature of the restaurant business—but Amelia
didn't like this whole situation.

Tessa hadn't been on the work calendar yesterday
because of school and Amelia felt bad, but she hadn't
thought much about Tessa not coming in for her last
shift. She'd had a lot going on at work, then with . . .
Nathan. *Not going to think about him right now,* she
ordered herself. Tessa missing her Sunday night shift
and now being late for her normal Tuesday morning
shift didn't sit right with Amelia.

"You worried about Tess?" Manuel asked, drying
his hands on his white apron as he joined her by her
door.

If this had happened a few weeks ago and she hadn't been aware of so many young women going missing— some who'd worked here—she might have chalked it up to teenage irresponsibility. Now . . . "Yeah. I'm gonna make a few calls, see if I can get the cops to check out her house. Sylvia told me she was dating Jonas?"

Manuel nodded. "Yeah, but I don't think dating is what the young people are calling it. I heard him tell one of the servers they were 'talking' and 'hanging out.' The boy was off yesterday, so I don't know if he's seen her."

"Okay, thanks. I'm going to shut the door while I make the calls." Amelia pulled out her cell and stepped into her office. She'd come in at the crack of dawn because she hadn't been able to sleep. Instead she'd replayed the conversation with Nathan in her mind over and over, obsessing over it and making herself sick. She wanted him to call and wasn't sure if she should make the first move. He'd left last night, clearly wanting space from her. She wanted to give it to him, but still, she needed to hear his voice.

No one else had been here, so she'd done all the scheduling for the next two weeks and caught up on a day's worth of paperwork. She worked fairly normal hours, so what she'd finished this morning would have taken all day because of the numerous interruptions she would have had. Normally she craved the chaotic atmosphere of her restaurants. There was always a mini-crisis to be dealt with. Right now she just wanted to go home, curl up on the couch with ice cream, and forget about the outside world for a while.

Of course she wouldn't be able to block out anything, not when her thoughts were consumed with Nathan and the pain and hurt that had radiated off him as he'd left last night. She laid herself bare and now he either forgave her or didn't. It had taken her a long damn time to forgive herself—and on bad days she still struggled with guilt—so maybe she shouldn't expect him to let go so easily. But that stupidly hopeful part of her had thought there was a chance he would. Hoped he would.

Sitting at her desk, she shook those thoughts off and scrolled through her phone to Joel Sinclair.

The detective answered on the third ring, his voice strained. "Hey, you know a girl named Tessa Hall?"

"Uh . . ." She paused, completely taken off guard. Alarm punched through her that a detective was asking about Tessa. "I was actually just calling you about her. What's going on?"

"I'm at her house now. Got a call from a neighbor who was worried about her, so she used the key Tessa had given her. When she didn't find anyone home, she called us."

She could hear the sound of papers rustling in the background.

"I found a pay stub from Plátanos Maduros and a uniform shirt from there. Tell me what . . ." He trailed off before he let out an annoyed curse. "Let me call you back." He disconnected before she could respond.

Screw that. Amelia scribbled down Tessa's address on a sticky note and stood. She'd plug it into her GPS and head over there herself. She knew Sinclair would need to officially talk to her anyway, so she'd save him a trip.

The location of Tessa's place was only about five miles away, but with traffic the drive took close to twenty minutes. By the time Amelia was pulling down Tessa's street, Sinclair had called her back. "Hey, I'm almost to Tessa's," she said by way of greeting.

"Amelia—"

"I'm literally pulling down her street."

He sighed. "Park at the curb across from her house. I'll meet you there."

As she steered down the street, she spotted Sinclair's Explorer in the driveway. A marked police car was behind it. On the curb in front of Tessa's house was a faded blue, older-model pickup truck. Some of the neighbors had come out of their houses and were standing on lawns. She noticed that almost everyone was in their fifties or older. She knew Tessa's parents had died and she still lived in her childhood home while going to school.

Leaving her purse in her Jeep, Amelia shoved her keys and phone in her pants pocket and started across the street. As she rounded the old truck, she spotted a uniformed police officer talking to Jonas. Though she was surprised to see Jonas here, she didn't have time to talk to him before Sinclair stepped out of the front door, his expression grim.

He strode across the front lawn, his long legs eating up the distance in seconds. "I've got another officer on the way here who'll take your statement, and a forensics team to sweep the place."

"You think she's been kidnapped?" Amelia's stomach twisted. Could it be by the same person or persons who'd taken so many other women?

He glanced around and kept his voice low when he spoke. "I don't know much of anything at this point, and what I am about to tell you is all just between us. There are subtle signs of a break-in. Her back door looks as if it's been picked, her bedroom is slightly disturbed, and we found heavy boot-print indents in her backyard. Could be nothing but a repair guy, but we're going to look into everything. A lot of women have gone missing, and if she's one of them we might have a jump on this case if we find physical evidence."

She nodded. They'd only discovered that the other women were missing after a lot of time had passed. There'd been no way to really search for any physical evidence or anything that might help the police discover who had taken them. Amelia was afraid for Tessa. "Why'd her neighbor call?"

"Guess she hadn't taken her garbage cans out to the curb yesterday even though her car's parked in the carport. And she wasn't answering her phone. She says that's not like Tessa, that she's very predictable, a friendly, sweet girl."

Yeah, that definitely sounded like Tessa. Real fear clawed at Amelia. "She didn't show up for work Sunday evening or this morning." Guilt threaded through her. She should have called Sinclair yesterday. One phone call could have had him looking into this sooner.

Sinclair pulled out a pad and started writing. "That's good info. It'll help establish a timeline of her movements. You know him well?" Sinclair jerked a chin in the direction of Jonas but kept scribbling.

She automatically glanced at her employee. Tall, a little lanky, he was a nice kid. "He works for me. He's a good kid as far as I know. Attends the University of Miami, works part-time, has never been late. You probably already know this, but I just heard from some staff that he and Tessa are semi-dating."

Sinclair nodded. "Yeah, already got that. Kid showed up looking for her because she hadn't returned his texts and freaked when he saw police cars here. Demanded to know what was going on, tried to rush into the house. She had any problems with anyone at work that you know of?"

"No . . . yes." Oh God. Why hadn't Amelia thought about that? "About a month ago I fired one of my chefs for harassing some of the girls. Tessa was one of them."

"Name?"

"Neal Gray. I gave you his info the other night."

Sinclair nodded, his expression grim. "I had him and the other one, Turner, pulled in for questioning about possibly hitting your Jeep."

She blinked, surprised by that. "And?"

"And nothing so far. Neither of their vehicles showed signs of damage either. Do you have his info on your phone by chance?"

"I can pull it up."

"I've got it on file, but give it to me now. I want to get someone over to his place asap."

With a sense of urgency, Amelia pulled her cell out of her pocket and logged in to one of her work accounting programs.

"What kind of harassment?" Sinclair asked as she searched.

"Vile sexual jokes targeted at specific girls, but only when it was just him and the girl. He cornered a few of them in the freezer but never actually touched anyone or did anything physical. Not that I care about that. As soon as the first girl came to me, I fired him. After that more girls came forward." She'd had a staff meeting after that, making it clear to everyone that they could come to her about anything. She wouldn't put up with that kind of crap. Ever.

"Here." She held out her phone, let Sinclair copy down all the information. "Can I talk to Jonas?" she asked when he finished.

"No, not yet at least. We've got to take him to the station and take his official statement."

"Oh, right." She watched enough TV that she knew significant others were often suspects. Jonas just looked worried and panicked to Amelia, but he could be acting for all she knew.

"Is there anything I can do?" She wanted to help in any way she could. Right now she felt so damn helpless. God, the thought of sweet Tessa being taken . . . It didn't matter if this was related to the other case or not; she wanted Tessa found alive and unharmed.

"Yeah, give me a list of any of her friends from work, anyone she's had an issue with, names, phone numbers, her work schedule. Basically anything you know about her that you think will be helpful. You can do it here or down at the station."

"Here's fine. Do you have something I can write on?"

"Yeah, just give me a sec." He turned, waved at the officer talking to Jonas, and called the man over.

It didn't take long for them to set her up with a pad and paper. She called both restaurants to let them know she likely wouldn't be by for a while and then let Sylvia know to find people to cover Tessa's shifts for the near future. She didn't give any other details, though, knowing the police wouldn't want her to. They'd probably want to question everyone who'd worked with Tessa.

As she jotted down names and phone numbers, she pushed back the nausea swirling inside her. It was hard not to think of the worst-case scenario in a situation like this. And she desperately wanted to call Nathan. She wasn't sure if Sinclair had done so already, but if the FBI was on this case, it stood to reason he'd have contacted them about it.

Just in case they hadn't, she decided to call Nathan too. Okay, she called complete and total bullshit on herself. She contacted him because she was desperate to hear his voice. She wanted to at least establish communication after last night because she wasn't sure when or if he'd call her.

He picked up on the second ring, his voice clipped. "Yeah."

Okay, then. Her stomach knotted, but she pushed all that crap back. Right now wasn't about her. "Tessa Hall, a girl who works for me, has gone missing. The police are involved. I'm at her house with Detective Sinclair right now. I don't know if it's related to your case and I have no idea if she's ever been to Maria's center, but I wanted to let you know."

He cursed quietly. "Thanks for letting me know. My boss might already be aware, but I'll pass the info on, make sure we coordinate with the Miami PD."

She didn't know how to respond as an awkward silence stretched between them. Sitting in the passenger seat of Sinclair's Explorer, she stared blindly out the window. She didn't want to give up Nathan without a fight. "Will you come see me tonight?"

He paused so long she wasn't sure he'd respond. "If I can."

Way too much relief slid through her veins. The cowardly part of her told her she shouldn't have opened herself up to him, shouldn't have been honest, because she'd known this would happen. Hell, she was surprised he was even thinking about coming over. "Okay."

Once they disconnected, she got out of the vehicle, feeling even crappier than this morning. He was probably just coming over so he could officially tell her he never wanted to see her again. He'd had time to think about it now and it was clear from his tone he hadn't wanted to talk to her.

"Are you done?" Sinclair asked as he approached her.

"Yeah. I left the info on the passenger seat."

He nodded once. "Good. If you think of anything else, contact me immediately. And I'm going to want to talk to your staff, but don't mention anything to anyone yet."

"I've covered Tessa's shifts, but I haven't said why and I won't. And I'll definitely call you if I think of something." She wanted Tessa found.

When she pulled away from the curb, she contemplated going home or back to the restaurant. It took her only a moment to decide on work. It would keep her busy. She could catch up on more paperwork. Unfortunately she'd have to field questions about Tessa's absence; that was inevitable. But the thought of going home, being alone, was too damn depressing.

All her friends worked during the day, so it wasn't as if she could call someone up either. Not only that, but she hadn't told anyone about what she'd gone through when she was seventeen. It was part of her past and she wanted it to stay that way. Now she wished she had someone to at least talk to. She contemplated reaching out to Maria, but her husband was friends with Nathan. That would be too weird.

By the time she reached the street to Plátanos Maduros, her stomach was even more twisted up. At least the parking lot was full, she saw, as she neared the turnoff.

Oh yeah, she'd be busy. She slid her hand down the steering wheel, ready to flip her turn signal on, when her Jeep jerked forward under an intense impact. Her head snapped forward, all the muscles in her body tightening. She flicked her gaze to the rearview mirror.

What the—

A truck slammed into her again, her vehicle shuddering as she gripped the wheel tightly. Not again.

Panic exploded inside her when she saw two women carrying shopping bags stepping out into the street in front of her. They weren't paying attention.

Without pause she yanked the wheel hard to the right, jumping onto the sidewalk to avoid hitting them. She heard screaming but couldn't look back as she maneuvered down the sidewalk, her Jeep tearing up the outlying grass. The outer sidewalk lined a parking lot, so there weren't any direct shops on it, but there were poles and freaking palm trees she couldn't maneuver around.

She looked in the rearview mirror again to see the same vehicle behind her on the sidewalk now. *Shit!* In front of her was a bus stop and to the right was a line of palm trees. She barely had time to decide which impact would suck less when the truck rammed her again.

Her Jeep jerked forward, the crunching sound of metal filling the air as her vehicle careened toward the empty bus stop. Barely in control, she yanked the wheel sharply so that the passenger side would take the impact.

Her muscles tightened as she braced for the impact.

Chapter 14

Analysts: people who take raw information from
HUMINT, OSINT, etc., and draw conclusions by
assessing its significance and by collating it with
other information.

Nathan nodded once at an agent he recognized but hadn't seen in a while as he strode down the quiet corridor of the NSA building. He'd already gone through multiple layers of security including more than one biometric scan just to get to this floor. He'd also been very careful not to be followed on the way over. It was impossible to know for certain, but he'd changed vehicles enough times and had gotten on the Metromover.

Twice.

He was new to the undercover part of his job but he knew that this op wasn't typical. On most of the ops agents got sent on, when they went undercover they might not have contact with Burkhart or anyone for weeks at a time. And even then it was usually via phone or e-mail. But this was a time-sensitive case. He wasn't infiltrating an organization; he was simply sliding on a persona to question suspected criminals. The meeting this morning had been a bust, unfortunately, he thought as he reached the halfway-open door to Burkhart's office. Well, one of them.

His boss had an office that was attached to their main command center in Miami, but this was another office he also used. Nathan wasn't sure why he had two in this building and he wasn't going to ask why. Though he guessed it gave Burkhart privacy when he needed to work with little to no interruptions.

Burkhart was on the phone but held up a hand and motioned for him to enter.

"Call me with updates," he said before setting his cell on the desk. "The meeting?" he asked by way of greeting.

"He's a criminal, mainly into low-level arms dealing. Seemed as if he'd be open to moving drugs, but when I mentioned moving people he shut me down. Got offended." Which was amusing in a fucked-up sort of way. Even criminals had codes they followed. Or at least a loose set of morals.

"What's your gut say?"

"He's not involved. From what we've found, his business is solid, and when I talked about moving heroin through his territory he was contemplative but didn't jump at it. He's doing well and if I had to guess, from his standpoint, he'll just bring more heat on himself if he gets involved with me. I think he didn't want to risk offending me, but he doesn't want to do business. He's making good bank per month and he's happy with his income."

"Yeah, that's what Elliott and Karen said too."

"Do the locals have any thoughts on him?" Nathan asked.

"Captain Nieto doesn't think he's involved either. I'm marking him off our list. We've taken three of the main suspects off so far."

It was progress at least. "How many more bodies did they find?" He could have called Elliott or Karen or anyone working the case, but since Nathan had known he was coming here, he had decided to hold off and find out from Burkhart.

"Three. They're still slowly moving all of the remains, but there are thirty-nine total." Burkhart's jaw clenched. "And every one in our custody gave birth before they died. Miami PD is finding the same thing."

Nausea rolled inside Nathan. "I can head back to the lake." He wanted to help, and after the undercover work he'd been doing, he found he liked doing stealth ops and hands-on work more. It was a startling thing to discover about himself. Months before the explosion, when Burkhart offered him more undercover work, he'd jumped at it, had thought he'd love it. Now . . . he wasn't so certain.

Seeing Amelia again had disrupted his life in more ways than one. He'd started to allow himself to imagine what it would be like if they started a real relationship. If they did he wouldn't do undercover work anymore. That thought alone should have disturbed him, but it didn't. He . . . cared for her. More than simply cared for her, but he wouldn't even think the words. Forgiving her wasn't the issue. It was about trust.

Which, maybe he didn't have a leg to stand on, but at least the things he couldn't tell her were because of national security. It was hard to swallow that she hadn't trusted him enough. Or maybe . . . she just hadn't loved him enough. He didn't know if that was his bullshit pride or what. But he'd loved her with everything he'd had, had known almost from the start, even at age seventeen, that he'd never meet anyone else like her. Over the years he'd wondered if he'd built up that attraction, that pull to her, but no such luck. So yeah, it stung that she hadn't trusted him enough to be there for her.

For them.

Burkhart shook his head. "I want you to set up a meet with another of our suspects."

Nathan nodded.

"Selene arrives tonight and has already set up a meet with Lopez. You're going with her tomorrow morning."

He nodded again. He'd be so busy with this case he wouldn't have time to obsess over Amelia. Right. He never stopped obsessing over her.

"Why'd you get back to your place so late last night—this morning?" Burkhart asked abruptly, his expression completely neutral.

This unexpected shift in topic was intentional. His boss clearly wanted to throw him off his game. Surprised by the question, Nathan kept his face just as passive. "You're having me followed?"

Burkhart sat back in his chair, his bright green eyes shrewd as ever. "No. When you key in the security code it's filed in the log. After you left the lab last night, it shouldn't have taken you long to get back to Miguel's place."

God, he just wanted to bury his alias. "I don't hear a question in there."

"You went to Amelia's." Also not a question.

No need to lie. "Yes."

"How involved with her are you?" Clearly he knew Nathan was involved in the first place. Not just friends with her as he'd alluded to.

Apparently Nathan hadn't been as stealth as he'd assumed. He didn't think Cade, Dax, or Elliott had said anything, but he couldn't know for sure.

"I don't know." Which was at least the truth. He had no idea what was going on between him and Amelia. He'd had a lot of time to think last night, and while he was pissed she hadn't trusted him, he didn't know how he could hold something against a seventeen-year-old girl who'd been in a lot of pain. The regret and agony on her face had been real; her apology had been raw and sincere. She'd clearly suffered as much as he had and she'd never had a solid family base like him. She'd had no one because her mother didn't count. He still cared for Amelia, had never stopped. Hell, he more than just cared for her. But he had no idea what their relationship was. Or if they could have one.

"She's been a help to us and we're going to need her inside Mercado's place again. Soon. We need to eliminate him or go after him hard. More women could go missing."

Nathan was going to go back to the part about Amelia infiltrating Mercado's again in a second, but for now . . . "I haven't had a chance to talk to the team. Do they think Tessa Hall is another victim?"

Burkhart's lips tightened for a moment. "She doesn't fit the socioeconomic profile, but she does fit the age group and she's an orphan. No parents, so she's technically alone in the world. And she's got a link to Amelia, which is a loose thread."

"No tie to the center?"

"Not directly, but she volunteered there when she was in high school as part of her community service credits."

Another connection to the center. "I'm guessing high school wasn't that long ago for her." Amelia had told him she was the hostess he'd briefly met, and she'd looked like a kid.

"It wasn't."

So there was a tie. It had to be the center. "Have Elliott or Karen found a link to the center yet?"

"Not yet, but they're ripping apart the online movements of everyone who works there. Maria's been a big help getting us info."

Good. Because his gut told him the center was the link. There were more missing women connected to the center. Maria had been the one to send the women to Amelia's restaurants. It wasn't as though Amelia had recruited them. Everything seemed to go back to that damn center. "Do you want me to talk to Amelia about getting another date with Mercado? I know he's called her since Sunday." Which was damn annoying even if it was good for the op. Not that Nathan could blame the guy for wanting to see Amelia again.

Sighing, Burkhart nodded and picked up a slim manila file from a mesh basket on his desk. He slid it across the desk. "She needs a date with him asap. Hell, tonight if possible. I want you to look at this, though. It's not the end of the world, but your girl got her start in business via . . . shady means. Thought you should know."

"I read her file." He knew she'd been suspected of borrowing money from loan sharks. Which wasn't something that even pinged on his radar. So what if she'd borrowed money from criminals? She'd have paid it back or she wouldn't be in business.

"I had Karen dig a little more. It's not just suspected, it's confirmed. I don't give a shit about what she did as long as she helps us now. Read it, do what you want with the knowledge."

Nathan realized his boss was giving him this information and it had nothing to do with work. Burkhart was just looking out for him. "Thanks, I will."

"I'm headed down to the command center. Come with me. You can—"

His cell phone rang, cutting him off. Burkhart didn't pause but answered immediately. "Burkhart here."

Nathan listened to half the conversation, which was mainly grunts and one-word answers. He jolted at the concerned look his boss shot him as he ended the call. Burkhart didn't do concern. "What is it?" Nathan asked.

"That was Captain Nieto. Amelia's been in an accident."

Amelia wanted to swat the paramedic's hand away as he shone a small flashlight in her eyes, but she knew he was just doing his job. She was sitting at the back of the ambulance with the doors propped open. Her heartbeat was still a little erratic and she was afraid she'd never stop shaking, but she was alive.

Sore, but alive, with no broken bones. Her chest

ached from the airbag impact, but it could have been so much worse.

Whoever had run her off the road had fled, thanks to a handful of Good Samaritans. The two women she'd avoided running over saw the whole thing and ran to her rescue immediately. A few customers from her restaurant's parking lot had also come to her aid, scaring the driver off.

She wasn't certain, but she thought one of the women had gotten a license plate. One of them had said something about it, but everything had been a blur with the police and paramedics showing up. She really, really wished it hadn't happened in front of her restaurant, but whatever, she was alive.

That was what mattered.

"Amelia!" Her heart jumped at the sound of a male voice calling her name. When she turned and saw Sinclair striding her way, that small spark of hope was snuffed out. She felt immediately stupid for hoping it had been Nathan. It wasn't as if she'd freaking called him, so how would he even know? And she definitely wasn't calling him. She didn't want him coming over here out of pity or duty or any combination of reasons.

The paramedic turned at the sound of Sinclair's voice and gave him a friendly nod and greeting before telling them he'd give them a couple of minutes.

"Hey, how'd you know about what happened?"

"Heard about it on the radio. Your name's red-flagged right now anyway."

She blinked. "What does that mean?"

"Just that if there's a mention of you I get a call. I'm

worried about you. More after today." He sat on the back deck of the ambulance next to her. "You get a look at who did this?"

"No." She'd already told the responding officers all this and didn't want to hash it out again. "Everything happened so fast, it was terrifying."

"You think it's the same guy who came after you Friday night?"

"I honestly don't know. I kinda hope so, though, because if there are two people out there who want to hurt me this badly . . ." She trailed off, wrapping her arms around herself. A shiver snaked through her and damn it if stupid tears didn't sting her eyes. Way too much had happened and she was pretty much at her breaking point. It didn't help that things between her and Nathan were all sorts of screwed up. She blinked the tears back, but they spilled over anyway.

"Aw, hell. Don't cry." Sinclair wrapped an arm around her shoulders and tugged her close.

She'd thought she could get through this without crying. She'd just wanted to finish making her statement, deal with the tow truck company, talk to her employees, then go home. That was the plan.

She liked having order in her life, and right now it seemed as if everything was all messed up. Her emotions were out of control, one of her employees was missing, and numerous women had been kidnapped for God knew what. And someone was apparently determined to kill her or at least hurt her really bad. "Sorry," she muttered, turning her face into his shirt.

"Don't apologize. You've dealt with a lot this past week. Hell, I—"

"Amelia."

Sinclair stopped talking and she looked up to find Nathan right in front of them, his arms over his chest.

He looked fierce and too sexy for his—or her—own good. He wore a dark suit that had to be custom-made for his gorgeous body. A mix of emotions played over his face, one of them most definitely annoyance, possibly jealousy—for Sinclair, who still hadn't dropped his arm from Amelia's shoulders.

And it didn't seem he planned to. Sinclair's grip tightened.

"What are you doing here?" she blurted, then felt stupid for it. And a little hopeful. The only reason he should have come was for her, unless he thought her attack was part of his case.

Nathan flicked a glance at Sinclair before focusing on her. "I heard you were in an accident. I wanted to make sure you were okay." His arms dropped and he took a small step forward, one of his hands slightly lifting as if he wanted to reach for her. But he shoved his hands in his pockets.

Disappointment flared inside her, bright and scorching. She wanted to feel the warmth of his touch right now. "I'm okay. Just a little sore, mainly from the airbag." She nudged Sinclair with her elbow, but he didn't move. Just sat next to her, arm securely around her. She knew he didn't have a thing for her—she was pretty sure he thought of her as a sister—so he must be feeling overprotective to act like this.

"What did the paramedics say?"

"They want me to go to the hospital to get checked out further."

Nathan nodded, the tightness in his shoulders loosening. "That's a good idea."

"Yeah, it's not happening." She wasn't going anywhere but home. After she took care of a few things.

"You could have a concussion or—"

"Sinclair!" a male voice called out, making all of them glance over.

Next to the half-crumpled bus stop, Captain Nieto stood with a man who looked about the same age as him, early to mid-fifties. He wore light-colored slacks and a button-down green shirt and was clearly in good shape. Since he had on sunglasses it was impossible to read him, but it seemed as if he was looking at her. But she was probably imagining that. Something about him was familiar, though.

Sinclair stood, but he leaned in as if hugging her and whispered, "Ask your friend who he really works for," before standing and kissing her gently on the forehead.

Surprise flickered through her. Sinclair had confirmed that Nathan worked for the FBI. That wasn't true? Then who did he work for and why would he lie to her? He couldn't be a criminal if Sinclair was working with him. As Sinclair strode over to his captain, she turned to Nathan, ready to ask him just that, but the words died in her throat at the dark look in his eyes. "What?"

"I don't like that fucker touching you." His words were raw and not a little jealous.

The hostility lacing his statement took her off guard. He was the one who'd taken off last night; he didn't have a right to feel jealous. She wasn't even going to go there right now. She also wasn't going to question him about who he worked for. Not now. She didn't want to give away that Sinclair had put the idea in her head to ask, and more to the point, she was freaking done for the day.

Done with everything.

Her body hurt, her brain hurt, and she was going home as soon as humanly possible.

Nathan moved lightning quick, sitting next to her. "You're sure you're okay?"

The concern in his voice pierced her. At least he actually cared. That knowledge broke something inside her. Without warning, the dam she'd been holding back burst free. To her horror, the waterworks started. Full-on, ugly crying. She managed to keep the sobbing noises to a minimum, but her body trembled from the onslaught of her emotions.

Before she could feel embarrassed, she found herself being tugged into Nathan's strong hold, didn't fight him as he led her . . . somewhere.

To a vehicle. When he opened the back door to an SUV, she started to protest. "My purse and Jeep—"

He held up her purse and said, "Jeep's being towed. I'll get all the info. Come on." His voice was gentle as he helped her into it and slid in after her. That was when it registered someone else was in the driver's seat.

Nathan gave him her address and they left, just like that. She wasn't even sure she should have gone. She needed to talk to her employees, and the police might still need to talk to her. But . . . screw it. She'd wanted to go home and now she was getting her wish.

Even though things were strained between them, and she wondered if they'd ever get past the divide, she still leaned against Nathan. Without pause he wrapped an arm around her shoulders, stroking a hand down her back as she curled against him.

Amelia jerked awake with a start as Nathan shifted next to her. Moving away from him, she saw that the SUV had stopped in her driveway.

Home.

"I'll call when I need a pickup," Nathan murmured to the driver before sliding out.

Even though she didn't need the help, Amelia savored the way his strong arm slid around her and held her close as he walked her to the front door. She didn't have to do anything as he pulled the keys from her purse and let them in. Inside he disarmed the alarm and reset it to stay mode.

His movements were precise and economical. It was weird to let someone else take over, but she was grateful to have him with her now. She couldn't believe she'd practically had a meltdown at the crash site. She usually held up in stressful situations but not today.

"You want hot tea?" He stood almost awkwardly in her foyer, watching her carefully.

She shook her head, touched by the question. His *abuela* had always made either of them hot tea whenever they'd felt under the weather or just had a bad day. "I'm okay. I think I just want to crash. You can call your friend or whoever that was to pick you up. Thank you for bringing me home, really, but you don't have to stay." She didn't want to be an obligation to him. Nathan had such an honorable streak, and she wasn't going to use that.

He just grunted what could have meant any number

or responses before bending down and scooping her into his arms.

She yelped, looping her arm around his neck as he strode for the stairs with determined strides. "What are you doing?"

"Taking care of you."

She appreciated it, but even so . . . "I can walk."

He did that grunt thing again, refusing to look at her as he hurried up the stairs. Once they were in her bedroom, he set her down at the foot of her bed while he pulled back the covers. Sunlight streamed in from the open blinds, bathing the gold-and-blue duvet and the oversize canvas of the Miami skyline that hung above her bed.

Too many emotions flooded her. Despite what had gone down with them, despite the fact that things were potentially beyond repair between them, he was still taking care of her. When he picked up the short pajama set she'd tossed onto her chaise, she wrapped her arms around herself.

"Nathan, you really don't need to stick around." It was almost harder with him here, being so damn nice that she just wanted to cry all over again. She understood why he'd taken off last night, but she was also a little resentful. She'd never kept the truth from him to hurt him or because she hadn't trusted him. She'd done it because she'd hated herself, had been drowning in ridiculous guilt. It had never been about him.

"I do." There was no room for argument in those two words. "Change. You'll feel better." Then, taking her totally by surprise, he stripped off his jacket, shirt, and shoes. He left his pants on, though, making it clear that he wasn't trying for more from her.

Instead of using the bathroom for privacy, she undressed by the chaise, leaving her clothes in a heap, even though she normally only left her pajamas out. She didn't have the energy to put them in the hamper.

Nathan stood rigid by her bed, not even pretending to look away as she changed clothes. Hunger simmered in his gaze, nearly scorching her. She felt her body flare to life, knowing that all that need was for her. But he didn't make a move for her as she approached the bed and collapsed onto it. Instead he rounded it and slid into the other side.

It depressed under his weight, but Amelia couldn't make herself turn around to face him. Why the hell was he here? She couldn't tell if this was obligation or maybe he was offering an olive branch between them. She hoped it was the latter, but that dark, bitchy voice in her head told her it wasn't.

She was just an obligation, a duty. Now her sheets and bed would smell like him. She craved him even as she silently ordered him to leave, to get the hell out of her home. The longer she was around him, the harder it was going to be to move on when he disappeared from her life.

When his solid arm slid around her waist, tugging her close, she couldn't even fight his hold. Didn't want to. She settled against him, soaking up all his strength.

"I know I said it, but . . ." She cleared her throat, her voice seeming overpronounced in the quiet room. "If I could go back and change things, I would. I'm so sorry, Nathan. If you can't forgive me, I'll understand, though."

He sighed, his grip tightening as his chin settled on top of her head. His masculine scent enveloped her. "It's not about forgiveness. I do forgive you. You were fucking seventeen and hurting. I'd have to be a monster not to be able to let that go. It just kills me that you didn't trust me. I would have done anything for you. Still would." He murmured the last part so low she almost didn't hear him.

Her throat tightened at his words. He forgave her, but it didn't sound as though that was enough. Had she ruined everything with her fearful decision twelve years ago? She was too afraid to ask if they had a chance at a future. Hell, maybe she didn't deserve one. More tears threatened, but this time she managed to rein them in. She would not cry again. At least not until she was alone.

"I need to ask you something." She wasn't sure how much time had passed when Nathan's voice cut through the silence.

"Okay," she whispered, feeling lethargic and beyond exhausted by now.

"We need you to get inside Mercado's house again. One more date and Elliott should be able to get what he needs. He was damn close last time." The steady cadence of his voice was normally soothing.

She went rigid in his hold. His words pissed her off. Maybe that was why he was still being decent to her. They still needed her. She almost let out a bitter laugh but held herself in check. A deal was a deal. Her jaw tightened. "I'll do it."

She figured after he'd gotten what he needed from her, then things would truly be over between them. Then she could move on for good.

Chapter 15

Babysitter: a bodyguard.

Sid paced in front of the faux fireplace in his condo. A fireplace in Florida was stupid, but it added to the ambience of his high-rise. At least that was what his bitch of a real estate agent had said. She hadn't even liked him, but she'd still fucked him right in front of the damn fireplace after he closed on the condo. He'd bought it free and clear, so she'd known he had money. Maybe she'd thought she'd get gifts or jewelry out of him. People were always like that, wanting to take, take, take.

Agitated, he shook his head. He had to think about the present, about what was important. Almost against his will his gaze strayed back to the muted television screen above the mantel. He unmuted it.

The same story was still playing. He needed to figure out what to do. He picked up the cold beer on his coffee table, took a swig.

Sitting behind the news desk on-screen, the brunette anchor stared at the camera, her expression sincere. "For those who are just tuning in, it's a shocking night in Miami. The remains of almost forty women have been found. The police haven't released the location or the causes of death, but it looks as if there could be a serial killer . . ."

Sid tuned her out and collapsed onto the couch. What he'd thought was a sleek and modern piece of furniture when he bought it now felt stiff and uncomfortable to sit on. Or maybe it was because he knew the FBI could be onto him now. Onto their whole operation.

What the hell was he going to do? He tugged his cell phone from his pocket and looked at the screen just in case he'd missed a call. Nothing. His boss had to have seen the news. The police had found one of his dumping sites. That place had been perfect too.

Private, owned by someone who lived out of state or something and didn't plan to return to Florida any time soon.

"We were careful, though," he muttered to himself. They'd sterilized each body before he dumped it. So there wouldn't be any evidence linking any of them. Well, the women were evidence, but it wasn't as if the police would be smart enough to tie the women to the babies they'd sold to rich people with more money than sense. No, things would be okay. They'd probably just figure a serial killer was on the loose. But still, they'd be digging into this case hard-core now. What if they caught him on a traffic cam and somehow figured out he was the one who'd dumped the bodies?

A chiming sound made him jump and he nearly spilled his beer. The downstairs security should have informed him he had visitors before anyone showed up here. Out of habit, he checked the weapon at the back of his pants and stood up. His heartbeat was erratic, so he took a deep, calming breath.

At his front door he turned on the video screen above the security keypad so he could see who was outside. Damn it, it was the doctor. He didn't see anyone with the doc, so maybe the people he worked with didn't want him dead.

Sid thought about ignoring it, but whatever the doc wanted, he needed to hear him out. If he had to kill the guy, so be it. He withdrew his weapon and opened the door. He didn't point it at the man just yet, but kept his finger on the trigger.

Dr. Phil Davis looked at his weapon with disdain. "A gun, really?" Without waiting for a response, Phil strode inside, his steps brisk. "I take it you've seen the news?" he continued.

"Yep. That lake is fucking secure! I don't know how—"

Phil held up a hand, his expression arrogant as usual. Something Sid found ironic, considering what a fuckup the guy was. He'd been fired from the hospital he worked at for too many malpractice suits. But the real kicker had been when he let a judge's daughter die on the operating table. The board had let him go almost immediately and he'd paid out the nose in a civil suit. "No one cares about the discovery. The police won't find any evidence on us. We were all careful." Phil looked at him pointedly, as if in question.

Sid nodded. "I'm always careful."

"Good. You need to get focused because you have three more jobs this week." He pulled a thin file folder from inside his jacket, handed it to Sid. "And burn this shit when you're done. We all need to be careful, now more than ever. No digital trail, nothing to link us to this."

Three? Sid blinked. "You want me to take more targets? *Now*?" No way. That was just asking for trouble. There had been a brief mention of a federal agency getting involved by that reporter, but nothing more. He was pretty sure the FBI got involved with serial killers. Maybe not every time, but often enough. Or that was what he'd seen on television. For all he knew the feds or even the locals knew about his other dump sites. The thought made a cold sweat spread through him.

Phil nodded, his expression hard. "You will do as you're told. We want the new acquisitions as quickly as possible. After we acquire them we won't be taking any more for a while. The media have caused a problem for us, but we can still make a nice profit if we bring in four more."

Sid frowned. "I thought you said three."

"I did. Boss will be taking one alone."

He started to ask why, but cut himself off. Whatever. One less job for Sid to worry about.

But he must have read the question in Sid's eyes because the doctor just shrugged. "I don't know and I don't care why." He turned and yanked open the front door. As he stepped halfway out, he turned and looked over his shoulder, his eyes shrewd—as if he knew what Sid was thinking. "If you think about doing anything stupid, you know what will happen to you." The warning note in his voice was clear.

Sid rolled his eyes and shut the door on him. Fucking doctor thought he could threaten him. But the truth was, a thread of fear slithered down his spine. It wasn't the doctor he was worried about.

After these next three targets, he was definitely out. Hell, if they were going to lie low after he took the women anyway, his employer wouldn't need him. That thought gave him pause. If they didn't need him, he'd be disposable.

Maybe he *should* split town before taking anyone else. He had a new ID already made, but he could get more aliases. Just disappear. He wouldn't have as much money as he'd planned on, but he could find new work.

Yeah, the more he thought about it, the more he liked the idea. He'd have to sleep on it. In the morning he could put his getaway plan into motion. Maybe he'd take one girl so no one would get suspicious and then he could split town and no one would realize, at least for a little while.

Amelia unlocked the back door to her restaurant and let herself in. She'd already stopped by La Cocina de Amelia first to see everyone. While she hired mainly college students at Plátanos Maduros, the first restaurant she'd opened was very family-oriented and had long-term, slightly older staff. Definitely not as much employee turnover.

She'd wanted to assure everyone that things would be operating as usual. Because she'd been in the business long enough to know that people would freak out, and the story of her accident—and she wasn't telling anyone it had been intentional—would morph into a tale of her going out of business and everyone losing their jobs. It was just the nature of gossip in this industry.

She didn't want to be here, though. Didn't want to face anyone. Nathan had left her house late last night, telling her that he had a meeting today. She had no idea if he was lying. Things between them had been awkward, and she didn't know what to do to make it right. She was afraid there wasn't anything she *could* do. He said he forgave her, but that didn't mean he wanted to have anything to do with her.

And now she had to worry about another date with Mercado. She wasn't nervous around Mercado, not after their last date, but she didn't feel like herself, didn't want to put on a fake smile and pretend to be happy. She knew she could say no, but she'd seen the news this morning and knew they'd found a lot of bodies—and she was hurt that Nathan hadn't said a damn thing to her about it. She didn't know for sure that the finding was related to his case, but she wasn't stupid. She wanted to help them either nail Mercado to the wall or clear him.

The scent of delicious fried foods wafted through the air as she shut the door behind her. It automatically locked, part of her security precautions. She'd taken a few steps down the hallway when she saw that her office door was open. No one should be in there.

Panic and paranoia pumped through her. After yesterday it was hard not to feel jumpy. She had reached into her purse for her pepper spray when her front-of-the-house manager, Sylvia, stepped out.

Her coffee-colored eyes widened as she saw Amelia. "What the heck are you doing here?" She took a concerned step forward and Amelia automatically dropped the pepper spray and withdrew her hand. "Shouldn't you be resting?"

"I'm fine, I swear." And wasn't she sick of saying that to people? Which made her feel a little bit like a jerk, considering that everyone was just concerned. "Everything okay here?" She tilted her head to her office door.

"What . . . oh yeah, just updating the floor plan for today and dropping off the receipt for yesterday's bank deposit. Sales were crazy yesterday." She leaned against the doorframe and shoved her hands in her pants pockets. "I compared them to last year and we almost doubled what we did on the same date one year ago. I bet we see more today too, especially after that news clip they did on you."

Amelia's heart rate increased. "News clip?"

"You didn't see it? Of course you didn't," Sylvia said, "or you wouldn't have asked. Yeah, it came on after that awful story about the remains of all those women being found this morning. Did you see that?"

Amelia nodded. It was why she'd turned the news off. One depressing story was enough for the day.

"It was on right after that. They just talked about how you'd been in a hit-and-run and there was a brief interview with two women who said that you avoided hitting them to your own detriment. We were all so worried yesterday, but the police wouldn't let us see you. And then you were just gone. Are you sure you're okay?" As usual, Sylvia was going a million miles a minute. She always seemed to have an unending supply of energy. It was one of the reasons she was so good at her job.

"I'll be so much better if you tell me there's fresh coffee made." There should be, this early in the morning. Her staff lived on the stuff. She'd had a cup at home, but she was still dragging. Lack of caffeine had little to do with it, though, and the truth was, she probably should have just stayed home.

"There is. I'll grab you a cup. Hey, how'd you even get here anyway? It looked like your Jeep was toast yesterday."

"Ah, rental." Which wasn't the truth, but Amelia had no problem lying. She wasn't going to say that the FBI—or whoever, per Sinclair's cryptic words—had let her borrow a vehicle until she got things straightened out.

When she woke up this morning, she'd had a text from Nathan telling her that she'd have an escort to work who would follow in another vehicle and that they'd left a mini-SUV in her garage. Which reminded her, she needed to call her insurance company and Sinclair. She wanted a copy of the police report so she could get a rental ASAP. She also wanted to grill Sinclair about who Nathan worked for.

She'd been a mess yesterday afternoon and last night. Nathan had been an absolute rock too. He'd just been a solid presence in her house, making her feel safe even though they'd barely talked. Of course that was probably because she'd been asleep more than half the time he was there. She tried to think why Nathan would lie about who he worked for and couldn't come up with anything.

And this wasn't the kind of conversation she could have with Nathan via text. Besides, he probably wouldn't even tell her the truth anyway. He hadn't told her about finding the bodies. Granted, he probably wasn't allowed to tell her, but if the freaking media knew, it should be okay to tell her *something*. She'd put her neck on the line by going over to Mercado's house.

Shaking her head, she stepped into her office and collapsed in the comfortable chair. Her neck and shoulders were a little sore, as if she'd run a 10K or done a bunch of push-ups. That was the least of her worries. Someone who wanted to do her serious harm was still out there.

And she had no idea who it was.

Neal Gray was a definite possibility. She hadn't even thought of him after the first time someone rammed into her Jeep, but now that Tessa was missing she was thinking twice. She'd already given Sinclair a list of women who Gray had harassed, but she needed to contact them directly herself. If she didn't and something happened, it would weigh on her forever.

Glancing at the wall calendar, she saw that two of the girls were on shift right now. Good, she could tell them later. Amelia nodded at Sylvia as she brought a cup of coffee in and picked up the office phone. She was calling the others now.

"Will you shut the door behind you?" she whispered as the phone started ringing.

Sylvia quickly ducked out. When Amelia was alone, she slumped back against the chair, not bothering to put on her happy face. After these calls she wanted to do the rounds at the restaurant and let everyone see she was fine.

Twenty minutes later, her calls were made. None of

the girls seemed particularly worried about Gray—
and that bothered Amelia. People never seemed to
think bad things would happen to them. Until they did.

She stood and tucked her pepper spray into one of
her pockets. She felt a little silly carrying it around,
but after the attacks on her she wasn't taking any
chances. She also wanted her cell phone with her, so
when she couldn't find it, she cursed. On the way to
work she'd called a few friends using her hands-free
system and had left the phone on her center console.

Her flat boots were quiet on the floor as she strode
down the short hallway to the open kitchen. The loud
blast of voices and clanking dishes filled the air, comforting her. It was an assault on her senses after the
quiet of her office, but she welcomed it. If anything she
needed it to feel a semblance of normal again.

"Amelia, surprised to see you here. You look good,"
Toni, a pixie-sized server, said as she hurried by Amelia in the direction of the walk-in freezer.

She didn't even have time to respond before a
cacophony of other voices mirrored the same sentiment. Smiling and feeling a hundred times lighter, she
snagged Mark, the nearest server. His order pad and
pens were tucked into the front of his long black apron,
but he didn't have any plates in his hand. "Can you
spare twenty seconds?"

"Sure, boss. What's up?" he asked as they started
back down the side hallway for the back door. "Thought
you got in an accident yesterday. Shouldn't you be resting or something?"

She was just going to hang a sign around her neck

that said "I'm fine." As soon as she had the thought, she felt ungrateful. She should be glad so many people cared. "I'm good, promise. Just need to grab something from my car and don't want to do it alone." Nathan had told her that her "escort" would be waiting in the parking lot and watching her all day, but she didn't have a way to contact the driver/temporary watchdog. And she sure as hell wasn't calling Nathan to tell him to tell the guy she was walking outside to get her freaking cell phone.

That sounded insane even as she thought it.

"Sure." He started walking with her. "So, what happened yesterday? I heard you were, like, hospitalized."

She snorted and shot him a glance. He was a foot taller than her, so she had to look up. "And you believed the gossip?"

He grinned, his expression boyish as they stepped out into the sunlight. "Wasn't sure what to think. We were all worried about you, though."

"I appreciate it. As you can see, I'm good, so spread the word." They were halfway across the back of the paved lot when she realized she'd forgotten her SUV keys. "Apparently I need more caffeine today. I forgot my keys."

Mark laughed lightly. "No worries."

As they started to turn back, a blur of motion to her left caught her eye. A medium-sized man wearing a mask jumped out from behind a row of vehicles, a gun in his hand! He was less than fifteen feet from them. Panic seized her lungs, making it difficult to breathe. Everything seemed to slow for a moment as he raised it toward Mark. She felt rooted to the spot, her gaze locked on the weapon in horror.

It wasn't a gun, she realized. *A Taser.*

The man fired, the dart flying straight for Mark. Her employee flew back, crying out in pain as he hit the ground.

Calling on all her strength, she started screaming at the top of her lungs, piercing the late-morning air. She pulled out her pepper spray and ran right for the guy.

Her assault seemed to take him off guard, because he stumbled back. She'd read up on Tasers and knew the shooting type could only fire once. She raised her arm, still screaming her head off, and fired a stream of liquid at the guy.

She nailed him right in the face.

A perverse sense of pleasure punched through her when his hands flew to his eyes and he bellowed in pain. She could hear Mark groaning but kept all her focus on their attacker. The weapon dropped from his hand, but she kept spraying. The man's knees hit the ground, his cries of agony music to her ears. She needed to get Mark away from here, but she needed to make sure this guy was down. For all she knew he had another weapon hidden on him.

Before she could think about her next move, another man raced from between another two vehicles. She barely had time to register that it was the man who'd escorted her to work this morning before he tackled the masked man.

Her pseudo-bodyguard—Dax, she remembered— had the crying, cursing guy on the ground, his hands and legs both secured in seconds. He whipped the mask off the guy and yanked his head up by the top of his hair. Recognition slammed into her.

Dax dug his knee into the man's back. "Shut the fuck up." His words were a low, angry order to the prisoner. "You know him?" he demanded of her.

Amelia nodded, feeling sick. It was Neal Gray. "He used to work for me."

Chapter 16

Agent: a person officially employed by an intelligence service.

"People are never going to want to eat here again," she muttered to Sinclair, who was leaning against her tiny desk in her matchbook-sized office. It seemed so much smaller with him in it, but there was nowhere else she wanted to be right now after the past couple of hours. Seriously her nightmare had better be over. She was tired of being attacked and dealing with the annoying police paperwork that inevitably seemed to follow.

Dax had been stealthy about calling Sinclair to come arrest her former employee—who'd screamed about police brutality as they hauled him away—and about sending an ambulance to pick up Mark. She didn't think he was hurt enough to warrant a trip to the hospital, but since it had happened on her property she'd insisted he go to get completely checked out. Nothing like the circus from yesterday.

Sinclair shook his head. "I wouldn't be so sure about that. You'll get more publicity if this ever hits the media, but I don't think most of your employees even know about what happened."

She rubbed her hands over her face. "You're right," she said, her words muffled. She dropped her arms. "I just want this nightmare over. Has he said anything yet?" Amelia didn't think she needed to be specific about who she meant.

"No, we're letting him stew. I'm going to interrogate that fucker myself, but I wanted to make sure you're okay first."

She had started to say "I'm fine" for what felt like the hundredth time that morning when Sylvia popped her head around the corner. She paused for a moment to give Sinclair a once-over before looking at Amelia. "There's a man named Iker Mercado here to see you. I told him you might have already left for the day because I wasn't sure if you wanted to see him or anyone."

Crap, she so didn't want to see anyone else right now. Not when her nerves were completely shot. But she nodded and stood. "I'll be out there in just a sec." But she was going to check her makeup first. If she wanted to snag a second date, she couldn't go out there looking as if she'd been run over by a truck. Even if that was what she felt like.

Sinclair blocked her way, his expression dark. "You're friends with Mercado?"

She blinked, surprised by his heated tone. "Uh, yes. I went with him to the auction last week. I told you."

"You didn't say a word about Mercado."

"Oh." Right.

"He's . . . not who you think he is." Sinclair's jaw tightened as he watched her.

Amelia bit her bottom lip. It was clear Nathan's team hadn't told Sinclair or maybe even the Miami PD about her involvement in trying to hack into Mercado's home system. She'd signed a confidentiality agreement, but she wouldn't say anything anyway. As Nathan had told her, she had to act completely normal about her and Mercado in public.

"Look, he's just a friend and I'm going to say hi. And you need to get down to the station and make that bastard confess to everything he's done." Because she knew Gray had been behind the other attacks. Or she really hoped he had been. It seemed insane that there could be more than one person randomly attacking her.

It was clear Sinclair wanted to argue, but he simply nodded. "I'll contact you as soon as I have news about Gray. I can tell you he's not going anywhere right now. He's going to do jail time. It's just a matter of how much we can pin on him. But about Mercado—be careful."

"I will." She walked Sinclair out, earning a frown from Mercado as the detective walked past him. Maybe he knew Sinclair was part of the Miami PD.

But Mercado's attention quickly focused on her, his eyes concerned. "I saw the news this morning and I've been trying to call. I . . ." He rubbed a hand over the back of his neck. "I've been worried."

If this man wasn't a criminal, he was incredibly sweet. She glanced at Sylvia, who was behind the hostess stand, pretending not to listen, and gently took Mercado's elbow. "Let's talk about this out here."

When they stepped out into the cool, early-afternoon air, she sucked in a deep breath, inhaling the crispness. She wasn't exactly nervous, but she felt weird around him. She nodded at one of the benches in front of the restaurant. They were between the morning and afternoon rush, so there shouldn't be too much foot traffic.

"Thank you for coming out here," she said when he sat next to her.

He took her hand in a comforting gesture, squeezed once, and didn't let go. She felt absolutely no spark. Yep, Nathan was definitely it for her. Unfortunately she probably wasn't "it" for him. "So, what happened? The news was vague."

"I . . ." She sighed, trying to find the right words. "I'm honestly not sure what happened. Or why I was attacked, I should say."

He stiffened, his gaze darkening much the same way Nathan's did when worried about a threat. "Attacked?"

She nodded and gently extracted her hand to rub the back of her stiff neck. "Yeah. Don't freak out or anything, but someone rammed into me while I was driving home from the auction the other night. I knew it was intentional and I contacted the police. My . . ." She started to say "friend" but stopped herself. "My contact with the police department just left."

Mercado nodded and something she couldn't define seemed to click into place in his eyes. As if he'd known who Sinclair was. That was interesting. And not in a good way. Why would he know who a police detective was? Unless maybe he'd seen Sinclair on the news. Or maybe he'd had run-ins with him. . . . No, Sinclair would have told her if so.

If Mercado really was a criminal mastermind—and apparently she was thinking in James Bond–movie terms now—then it made sense he would know who some of the police were. Now she was very thankful that Nathan had kept her involvement in all this very quiet. The fewer people who knew, the safer she was.

"Yesterday I was attacked in a similar way, but it was more brazen. I had to pretty much crash to avoid hitting innocent people. The guy got away, but this morning a man . . ." She swallowed hard. Damn it, she'd been keeping it together, but talking about it was making too many emotions surge to the surface.

Mercado took her hands again, and a small part of her was grateful to be able to hold on to someone. "You don't have to tell me. I was just worried, but you shouldn't upset yourself."

"No, it's okay. It just hit me harder than I realized. Long story short, a man I fired not too long ago attacked me and another employee in the parking lot this morning. I thought I was being smart bringing someone with me, but the man Tased one of my waitstaff." Which she still felt guilty about. "I managed to disarm Neal—that's his name—with pepper spray and a lot of screaming." She let out a short laugh. "It was absolutely terrifying, but I'm hopeful they'll be able to prosecute him for everything."

Mercado's jaw had tightened and for the first time she could see more to him than the sweet, potentially possessive man. There was a rage simmering beneath the surface. It flared like a bright meteor before dimming and the polite man she knew was back. "I'm so sorry this happened to you."

"Thank you, truly."

His brow furrowed. "Are you headed home?"

She nodded. "Yes, and I think I'm going to take tomorrow off. Maybe."

The ghost of a smile tugged at his lips. "You're like me. Work, work, work. If you'd like to be alone, that's understandable, but if you want company I'd like to spend time with you."

This was pretty much the perfect opportunity. She desperately wanted to go home and crash, but she smiled. "I don't really feel like going home and I definitely don't want to go somewhere public. We could . . ." She gave him the most sincere smile she could muster. ". . . kick up our feet by your pool with a couple drinks. I wouldn't mind the company."

His smile was easy. "That sounds like a plan. Do you want to go home first for anything?"

"No, just let me grab my purse and let my staff know. Should I drive or will you be able to bring me home later?"

"My driver will take you home whenever you wish."

If it wasn't for Nathan's reentry into her life and the whole "potential psychopathic criminal" thing, Mercado would be a catch. "Perfect. Just give me a few minutes."

Amelia kept her movements steady and normal as she headed back into the restaurant when in reality her heart was racing triple time. She'd gotten the invite to Mercado's house again and all because of a deranged ex-employee. She was going to take full advantage of it and she sure as hell wasn't going to his place without backup.

She ignored everyone and made a beeline to her office. Once inside, she locked the door and with trembling hands dialed the number Elliott had given her before.

He picked up almost immediately. "Hey, Amelia. You okay?"

She could hear the soft clicking of a keyboard and other voices in the background. "Fine. I don't have time to get into it, but I got what you needed. I'm going there *now*." She wasn't sure how much she should say over the phone.

There was a brief pause. "Right now?"

"As soon as we're done talking. I'm not going without backup." Again, this was apparently her new James Bond dialogue. For her, backup had only ever meant a wing-woman when headed out for drinks with a friend. Someone to save her when an annoying guy was chatting her up. Not someone with a gun waiting nearby to infiltrate Mercado's house in case he wanted to kidnap her.

"You'll have it. Think you can stay an hour?" His voice was clipped.

"Probably longer." It was afternoon. She could stretch out a few drinks with him and then beg off with a headache. The thought absolutely exhausted her, but she'd be potentially helping find Danita and a lot of other women. Being tired was nothing compared to what they could be going through.

"Do it. We've got your back."

She desperately wanted to ask if Nathan would be part of the backup, but she still had some pride left. Instead she said, "I'm trusting you because Nathan does."

"I know."

And that was that. Because it was absolutely the truth. She *was* trusting that they'd have her back if she got tossed into a dangerous situation, because Nathan did. And that was good enough for her.

The comm van slowed to a stop and after a moment's pause for Elliott to check out the surrounding neighborhood via their exterior cameras, Freeman, one of Burkhart's field agents, slipped out the back door. He closed it behind him with barely a sound.

Their command center today looked like an electrical company truck. Everything on the exterior was authentic, as were Freeman's uniform and credentials. They didn't belong to him, but they were real. Not that anyone would question them anyway. Not in a ritzy neighborhood like this. Freeman was part of the working class, which basically made him invisible to the wealthy who might be curious enough to check out the electric company van.

Burkhart slipped his earpiece in and stepped behind Elliott and another analyst he'd pulled in for this backup op. There were also two other agents in the van, including Dax, who joined him behind Elliott.

"She's in," Elliott said, clacking away at the keyboard, even though they could all hear Amelia's conversation with Mercado.

"She was a fucking champ today," Dax said quietly, his comment directed at Burkhart.

He simply nodded. "I read the report." The way she'd reacted to being attacked had no doubt saved her life and her employee's life. Instead of running or panicking, she'd full-on attacked, taking that psycho off guard.

"Any news from Nieto about her attacker?"

"Not yet. Guy's got a lawyer, but I think they'll get him to talk."

"We're in!" Elliott's voice was excited as code started streaming across his computer screen and the two above his main one.

"Thanks again for having me over. Today's been rough," Amelia said to Mercado, her voice clear. The connection they had to the microphone in her cell was strong.

"She left her purse in the kitchen like we instructed." Elliott was talking more to himself than anyone else at this point. "The phone's stopped moving."

Burkhart had worked with him long enough to know when he was in the zone.

"She seems to be a natural at this. Maybe we should recruit her." Dax's voice was only partially joking.

Her voice grew fainter, as did Mercado's. They were moving to somewhere else on his property, which meant there wouldn't be any audio for her right now.

Burkhart just laughed even though he *was* worried that she was a naturally good liar. It was good for the op, only he couldn't help worrying about Ortiz. His man was very adept at covering his emotions, as were most of his agents, but Amelia Rios meant something to Ortiz.

Burkhart had noticed it the first time Ortiz talked about her, even though he'd covered it well. She'd been more than a friend to Ortiz. A lot more. Burkhart still wasn't certain what to make of their relationship.

"You tell Ortiz about this?" Dax asked quietly.

"No. Didn't want to distract him." Ortiz was in a potentially important meeting right now, and if he knew Amelia was inside Mercado's house—or had been attacked earlier—it could screw with his concentration. Especially since they didn't currently have audio on her.

Burkhart didn't like it, but it was the way it had to be. They had eyes on the house too, so if anyone left, they'd know. "How're you coming along?"

"Much faster this time since I already got a crack at his system once. There are still a few layers of encryption to slide through."

Good. The sooner the better.

"Come on, he'll never know. Don't be such a baby," a female voice streamed over the line.

"Who is that?" Burkhart demanded. He guessed it was Mercado's daughter, since she lived at the palatial estate.

Eugene, the other analyst, pulled up another program on one of his screens. "Voice recognition says . . . Collette Mercado."

"We shouldn't disrespect him in his house," a deep male voice said.

"It's my house too. You used to be fun," she snapped.

"Collette—"

There was a groan. Then another, longer one. Definitely sexual in nature.

Oh hell, they were having sex in the kitchen. Just great.

"Voice recognition says that's Santino Luna, Iker's head of security."

Burkhart raised his eyebrows but didn't respond. That was interesting and he made a mental note of it. If Mercado was involved in the kidnapping of all these women, maybe they'd be able to get to him through his daughter. Or his head of security. Burkhart had done thorough checks of all of Mercado's people, so if Collette and Luna were having an affair, they were very secretive about it. Maybe he could use that against Luna. Burkhart never ruled out any option when it came to saving the innocent.

"I'm fully in," Elliot announced quietly.

Burkhart's heart rate increased a fraction, but he remained immobile. Years in the Navy had taught him to always remain calm and in control on the outside. His job now demanded it. "How long will it take to copy everything?"

"Few minutes, max."

"Good work." He glanced at the screen with the video feed of Freeman "working" on a light pole a few houses down from Mercado's place. Everything looked clear on his end too.

Soon they'd have the information they needed. If Mercado was involved in any way, they were going to go after him fast and hard. And rip his life apart.

Chapter 17

Solid intelligence: the gold standard of information gathered from data processing.

Nathan let his hands drop to his sides as Alexander Lopez's guard finished searching him for weapons.

Next to him, Selene did the same. Her real name was Selene Lazaro, but Lopez knew her as Selene Silva, a high-priced assassin.

They'd already had their vehicle searched and had been scanned with a metal-detecting wand. Nathan was surprised, since Selene and Lopez had a good relationship—the arms dealer had invited her alias to his wedding. The precaution was likely because she was bringing a stranger to his home—well, one of his homes.

"They're clear," one of the guards said quietly into a communicator Nathan couldn't see.

Moments later Lopez strode out into the marbled entryway wearing flip-flops, green cargo pants, and a T-shirt that said FBI: FEMALE BODY INSPECTOR on the front.

Next to Nathan, Selene started laughing. "I can't believe Allison let you wear that!"

Lopez just grinned. "She bought it for me."

Selene laughed harder, shaking her head once. "At least she made you get rid of that awful statue out here."

"You didn't like it either?" Lopez sounded truly surprised.

Selene's eyebrows lifted. "It was of a naked woman obscenely cupping herself between her legs and groping her breasts." *What do you think?* was the implied, silent question.

Lopez shrugged, the ghost of a smile tugging at his mouth. "What's not to love?"

Selene simply sighed and held out a hand to Nathan. "Miguel, this is Alexander. Alexander, Miguel. We appreciate you meeting with us today."

After brief greetings were made, Lopez tilted his head toward a hallway. "Come on, let's talk in my office."

Two guards flanked them but stopped when Lopez opened a polished wooden door. Selene went ahead of Nathan, her heels making an insistent *click-click* sound as she moved. She'd dressed in all black today and looked sleek. Like an operator. Snug pants, strappy fitted top with a black custom-made jacket over it. No jewelry except for small earrings and a watch he knew turned into a garrote wire. She'd pulled her pale blond hair back into a sleek ponytail at the nape of her neck so that it spilled down her back.

"Would either of you like something to drink?" Lopez motioned to a Chesterfield.

When Selene sat, so did Nathan. And when she

declined a drink, he did too. Today he was following her lead. This was his first meet with Lopez and potentially the start of a relationship with the gunrunner who was always good for information.

Lopez poured a glass of scotch for himself before perching on the edge of his desk. In his early forties, the man was fit and muscular. His clothes were on the goofy side, but Nathan could see the man was prepared for an attack. It was likely a subconscious thing, but even as he sat, seemingly casual, all the lines of his body were pulled tight. "As usual, you were annoyingly vague," he said to Selene. "So talk. And explain why you brought a friend."

Selene crossed one long leg over the other and leaned back against the couch, the picture of casual elegance. "I brought Miguel because he's in the same business as me. I simply wanted you two to meet, since I thought you could potentially be beneficial to each other in the future."

Lopez shot him a glance, his expression neutral, before focusing on Selene again. "Okay. Why are you here?"

"Iker Mercado. Is he taking over the skin trade now that Paul Hill's out of the way?" Her voice was crisp.

Lopez's dark eyes narrowed. He set his tumbler down on the desk behind him. "Why are you asking?"

"I'm interested in doing business with him but not if he's in any way like Hill." Her answer was immediate.

So was Lopez's relief. It was subtle, but Nathan noticed the way the man's shoulders relaxed. Lopez was in a serious relationship with a former escort and had a general dislike for anyone who was involved in the sex or slave trade.

Lopez cleared his throat. "It's not gospel, but as far as I know, he's clean—as far as human trade goes. He deals mainly in antiquities and art. I didn't know you were interested in that."

Illegal antiquities and *stolen* art. One piece could fetch millions. And Mercado was suspected of heavy-duty smuggling as well.

"I'm not, exactly. Have you seen the news recently?" she asked.

A brief nod. "I'm always tuned in."

"You saw the piece on the female remains found."

He pushed out a sigh. "Yeah. Fucking serial killer in Miami."

Selene was silent for a moment, as if weighing how much she wanted to say. It was all part of her cover, as Nathan knew. "I have a new client who wants me to find who killed those women." *And kill whoever did it,* was her unspoken sentiment. "My client had a relationship with one of them."

Lopez's eyes narrowed. "Names and identities haven't been released yet."

Selene snorted, as if that didn't matter. To someone like Selene Silva, it wouldn't. If she wanted the names of the victims, her alias would get them.

Lopez continued before she could. "That's why you're here. You think Mercado might be involved? And you think or know those women were part of the skin trade?"

"Yes to the first and I don't know to the second. My

source says the police aren't certain what happened to the women before they died. They could be victims of the skin trade or one sick fuck. Either way, I don't care. I want to know who's in charge." Apparently she wasn't going to mention the black-market-babies angle to him.

"I'll see what I can find out. I don't think Mercado's your guy, though. He's kind of . . . old-fashioned, I guess. A gentleman criminal, I've heard him called. We don't run in the same circles, but I know a lot of people he interacts with."

"Thanks. I'll double your normal fee if you can get me solid intel in the next couple days. My client is anxious."

Lopez stood. "I'll try."

They talked for a few more minutes before leaving. Nathan kept his disappointment in check even when he and Selene were alone in the SUV. He'd been hoping for something solid and incriminating against Mercado. The darkly jealous part of him wanted the guy to be involved simply because of the way he looked at Amelia, but Nathan really wanted to find out who the leader of this operation was. And if someone was impregnating women and selling their babies on the black market, it would be more than a one-man show. It would be funded and organized.

If Mercado was their guy, they could stop looking and take him down. If he wasn't, they still had to pin down a monster. Unfortunately there were a lot of them in the world. Finding one was like finding a needle in a stack of needles.

Once they were on the road—headed to a warehouse where they'd ditch this SUV and pick up another in case Lopez had them tailed—Nathan turned his encrypted cell back on. "Gonna check in with home base," he murmured.

Selene just nodded and continued driving. She'd be heading out of town in a few days if Lopez didn't make further contact with her. As far as Nathan knew she'd only come down to Miami because of her relationship with Lopez, but she wasn't going to be part of this op long-term.

He had a few messages and two texts. The first was from Elliott. *Rios got the date and we got the info. Job done.*

Amelia had gone on another date with Mercado? When the fuck had *that* happened? He'd just seen her last night.

Frowning, he scrolled to the next text. From Dax. *A attacked but fine. Guy caught. Former employee in custody. Check e-mail for full report.*

His blood chilled as he reread the text. Amelia had been attacked again. She had to be okay, because she'd gone on a freaking date with Mercado according to when these texts were sent. He could speculate all he wanted about what had happened, but he decided to call her directly. When she didn't answer he contacted Burkhart next.

"How'd it go?" Burkhart asked after two rings.

"Potentially good." He quickly relayed everything, then asked, "So we got the intel from Mercado?" He wanted to find out what had happened to Amelia, but he didn't want to act too eager.

"We're going through everything from his files now. He's into some shady stuff, but we haven't found anything to indicate he's into either the skin trade or selling babies on the black market."

That was good and bad. They needed to nail whoever was behind this. "How's Amelia?"

"Good. She held up well, stayed at Mercado's for a couple hours. Then he took her to the hospital to see her employee who was injured in the attack this morning. She's home now, alone. I've got one of my guys watching her place just as a precaution."

Relief flooded his veins like a tidal wave. Knowing she was home safe smoothed out most of his edges. Even if he was pissed she hadn't contacted him about what had happened.

He wondered if that bastard Mercado had kissed Amelia again. The thought of another man's lips on hers had all the muscles in his body tightening. It took a moment for him to find his voice. "What happened?"

"Guy she fired about a month ago ambushed her behind her restaurant. Tased one of her employees, so she pepper-sprayed him until he went down. Dax restrained the guy and the locals have him in custody."

Nathan wanted to know the bastard's name but reined in his anger. Burkhart didn't need to know the scope of his rage. Nathan would just read the report as soon as they disconnected. "Are they going to be able to hold him?"

"Think so. Nieto's personally involved in this case now."

Good. If the former employee was let go from police custody, Nathan didn't want to think about what he'd do. The thought of someone hurting Amelia made something dark twist inside him. He wanted to head directly to where she was and take care of her. Didn't matter that it was impossible right now; his heart was telling him to get over to her place.

"You two headed back to base?" Burkhart asked.

"On our way."

"Is your friend okay?" Selene asked as soon as he and Burkhart had disconnected.

"She's good." He didn't say more, but Selene didn't seem to mind, thankfully. Right now he just wanted to get through the rest of the day and go see Amelia.

He needed to see with his own eyes that she was truly fine.

Leaning back in his office chair, Wesley speed-dialed Karen as soon as he ended his call with Ortiz. "You find anything?"

"I was just about to call you." She sounded smug, a sure sign she'd most definitely discovered something to help their case. Right now he had her digging up everything she could to find out who'd hurt Amelia. "I did a run scanning CCTVs for license plates or vehicles that showed up around the same time Amelia was attacked the night of the auction, then yesterday. One license plate showed in the exact same vicinities."

"Gray?" The truck Neal Gray had been driving that morning hadn't been damaged, so if he'd attacked Amelia the day before, he'd done it in a different vehicle. They needed evidence to link him to the previous attack to show a steady escalation of violence toward her. Then they'd be able to get him on multiple offenses.

"No, but I found something very interesting. The plate of the truck used belongs to a Lorna Torres. According to the DMV she's eighty-two years old. From what I've gathered through her insurance records, the truck belonged to her deceased husband and she just keeps it in storage in her garage."

"The point, Karen."

"I'm getting there. You need to appreciate my brilliance first. Guess who Torres lives next door to? Gray's mother—and Gray had to move back in with her when he lost his job at Amelia's restaurant. That's not a coincidence."

So Neal had stolen his elderly neighbor's truck for the attacks. Stupid to steal so close to home. "Good work. Send all the info to Nieto. I'm going to call and give him a heads-up."

"Already done. I blind-copied you."

Of course she had. He swore Karen could read his mind some days. "Thanks." Once he disconnected he pulled up his e-mail and scanned the info before calling Nieto.

"Yeah?" Nieto answered immediately.

"You checked your e-mail in the last five minutes?"

"No, I'm fucking busy over here."

A smile tugged at Wesley's mouth. "Well, check. One of my people just sent you a Christmas present. Has Sinclair gotten Gray to confess to the other attacks on Amelia yet?"

"No, he's back in holding right now."

"Well, get him out. With the new info you've got, Sinclair should be able to make this guy talk. Especially if you try to nail him for taking Tessa Hall." Wesley didn't think he was involved with that. According to Detective Sinclair, Neal Gray was pissed at Amelia for losing his job and giving him a bad evaluation when potential employers had called to check up on his references. Wesley couldn't believe the guy had even listed her, considering why he'd been fired, but the stupidity of people never ceased to amaze him.

"You don't really think he's involved with Hall's disappearance," Nieto scoffed.

"No, I don't." But if they scared him enough into thinking he could be charged for the disappearance of Hall, hopefully he'd confess to everything else.

"Ah, gotcha. Thanks for the info. I'll let you know what happens, but he's in holding for now and he's not going anywhere for the next forty-eight hours regardless."

"Good." At least that was one problem out of the way.

For now. It seemed clear that Gray had been the one to go after Amelia. And as long as he was in jail, she was safe. But Wesley figured that with Sinclair's stellar record, he'd be able to break Gray soon. When that happened, it just depended on the right judge revoking Gray's bail if he decided to take things to trial. But if he took a deal he'd skip a trial and go straight to prison.

That was what Wesley was hoping for. If not, he'd pull some strings and make sure that bastard got in front of the "right" judge.

Chapter 18

Shock and awe: a military doctrine meaning rapid dominance. A technique using an overwhelming display of force to paralyze your target's perception of the battleground.

Nathan's gut clenched as Amelia opened her front door and stepped back. He'd called ahead and told her he had good news and wanted to tell her in person.

But the divide between them was so thick it might as well be tangible.

"Did I wake you?" he asked as she shut the door behind him.

She was wearing lounge pants, a tank top—no bra, something he was trying hard not to pay attention to—and had bare feet. Her toes were painted a teal color today. "No, can't sleep." Her words were clipped, her gaze shuttered.

When she wrapped her arms around herself and didn't invite him any farther than the foyer, he shoved his hands in his pockets. If he tried to reach for her, he knew she'd reject him. "I'm sorry about what happened this morning. How are you doing?"

Her shrug was jerky. "Good, I guess. Thank you for asking."

Her response was ultra-polite, like something she'd say to a stranger. Which was what they felt like right now. It grated on his nerves. He wanted to pin her up against her front door and kiss her senseless. "Gray confessed to all the attacks on you. He's going away for six to eight years." He'd probably get out sooner thanks to their fucked-up system, but at least he was off the streets for now.

Amelia's arms dropped, her bright eyes lighting up with hope. "For real?"

"Yeah, he confessed and took a deal. He was scared the cops would try to pin the disappearance of Tessa on him." Not to mention he had a few priors so he knew how the system worked. If he hadn't taken the deal and then had gone to trial with those priors on his record, he would have likely been found guilty. And a jury would have potentially, and probably, given him a harsher sentence than what he'd gotten. The guy was playing the odds that he'd get out of prison early.

"Thank God." She raked a trembling hand through her hair.

He wanted to pull her close, to comfort her, but held back. "I . . . found out after the fact that you went to Mercado's." And he was trying to get over being pissed about it. "The team got everything. He doesn't appear to be involved. Not with the kidnappings anyway. He's definitely into some illegal stuff, but it doesn't look as if he's into moving or selling people." Or if he was, there was absolutely no evidence to indicate it.

"Thank God," she murmured. "I thought my psycho-detecting radar was screwed up." Her lips twitched a fraction, making him smile in return.

"You shouldn't see him anymore, regardless."

She cocked an eyebrow at him. "Is that an order?" He'd started to respond when she shook her head, cutting him off. "I don't know why I said that. I'm not going to see him anymore."

He nodded once, that awkwardness between them expanding again. He wished he knew how to fix it. "I don't want to walk away from us," he blurted.

It was clear he'd surprised her. She took a step toward him, her blue eyes filled with anguish. "I don't either, Nathan."

God, he loved when she said his name.

"But I feel like there's this chasm between us and I don't know how to fix it," she continued. "And I'm not saying you will, but I have this fear that you'll always resent me or hold it over my head that I didn't tell you. I don't want to live like that, feeling guilty all the time. It took me years—and a lot of counseling—to get to where I am, to a good place where I like myself again."

Anger flared inside him even if he knew he deserved her reaction. He'd walked out, but only so he wouldn't say something he'd regret. "I'm right here, telling you I want to try. You're not even going to give me a chance?"

She started to reach for him, let her hands drop instead. "I didn't say that. I just . . . I want to try a relationship with you. So much. Being with you again has reminded me how much I . . ." She cleared her throat.

"How much I care for you. But it feels like we're doomed to fail."

Screw that. He wasn't giving her up. He closed the distance between them and in a completely dominant move grabbed her hips and tugged her close. Her hands flew to his chest and slid over his pecs. "We can start fresh, be honest with each other about everything."

Something flared in her eyes and she watched him for a long moment. "You mean like telling me who you really work for?" There was no anger in her words.

Shit. He didn't respond. He *did* want complete and total honesty between them, but his cover was part of his job. He'd grown accustomed to it, but lying to Amelia twisted him up inside. Especially since he'd just talked about starting fresh. Who the hell had told her? Or maybe she'd just figured it out on her own.

"Are you going to say anything?" she asked quietly.

He wanted to tell her the truth. Desperately. "I can't."

"Can't or won't?" Her voice was flat.

"Can't." He absolutely couldn't tell her who he worked for without authorization.

"Right." Her lips pulled into a thin line. She took a small step back, forcing him to drop his hands from her hips. The step might as well have been as big as the Grand Canyon for how wide he could feel it stretching between them. "Is this like some sort of punishment? I don't trust you, so you don't tell me something?" Her question wasn't bitter, just . . . full of anguish. Once again she wrapped her arms around herself in a clearly protective gesture.

He'd never do that, and it pissed him off she could think it. He physically ached to hold her. "No," he gritted out. He started to say more, but his phone buzzed in his pocket. It was close to midnight, so this wouldn't be good. Jaw clenched tight, he whipped his cell out, winced.

It was Burkhart. *Infil in one hour. Get to base now.*

No details because they weren't necessary. They'd be infiltrating somewhere and he'd better be ready to gear up and go. "I've got to go." Talk about perfect fucking timing.

Amelia simply nodded, her expression one of complete remoteness.

Well, fuck that. He covered the distance between them and crushed his mouth to hers. Her palms flattened against his chest. He thought she was pushing him away and started to back up, but then her fingers curled into his shirt.

Consumed with the need to taste her, he invaded her mouth with his tongue, teasing his against hers. When she moaned and lifted a leg to wind around his waist, grinding her body against his, it took all the strength he possessed not to stay and finish this.

With effort, he pulled back. "I've gotta go."

Breathing as hard as he was, she simply nodded and let her leg drop. She didn't ask if he'd call, didn't ask anything at all. Just nodded. And there was a hint of resignation in her gaze, as if she expected that to be their last kiss.

No fucking way. Whatever had happened between them, they could move past it. He refused to believe otherwise. "I'm not letting you go," he growled before turning and shutting the door behind him.

After whatever this op was, he was talking to

Burkhart. He needed to be honest with Amelia if they had a shot at moving forward. He couldn't ask for pure honesty from her and give her less. But it went both ways. They needed to start their relationship with nothing between them. There was still the matter of the information from the file on her that Burkhart had given him. Nathan didn't care about how she'd gotten her start in business, though, only that she came clean with him about that too.

If she trusted him enough to tell him, maybe they had a real shot.

"No more movement along the perimeter," Nathan said quietly into his comm as he looked through his NVBs— night-vision binocs. From his position on top of the abandoned warehouse across the street, he had a good visual of their target's exterior. "Everyone report."

Bell, Freeman, Dax, and the other men in his twelve-man team reported that they were in place and all saw the same thing he did.

As of twenty minutes ago, there had been no move-ment along the gated perimeter of a warehouse the NSA suspected of holding kidnapped women and children. Burkhart wasn't certain if this was related to the operation they were trying to bring down, but they weren't going to turn a blind eye to it regardless. Lopez had given Selene a tip that some Russians had been running a small slave trade and using this warehouse as their base of operations.

Fuckers were about to go down.

"Ten-four, headed down. Elliott, what's your visual?"

"Except for a few homeless people, you're clear for

three blocks surrounding the target." Elliott, as usual, was in the command center, keeping watch via CCTVs and other cameras he'd hacked into.

"I'm on my way down to ground level. In fifteen seconds we move in. Everyone knows their positions." They'd put this tactical team together quickly, gearing up at home base and moving out in company-owned SUVs. They'd studied the blueprints of the place and, since it was basically a giant warehouse, it wasn't hard to decide where to infiltrate.

With twelve of them, they were working in tandem, each pair entering together in a hard entrance.

"Explosives are in place," Dax said quietly. He was the only one who'd already breached the fenced perimeter, using the cover of darkness to evade detection—and thanks to Elliott, who'd fucked with the video capabilities coming from the warehouse, it was a lot easier.

"Our guys just got off the phone with their 'security provider,'" Elliott said, laughter in his voice. "They think it's a widespread malfunction across a grid in the city. You guys are good to go."

Nathan smiled to himself as he stepped out onto street level across from the abandoned building. The Russian thugs they were about to infiltrate had called their security company when their system went haywire, but Elliott had intercepted the call.

Now it was up to Nathan and his guys to do the rest. "Freeman and I are going through first. The rest of you follow in ten-second increments."

After disabling the alarm system, they'd created a

breach in the ten-foot fence line. Now they'd go inside in twos, fanning out to their designated position.

They'd all done enough ops similar to this that it was standard operating procedure, but Nathan never let his guard down.

M4 in hand, he slipped through the cutout in the fence, Freeman right behind him. Their soft-soled boots barely made a sound over the pavement as they moved quickly across the open space surrounding the warehouse.

Moonlight and the natural illumination from the city gave them enough of a visual that they didn't need their NVGs.

There was no outer movement that he could discern as he raced to the far west corner of the warehouse. High along the building were a few windows. Light streamed out from them. Once he and Freeman were in place, he mentally ticked off the time, waiting for his last guy to check in.

Barely two minutes later, Dax murmured, "In place."

He was the last one Nathan was waiting for. Their intel told them that they should expect a dozen armed men inside. He knew his guys could take triple that and still come out on top, but he liked these odds. He pulled his custom-fit gas mask down over his face. They all had on full headgear, covering their heads and faces except for eyes, nose, and mouth, but the gas mask was necessary for their next move.

"Everyone ready?" he asked as he pulled a canister from his utility belt. He and Freeman plastered themselves back against the outer wall.

"Affirmative," came the replies from everyone.

"Hit it, Delta." Delta was Dax's call sign for this op. He'd set the charges; now it was time to blow everything.

A second later multiple explosions ripped through the air. The ground rumbled slightly beneath them. Excluding the rolling door at the front, there were four regular doors on each side of the building. Or there had been.

They'd all been blown free.

Adrenaline pumping hard, Nathan tuned out the shouts from inside as he tossed in a canister of tear gas through the newly created hole. Freeman did the same.

They entered hard, their weapons up as they pushed through the haze of smoke.

The shouts were nonsensical, mainly just "police" and "run." A burst of staccato gunfire went off, then ended just as quickly.

"Gunman down," Dax said through the comm line.

As the smoke cleared, Nathan spotted two men hunched over on the floor near a foldout table. Beers and playing cards were scattered over the top. He couldn't see any civilians, just huge containers backed against one wall. He had a feeling he knew what was in them.

One of the men clawed at his eyes with one hand and blindly groped at his back for a weapon tucked into his pants.

Nathan shoved his M4 into the guy's spine. "Face down, hands above your head!" He retrieved the weapon, shoved it into one of his pockets as he secured the groaning man's hands and feet into flex cuffs.

"Got your six," Freeman said over the comm.

There were always a few precious seconds when an operator's back was exposed in situations like this, usually when securing a target. He'd worked with Freeman enough to trust the guy with his life. Hell, they'd almost died together not too long ago.

"Two targets secured," he said into his comm after cuffing the next groaning man.

Less than ten minutes later, the smoke had cleared and a dozen men with ties to a local Russian gang were facedown on the floor in a single line with their hands and feet secured.

Nathan's team had found two locked containers of women and children, all in various conditions of shock or terror, though they were all malnourished to an extent.

And none of them seemed to speak any English.

His gut tightened as he radioed Burkhart. "Targets all secure and we're gonna need a Russian translator." He assumed the women and children were Russian, given some of the phrases, but he couldn't be certain.

In that moment, the darkest part of him wanted to line up the men on the floor and execute them all. No one had a right to own or sell another human being. It was one of the most deplorable acts in the world.

For now he compartmentalized what was going on and kept his game face on. They'd been able to save a lot of people tonight. He'd take the win.

Very soon, he planned to take the biggest win of all, Amelia's heart.

Chapter 19

Burn phone: prepaid disposable phone.

"Thanks for walking me out," Amelia said to Manuel as they left the restaurant. From now on she was going to make sure everyone had an escort when they walked to their vehicle, regardless of the time of day.

"Of course. I just hope things will settle down." He glanced around the full parking lot.

"Neal confessed, so hopefully things will." That had nothing to do with Tessa's going missing, but Amelia kept that thought to herself. She paused along a row of vehicles as a BMW with tinted windows turned down the parking aisle they were about to cross.

Manuel frowned and actually held out a hand in front of her, to protect her. The likely subconscious protective motion was ridiculously sweet, warming her from the inside out. Considering she felt like crap at the moment, it eased some of the stiffness in her shoulders. Not by much, though.

When the sleek silver car slowed and the window rolled down, she tensed until she saw Collette Mercado behind the wheel. Wearing Fendi sunglasses with amber lenses, the woman smiled widely. "I must have perfect timing. Are you leaving?"

Amelia nodded before laying a gentle hand on Manuel's forearm. "You can head back in. My rental's right there." She tilted her chin to the next row across from them.

"You're sure?"

"Positive. I'll see you tomorrow. Afternoon, though. I'll be at Amelia's in the morning." Amelia's was short for La Cocina de Amelia.

He nodded once before heading back through the throng of parked vehicles. She turned and smiled at Collette, even though she was certain the look didn't meet her eyes. She was too damn tired to paint on a happy face. "How are you?"

"Good, but I should be asking you that. I'm surprised you're at work so soon." Her voice was sincere enough, but something about Collette bothered her. It was subtle, but she had an entitled air that rubbed Amelia the wrong way.

Or maybe she was just projecting her own insecurities. Amelia had seen her the day before at Mercado's, but Collette had disappeared after saying hello to them. "Staying active keeps me sane," she said, lightly laughing. It was the truth. She needed to keep busy, though this had more to do with Nathan than anything else. When he'd come by late last night, she hoped they might be able to work through some of their stuff. Instead she just felt even worse today and they'd resolved nothing. Which wasn't anyone's fault. She understood that he'd been called away to work.

"I understand that. Listen . . . I have a favor to ask and it's okay if you say no. I took a chance coming to see you today, so I'm hoping it's fate I ran into you." She smiled that wide smile again and for a moment it reminded Amelia of a shark. "I, God, this is a little embarrassing, but I'm thinking of investing in a new restaurant. Well, a potential one. I could ask my father, but you're the expert, so I was hoping you could come look at the property. My friend is actually buying the building and will be starting his own business, but he approached me with a business proposal. It looks solid to me, but . . . I was really hoping you'd check out the area and just give me your general thoughts. I know location matters as much as anything else. I'll buy you lunch," Collette added, almost as an afterthought.

Amelia so didn't want to do this now. "Is it far from here?"

She shook her head, hopeful smile in place. "About fifteen minutes away."

Amelia wanted to say no. It was on the tip of her tongue, but guilt pushed at her. She'd basically used Mercado—for very good reasons—and since he wasn't the criminal mastermind Nathan and his team had thought, she couldn't help the sliver of guilt that wormed its way into her. "Okay, as long as it's not for too long. I've got a lot of paperwork to catch up on." A total lie, but she'd use work as an excuse any day. "I'll take a rain check on lunch." Now she forced a smile out. It wasn't the woman's fault she'd been having a crappy week.

"Thank you." Collette nodded at the passenger side. "Hop in."

Amelia thought about telling Collette she'd just

follow her, but she didn't want to drive even an extra fifteen minutes in Miami traffic. Hell, it would end up being thirty minutes at least, with the return trip. Amelia slid into the smooth seat, somehow not surprised that Collette had classical music playing.

Collette's long honey brown hair was down in soft waves. Small gold hoops peeked through her hair when she turned to Amelia. "I can't thank you enough for this."

"No problem. I know how stressful it is to invest in something." Mainly because she'd invested in herself. She doubted Collette had any clue what it was like to put her heart and soul into something and fear what would happen if she failed. To sacrifice any extras for years just to make ends meet. No, the woman would have a buffer with her father's money to back her.

"It really is, especially in such a difficult industry. Oh, I have an extra water bottle if you want." She tapped one of the bottles in the drink holder between them.

"Thanks." Mainly to keep her hands busy, she took it. When she heard the buzz of her cell phone, she pulled it from her purse. As she looked at the screen she said, "What type of restaurant is this going to be?"

"Asian fusion. . . ." Amelia tuned her out as Collette chatted about the type of decor her friend planned. She felt a little bad, but she really didn't care and something about Collette bothered her.

Her heart skipped a beat as she looked at Nathan's message. *You can't ignore me forever. I want to see you tonight.*

She wasn't ignoring him. Not exactly. Okay, maybe that was what she'd been doing. She'd been at work, though, so it wasn't as if she'd had time to talk. But she did now. And no matter what, no matter how hard it might be, she *did* want to see if they had a shot at something real. She'd never gotten over him, not truly, and he'd clearly never gotten over her. That had to mean something. If he said he couldn't tell her who he worked for, then she needed to believe that he'd tell her when he could.

Half listening to Collette, she texted him back. *Not ignoring you. Was busy at work. Leaving now, about to run an errand then headed home. Should be there in a couple hours. Come by whenever.* Her finger hovered over the keyboard for a moment and then she added another message. *I'm not letting you go either.*

At least not without a fight. If he could fight for her, she could for him. They had to be able to make things work. She was too stubborn to believe otherwise. Feeling better, she set her phone on her lap and opened the water bottle. "It all sounds like a really exciting venture," she said to Collette before taking a sip of the water. Or the bits and pieces she'd heard did. Fusion restaurants tended to be popular because there was often something for everyone. As long as the food was good, the prices were right for the target audience, and the location was decent, in the end it often came down to money management and in-house management.

It was where so many people failed when running restaurants. She wasn't about to get into that, though. She took another sip and then set it in one of the cup holders when a wave of dizziness swept through her.

"I think so." Collette glanced at her as she pulled up to a stoplight.

Dang it, maybe she'd been more tired than she thought. Amelia blinked and tried to clear her thoughts as a haziness descended on her. Her phone buzzed again, but she couldn't find the energy to swipe in her code. "I don't feel very good." Were her words slurred? Jeez, what was wrong with her?

"That's the whole point," Collette murmured, glee in her voice.

Fear jolted through her. Amelia tried to respond, but her eyelids weighed heavily, drooping until she couldn't force them open. The last thing she thought she heard Collette say was "finally" before darkness engulfed her.

Amelia struggled to open her eyes, a sense of panic pushing at her chest, but she couldn't remember why. Where was she? Sheets rustled beneath her as a wave of nausea swept through her.

Her eyes finally cracked open to fluorescent brightness. She wasn't at home or at work. The hospital? Had something else happened?

She took a deep breath, the inhalation of air steadying her. *Think, think, think,* her mind ordered.

The last thing she remembered was leaving the restaurant. Then Collette had been there, which seemed odd. She'd wanted Amelia to look at . . . a building for a potential restaurant. She hadn't wanted to go, but had done so anyway. Stupid guilty feelings . . .

The water. *Shit, shit, shit.*

Realization slammed into Amelia. There had been something in that water bottle. Full-blown fear slid through her, the rush of terror and adrenaline giving her the energy to move.

She sat up and swung her legs off the bed. The sudden action made her lose her balance and pitch forward onto a linoleum floor. She cried out as her knees slammed into the floor. The jolt of pain grounded her a little more. Everything was wavy and hazy, but she pushed onto all fours.

Have to get out of here. Have to call Nathan. Those were the main two thoughts she focused on. She looked around the stark room from her position on the floor. There was the bed she'd just fallen off, a mini-fridge, a table. No windows. The room had an antiseptic scent to it. Fresh but also very sterile. Like a hospital.

She tried to push herself up but couldn't manage it, so she turned back around and held on to the mattress, using it to stand. On wobbly legs she stood, leaning against the bed to hold herself in place. Before she could think about moving any farther, a door opened.

A man stepped inside. He was taller than her, but not nearly as tall as Nathan. Likely in his early fifties, he had dark hair and a clean-shaven face. He looked nice. Was he here to help her?

"Feeling a little shaky?" the man asked, stepping toward her almost cautiously.

"Yesh." She slurred the word. Too late she saw something in his hand.

A syringe.

She tried to ward him off, but her arms just Kermit-flailed. All her movements were in slow motion while he moved at warp speed. "No." The word rasped from her as the syringe pierced her upper arm.

She didn't even feel the sting, but that haziness was back, sweeping her into darkness once again.

* * *

Out of habit, Sid checked the pistol he had tucked into the back of his pants. He'd been called in for a "friendly check-in" as Collette had put it. Bitch thought she had him on a leash. He nearly snorted to himself as he strode down the hall of the warehouse she'd turned into a covert medical center. Maybe she did have him on a leash, because here he was.

She was sexy as fuck and ruthless. He wouldn't ever admit it aloud, but something about her scared him. He could take her in a one-on-one fight, though, so it was the only reason he'd agreed to meet her in her office alone.

As he strode down the quiet corridor, the only sounds he occasionally heard was weeping from some of the locked-up women. What the hell were they crying about? It wasn't as if they were being abused. They got the best food and vitamins and got to lie around on their asses for months.

When he reached the wooden door with no identifying markers, he knocked once.

"Come in," Collette called out.

He stepped inside, fully ready to defend himself, but stopped dead in his tracks. Collette was sitting on the front of her desk, legs spread—and completely naked. He swallowed hard, his gaze traveling down to her bare mound. He already knew she got everything waxed, but it had been months since she let him fuck her.

"You've been a bad boy," Collette murmured, her voice silky smooth and seductive.

His dick immediately stood at attention. He knew that tone well, knew what she wanted.

"Shut the door unless you want to give the doctor

a show." She threw her head back and laughed, loose tendrils of her honey-streaked hair escaping from the messy bun she'd pulled it up into. She had a year-round glow and a perfectly toned body.

Without taking his eyes off her, he reached behind him and shut the door with a barely audible click. "What are you doing?" She had to be pissed at him. This could be a trap.

On guard, he turned and locked the door behind him. Maybe she thought she could distract him with sex and let one of the security guys ambush him. No way in hell. He leaned against the door, keeping distance between them. "Why am I here?"

"You've potentially cost me a lot of money." Her gaze sharpened then.

Knowing it would piss her off, he lifted one shoulder. "No one will track the bodies back to you."

"Still, we're going to have to stop bringing in any more women until the heat's passed."

Yeah, and he planned to be long gone soon. He hadn't been willing to split this morning, though. Not when she'd personally called him in. He'd seen one of her guys watching his condo and figured it was a test. She wanted to see how loyal he was. He'd prove his loyalty, or at least give the appearance of it, then run when the time was right. "We've already made a big profit. It's just part of business."

Her dark eyes narrowed. "So what? You still cost me money because of your carelessness. Now you get to make it up to me." She stroked a hand between her legs, slid a finger inside herself before slowly drawing it out. "On your knees," she ordered.

Of their own accord, his hips jerked forward. He remembered how tight she was, how they'd screwed for practically weeks on end when they first met. Looking back, he realized that was how she'd recruited him. He'd have worked for her anyway, especially with the money he made, but the sex had been a nice bonus.

He'd missed fucking someone as free as her. She had absolutely no hang-ups when it came to sex.

Raging hard, he strode across the office and slid between her open thighs. He tugged on her hair, pulling her neck back so she had to look at him.

Pleasure flashed in her dark eyes. She liked a bite of pain and he was more than willing to deliver. But first, he needed to make sure this wasn't a trap. "You had someone watching me this morning," he growled.

"Yeah, so?"

He swept a hand out on the desk, shoving the small container of pens and a scissor to the floor. It was the only potential choice of weapons on the desk and he wasn't taking the chance she'd try to attack him when he went down on her. "I'm not your lapdog."

She scored her nails down his chest. "I thought you might try to run."

He tugged on her hair once. "Do I have a reason to?"

"If you want to go, get out. No one's keeping you here. I just wanted to make sure you didn't go to the cops." She shoved lightly at his chest. "Leave if you want. I'll find someone else to please me," she murmured.

He cupped between her legs, shuddered when he found her soaking. "I'll leave when I'm good and ready." He yanked on her hair one more time, smiled when she sucked in a sharp breath, then went to his knees. He had no problem tasting her before he bent her over the desk.

She grabbed on to the back of his head with one hand, her grip tight as he buried his face between her legs.

"Oh yeah," she moaned, grinding against him.

At a soft *snick*ing sound he started to jerk back, but a sharp pain exploded in his skull, and darkness engulfed him.

"Wipe that goofy grin off your face before we head inside," Selene murmured.

Nathan realized he was smiling as they pulled through Lopez's security gate for the second time in twenty-four hours. "I wasn't grinning."

She snorted. "Please, I recognize that look. I've *had* that look. It's the Rios woman, right?"

Nathan cleared his throat, not wanting to talk about him and Amelia. At least not here. Thinking about her as he had to slip on his Miguel persona felt wrong for some reason and he wasn't certain why. He had erased her last text from his secure phone, not wanting any trace of their messaging on it. He didn't need to reread it anyway. That message was burned in his brain.

I'm not letting you go either.

Good, because he couldn't let her go. As soon as this op was over, he was making some changes and putting in a request to be transferred to the Miami location permanently. And no more undercover work. It might piss Burkhart off, but if he wanted to choose having a life and happiness, Amelia was going to win.

"Is it hard doing what you do and having a family?"

He kept his question as vague as possible as Selene pulled up to the front of Lopez's house. Nathan knew Selene's husband, had served with the guy back in their Marine Corps days. Now Levi was a civilian with no ties to the NSA other than Selene.

"Some days. The traveling sucks, but you do what you have to do and you make it work. If you love someone and they're willing to put up with your bullshit hours, then you don't lose sight of that." Her words were blunt with the sharp ring of truth.

Nathan had no doubt Amelia would put up with his hours. She didn't exactly have a nine-to-five job anyway. That was the least of his concerns, though. His only issue was their past. But that was quickly fading as a concern too. She'd been seventeen. Yeah, he was pissed she hadn't trusted him, but twelve years had passed. He would only focus on who they were now and move forward.

He never got a chance to respond, because two of Lopez's guys opened their doors. He and Selene went through the whole pat-down and scanned-weapons check again before being escorted through the massive house to the pool area instead of the office.

Today Lopez had on cargo pants and a hideously bright Hawaiian-style button-down shirt. He immediately dismissed his guards and motioned for Nathan and Selene to sit in one of his covered cabanas. The white billowy curtains giving them privacy rippled in the breeze.

"You have what we need?" Selene asked, not bothering with niceties.

Lopez nodded, his expression grim. "I started

asking around about Mercado, but got stonewalled when it came to Iker. But not his daughter. She's been into some nasty shit, apparently."

Nathan straightened slightly. Collette wasn't even on their radar. They'd looked into her initially because of her father—but apparently not deep enough.

"Some of this is just rumors, so take it with a grain of salt. Allegedly about three years ago she got involved with some wannabe gangbanger. Guy cheated on her and his life did not end well." Lopez shuddered. "Supposedly he was found with his throat slit and his cut-off dick in his mouth. I don't know if that's true, but a few months later she started moving drugs with a small team of former military guys. She had the capital and a lot of contacts to get an operation off the ground and they were turning a tidy profit. I know that's true because I heard about it back then. Her father got angry and worried that she'd piss off one of the cartels so he used his influence to get her shut down by another outfit."

"The cops or DEA never knew about her?" Nathan asked. Because she hadn't been on *anyone's* radar.

Lopez shook his head. "No. She hadn't been in the business long enough. About seven months after that she very quietly—so quietly I didn't know about it until I started making inquiries yesterday—bought up abandoned properties all over Miami. Not sure what she's using them for, but I heard she had some of her guys trolling clubs and homeless hangouts for young girls. That part is just a rumor because she's been very quiet the past two years. But if she was looking to scoop up young girls and women . . . I can think of a lot of reasons for that. None of them good. She could be using her properties for . . . hell, I don't even want to think about it."

Yeah, neither did Nathan.

Lopez's expression darkened as he continued. "She might be who your client is after. It's only a potential lead and I'm going to keep pushing my contacts for more, but I wanted to tell you this now. If she's behind all those women being found—shut that bitch down."

Selene glanced at Nathan. He kept his expression neutral even as inside his blood had turned icy. Amelia had been around Collette on more than one occasion. Just yesterday, in fact.

"I'll wire your normal fee if this pans out," Selene said, standing. Nathan stood with her.

Lopez shook his head and followed suit. "This one's on me."

"Thanks," Nathan said quietly as Selene murmured the same thing.

Once they were on the road, Nathan tried calling Amelia to check in. He needed to hear her voice and to make sure she was headed home. He needed her safe.

When it went straight to voice mail, he called Elliott and relayed everything. If Collette was involved in kidnapping so many women, they'd figure out where she was keeping them. Once they had that, ripping apart her life should be easy enough, especially for Elliott.

"Can you ping Amelia's phone?" Nathan asked Elliott as Selene pulled onto the highway. He didn't care if he was being paranoid; he wanted to know where she was. She'd told him in her text she'd be heading home after errands. Didn't matter, he needed to *know* she was safe. And it bugged him that her phone had gone to voice mail right away. As if it was turned off.

"Yeah, just a sec . . . Her phone's not pinging." He could hear the slight confusion in Elliott's voice.

"At all?" That was *not* good. His heart rate kicked up and he swallowed back the sharp taste of fear.

Elliott was silent for a moment, the soft clicking of fingers over a keyboard the only sound coming over the line. "No. Her battery has to be out. I can't get a signal."

Nathan looked at Selene. Panic gripped his chest, the talons digging in and making it difficult to draw breath. "Get off on the next exit." They were headed to Amelia's restaurant now.

He knew her last location, so he'd work from there. Maybe he was being completely paranoid, but Amelia wouldn't just turn her phone off, much less take her battery out. Not with everything going on.

A gnawing feeling in his gut told him something else had happened. "Try tracking her credit cards and run her face through—"

"Already on it."

"Run Collette's phone and—"

"Running that too. Not getting anything. She's probably using a burner."

Of course he was on it, Nathan thought. Elliott wasn't an amateur. "I'll call you back in a sec." He hung up and dialed Detective Sinclair. The last place he knew Amelia had been was her restaurant. Since Sinclair had already questioned all her employees once before, he was going to get the detective to do it again.

Nathan could go in and start questioning everyone, but Sinclair already had a rapport with a lot of the people who worked for her. While Nathan hated asking for outside help, he'd do anything to find her.

As the phone rang, he tried to tell himself that this was just a mistake. Maybe she'd dropped her phone in water and shorted it out. Even as he had the thought, he knew it was utter crap.

If Collette was kidnapping women, some from Amelia's restaurant, it wasn't out of the realm of reality that she'd make a play for Amelia. Maybe out of revenge. The reason didn't matter.

If she had, she was going to pay. No matter what, he was going to find Amelia.

Chapter 20

Infiltration: the secret movement of an individual (or small group) penetrating a target area with the intent to remain undetected.

"Have you done a thorough sweep yet?" Wesley asked Cade as he glanced down at the dead body on the kitchen floor. The woman's pale eyes were open in shock and her limbs stiff, rigor mortis having set in. As far as dead bodies went, he'd definitely seen worse. Her clothes were on and there was no blood. A slight puncture wound on her neck told him she'd been poisoned with something. At this point it didn't matter what.

"As thorough as possible." Cade pointed behind Wesley with his gloved hand. "This way."

He fell in step behind Cade. Cade and the rest of the team had been following up various leads, specifically people from Maria's center or Amelia's restaurants who'd had contact with multiple missing women. Lita Clark had been one of Maria's volunteers—and she'd abruptly quit yesterday after two years of steadily putting in hours at Bayside.

Burkhart didn't like the time frame and Elliott had confirmed some interesting financial data on Clark. Her husband had left her three years ago for a much younger woman, screwing her out of decent alimony, yet she'd somehow managed to pay off her house and continue volunteering regularly without much extra income. They'd missed some of the info on the first round of digging because she had no red flags and she paid for a lot of stuff in cash.

"There was either a safe inside or stacks of cash." Cade nodded at the giant cutout hole in Clark's walk-in closet.

Wesley nodded. "Yep." He'd seen the same thing too many times. Drug lords and various criminals liked to keep their cash close at hand. Hiding it in walls or burying money underground was a favorite. "Explains why there wasn't a digital link to her and whoever's behind this," he muttered more to himself than Cade. Cash was damn hard to trace.

Whoever had set up this operation was careful. There'd been no unusual phone activity on Clark's line, no large deposits into her bank accounts, and her lifestyle had been anything but extravagant.

"What do you want me to do?" Cade asked.

"Call Nieto, get the locals down here." They could deal with the body and cleanup. Wesley had the information he wanted. Clark was clearly dead because whoever was in charge was cleaning house. Or that was what his gut told him. His instinct was almost never wrong.

As Cade pulled out his cell and strode from the walk-in closet, Wesley's own phone buzzed in his jacket pocket. He answered when he saw Ortiz's name. "You find out anything from Lopez?"

"Yeah. Amelia's missing and we're pretty certain Collette Mercado took her. She's behind this operation, and from the look of it, her father has no clue what she's been doing." Ortiz's voice was tight and grim.

His jaw tightened. Wesley knew there'd be more details to catch up on, but for now he focused on the most important facts. "You're sure Amelia's been taken?"

"Yeah. Her phone's not pinging and I got Sinclair down to her restaurant to question the staff. One of the cooks walked her to her vehicle, but she got into a BMW with Collette. That was two hours ago. Elliott can't fucking track Collette either. Her vehicle GPS is disabled. She had to have had it done professionally. No ping on her phone either, but she's probably using burners anyway."

Damn it. Ortiz sounded in control, but Wesley knew he cared for Amelia. "Where are you?"

"Base."

"I'm on my way." He disconnected and headed out. Cade could handle things here and they had their first solid lead. He hated that a woman Ortiz clearly cared about had been kidnapped, but the shitty silver lining was, these women were being killed months after their abductions. Amelia had a shot at surviving this.

Unless Collette had taken her because she suspected Amelia's involvement with the police. If that was the case . . . He steeled himself against that thought. He couldn't think about that now. He had a job to do.

* * *

Nathan swiped the stylus over his screen, adding a blueprint to it. On the oversize screen on the wall, the same image popped up for everyone in the conference room to see. It was a small team so far, with him, Dax, Freeman, Bell, and of course Elliott. Burkhart should be in soon, and he knew his boss would pick a team to send for their infiltration, but for now he wanted to start going over the details with his three guys.

They'd worked together enough and he'd be requesting to work directly with them for the upcoming op. And Burkhart better not fucking bench him for the mission to save Amelia. He couldn't just sit on his ass and do nothing.

"This is a former medical testing facility," he started, only pausing when he heard the sliding glass doors whoosh open behind him. Nathan turned to see Burkhart stride in, but his boss just nodded at him to continue.

He turned back to the screen. "It's one of the many places that Collette Mercado scooped up a couple years ago when it went into foreclosure." Nathan swiped the stylus across his screen again, motioned to a new image. "And this is a shot from a satellite that Elliott managed to hack into."

Nathan continued. "It's not the clearest shot, but you can see two pregnant women in this courtyard area. An armed guard is near them at all times. Combined with the huge perimeter privacy fence, this might be where the women are being held." He refused to think about what might be happening to Amelia right now. His only focus had to be on finding her.

"Amelia's phone lost its signal two blocks from here," Elliott added, looking back at Burkhart.

Their boss stepped forward, his expression dark. "I read the intel you sent me on the way over here," he said to Elliott before turning to all of them. "I agree—this is likely where they're being held. It'll be sunset in a couple hours, so we move in then. I've already called three more teams together. Ortiz, you're going to lead the group here, but I want to talk to you in private. Now."

Everyone filed out without a word. Nathan wanted to protest waiting until sunset even though he knew that was the smart choice. He hated the idea of Amelia being injured or worse. He flat-out refused to contemplate that she wasn't okay.

Burkhart crossed his arms over his chest, looking every bit the lieutenant general he'd been. "You okay for this mission?"

Nathan wasn't even going to pretend not to know what his boss meant. "Yes. I care for her." More than care, but he wasn't telling Burkhart that before he told Amelia—and he *would* tell her. "My objectivity right now is the same as it would be even if she hadn't been taken. I want to save her and the women. I'm trained and when we go in, there could be mass confusion or hysteria with the women. We don't know what they've been through, but a bunch of guys armed to the teeth storming their facility is going to be terrifying no matter what. Amelia knows me and some of the others. She'll be able to relay her trust in us to the women. It's a better choice to have me go than to let me sit on the sidelines. But I'll respect your decision," he added grudgingly. Okay, the last part was bullshit. If he got sidelined . . . he might lose it.

Burkhart raised an eyebrow. "You practice that little speech?"

"I did, sir."

A real smile tugged at his boss's mouth, for just an instant. "Stand down. You're not in the Corps anymore. And I agree with everything you said. You'll head up the team for Bell, Freeman, and Dax. Unless you have any arguments?"

The tension in Nathan's shoulders loosened. "No."

"Good. I've already put in an order to have a drone fly over the area, see if we can get some better images. Until then, gear up and meet back here in thirty. We're going to nail down a solid infiltration so there's no question of who does what. I want to put an end to this operation tonight."

"What about the other properties Collette bought up?"

"I've got Karen looking into them and seeing what she can find via satellite. I'll put a few men on the ground to do visual sweeps, but this place"—he nodded at the screen—"is the most likely for what we think she's doing. We'll have eyes on it until we move in."

"Okay." Nathan nodded, agreeing completely. Now it was go time. He just prayed that Amelia was okay. She was strong, one of the strongest women he knew. She'd make it through this.

Blinking to clear away the fuzziness, Amelia wrapped the pillowcase around her fist multiple times and stood up. She'd been awake for maybe twenty minutes and had already gone to the bathroom. She kept expecting someone to come into her room and knock her out again or something. Since that hadn't happened, she was going to take action.

Yeah, she might feel woozy, but she could take on that prick of a doctor if he entered her room alone again. She just needed to get a weapon. The bathroom door squeaked as she opened it. There was a shower area, a toilet, and a small mirror hanging over a white sink. It was all very sparse.

She slammed her wrapped fist against the mirror, once, twice . . . *crack*. The glass splintered, sending a jolt of adrenaline ricocheting through her. She could do this.

With trembling fingers, she pulled on one of the pieces until it broke free from the broken mirror. She set it on the sink ledge before pulling off another jagged piece. A few shards dropped, falling onto the sink and floor.

Careful not to move near them, since her feet were bare and she was still unsteady, she took the first piece and cut the pillowcase in half. She sliced part of her palm but barely felt the sting. Her adrenaline was pumping too fast, her heartbeat out of control. If someone had heard her banging on the mirror, they could be here any second. Or maybe they were recording her room. She hadn't seen any overt cameras, but that didn't mean jack.

She wrapped both jagged pieces on one end with the pillowcase strips. Now she could hold on to the glass without slicing herself up and actually use them as a weapon.

On shaky legs, she stepped out of the bathroom and

pulled the door closed behind her. She didn't want to risk anyone seeing the broken glass. Chills racked her, more from terror than anything else. The adrenaline surging through her was good, though; it was pumping her up more. She had a feeling she'd only get one chance at attacking and escaping. She kept her make-shift weapons close to her body, hoping to hide them in case someone was watching her. After tucking them under her pillow, she opened the mini-refrigerator.

There were juices and various fruits on the shelves, but she didn't trust anything these people provided not to be drugged. Shutting the door, she strode back to the bed. No one had stormed into her room yet, so she lay down on it and stretched out. She needed to regain her strength.

If that doctor—

The door handle jiggled, then a second later opened. Collette strode in—alone—wearing different clothes than earlier. She even looked different. In boots, black pants, and a black sweater she looked a little like the Grim Reaper. Her hair was pulled back into a sharp bun, and her eyes were cold and flat.

On instinct, Amelia sat up. She kept her pillow behind her, wanting to keep her weapons hidden. Collette was too hard to read and Amelia couldn't tell if the woman knew what she was hiding.

"Glad to see you're awake." Collette flicked a semi-interested gaze over her as she leaned against the wall right next to the bathroom door.

Amelia didn't respond, just watched her warily. Her fingers itched to slide back and grab the blade, but she didn't want to give herself away.

Collette raised an eyebrow. "No questions about why I took you?"

"'You're a psycho' seems like the most obvious answer." Amelia probably wouldn't be so bold if Collette had come into her room with backup, but if she could goad the woman into getting closer, maybe she'd have a chance to strike out. And she figured she'd only have one shot at this.

Collette's gaze narrowed. "I'm surprised my father ever took an interest in you. You're so unpolished."

"Is that why you took me? Daddy issues?" Her voice was dry, but she couldn't keep the slight tremble out of it.

Collette snorted and pushed off the wall, real amusement in her laugh, but she only took a single step forward. Not nearly close enough. "I took you for a profit. Fucking over my father was just a bonus. Besides, I heard you'd been getting friendly with a detective. Why?"

Amelia blinked in surprise. Was that why this psycho had kidnapped her? "Why have I been talking to a detective? Um, because one of my employees attacked me multiple times." She wasn't certain of the line of questioning, so it wasn't hard to feign confusion.

"You sure that's the only reason?" Collette's voice had a deadly edge as she took another step closer. She was near the foot of the bed now.

"What other reason would there be? Why am I here?" she demanded, wanting to shift the topic of conversation.

"I told you, profit, though to be fair that's a secondary reason. For the last two years I've sold over a hundred and fifty babies on the black market." She sounded positively smug as she admitted to the atrocities.

Oh God. The remains of all those women who'd been found. *That* was why they'd been killed. For their babies. Amelia's stomach pitched as she stared at Collette. She'd never used the term "evil" lightly before, but right now she knew she was looking into the face of it. "You kidnapped pregnant women?" Amelia slowly slid her hand behind her back and grasped one of the makeshift blades.

Collette rolled her eyes and stepped over to the minifridge. She ran a manicured fingernail over the top of it. "Of course not. We take them, impregnate them through IVF, and give them a happy, healthy life for nine months. They should thank us, really. No one cares about them and we're doing the world a service, selling children to rich families who can take care of them."

She turned all her focus on Amelia then, her smile glinting dangerous and sharklike. "You're a little different from them, since you're established in the community, but I couldn't take the chance you were talking to the police. So I decided to kill two birds with one stone. Now you're out of my way and I'll make a very nice profit off you. A win-win for me. Besides, knowing it'll hurt my father makes it worth it. I'm going to have someone move your car so it looks like you returned to the restaurant after I brought you back. So no ties to me."

"Why would I even suspect you were involved in anything?"

"You came over to my house twice, and I know you weren't fucking my father. Most women throw themselves at him, but not you. Something about you is off. I just can't decide whether you're lying to me or not."

Freaking crazy bitch. "If I was working with the police or suspected you of pretty much the worst crime I've ever heard of, would I have gotten in your car?" Not giving Collette a chance to respond, she continued. "Unless you plan on letting me go, then get the fuck out of here. I'm tired of listening to you talk."

Rage flared in Collette's gaze. She stepped closer, mere feet from the edge of the bed now. Energy hummed through Amelia and she hoped it didn't show in her eyes.

"I don't let my men touch the product, but I might make an exception for you." Her words were silky smooth. It was disturbing to see the manic glee in the woman's eyes. She took another step forward now, her breathing more erratic, as if she was getting pleasure out of telling her. "Maybe I'll just keep you around as a toy for them. I'll watch as you—"

Amelia lunged forward. She flew off the bed, lifting the blade in an upward arc.

Surprise flared in Collette's eyes, but she raised an arm, deflecting the blow from striking her in the chest. She cried out as the jagged edge sliced along her forearm.

Fear detonated inside Amelia. She needed to take Collette down as quickly as possible, before anyone heard them struggling.

Grunting in anger, Collette swung out with her fist, aiming for Amelia's face. She ducked the blow and kicked at Collette's knee. The jab from her foot wasn't as effective as it would have been if she'd been wearing shoes, but Collette's leg buckled under the pressure.

She fell to her knees, an agonized cry ripping from her throat. Moving on pure instinct, Amelia slashed out with the makeshift blade.

Collette rolled to the side, avoiding the strike. As she moved, she kicked out with her good leg, swiping Amelia's feet out from under her.

All the air whooshed from her lungs as she fell hard against the floor on her side. Before she could move, Collette was on top of her. Amelia felt a blow to her ribs, then a slap to her face. Her ears rang from the shocks of pain.

She was vaguely aware of the woman snarling something at her, but she tuned it out. She reared back and head-butted Collette. The loud crunch of bone breaking filled the air.

"Bitch!" Collette's hands went to her face.

Using the only opportunity she might get, Amelia jerked the blade up in one swift strike. It slammed directly into Collette's chest.

For a moment Collette froze. Her hands dropped and she stared at Amelia with wide eyes. All Amelia could do was stare right back. Then she looked down at the jagged piece of glass deep in the monster's chest.

She shoved Collette off her. The woman rolled onto her back, gasping sounds escaping her throat, until she simply stopped moving. Amelia scrambled back toward the bed, wanting to put as much distance between them as she could. Then reality crashed over her. She couldn't wimp out now. She had to get out of here, get help.

Pushing back the bile that threatened her, she stepped around the blood pooling on the floor and patted down Collette's pockets. No phone and no weapon, but she came up with a set of keys.

Her heart was a staccato drumbeat against her chest, her fingers trembling as she shoved the keys into her pocket and then tugged off Collette's boots.

When Amelia was dumped in here, they'd taken her shoes, and she might need them in her escape. The boots were a little loose, but they'd do.

Right now she needed to find a phone and get help. If other women were being held here, she had to save them all. Unfortunately she had no idea what was waiting for her outside the door. There could be guards, cameras . . . She shuddered.

Well, there was only one way to find out.

She snagged the other makeshift weapon from under the pillow and crept to the door. When she pulled it open, all she could hear was blood rushing in her ears.

She pushed out a quiet breath when she saw an empty, dimly lit hallway. The rubber-soled boots were silent when she stepped out. There was a line of doors, all shut, in both directions. Since she had no idea which was the right way, she moved to her right and tried the first door she came to.

Locked.

Sweat soaked her back as she tried various keys. On the fourth try, it snicked open. Holding her breath, she opened the door. The lights were off, so she reached for a switch. When her fingers touched a dimmer, she turned it.

A blond woman wearing scrublike clothing rolled over on a bed, clearly a few months pregnant. She covered her eyes with her arm as she sat up. "What's . . . who are you?" she whispered.

Amelia looked out in the hallway again, glancing both ways before she stepped inside and closed the door. There was no time to sugarcoat any of this. "I was taken, but I just killed Collette."

The woman gasped and stood up fully, clearly taking in the blood on Amelia's shirt and the jagged blade in her hand. "She has guards."

"I figured. How much do you know about this place?" Amelia could practically hear a clock ticking in warning, telling her to hurry, hurry, hurry.

"Enough, I guess."

"Are there other women on this floor?"

She nodded.

"Can you let them out?" Amelia held up the keys.

Hope bloomed in the woman's gaze before it dimmed. "The guards have guns." She sat back on the bed and placed a protective hand over her belly. "I don't want to die."

"Fine. I'm leaving your door unlocked. Do what you want. I've gotta find a phone. I know people who will help us." She didn't have time to beg the woman to make a run for her life. She had no idea what this woman had to be feeling right now, and while she wasn't judging her, she needed to get help for all of them.

The woman popped up again, that hope back in her gaze. "This isn't a trick?"

It sickened Amelia that the woman thought it might

be. She shook her head and stepped forward, pulling the key she'd used off the key ring. "No. There aren't enough keys on here for the rooms to have individual keys." She was hoping they used a universal lock for all the rooms. "Is there anything you can tell me about this place, like where a phone might be?"

The blonde took the key. "Maybe. If you head down the hallway, that way"—she pointed to the right—"then make a left, I saw Collette going in and out of the first door on the left more than once. Is she really dead?"

Amelia nodded and lifted her makeshift weapon. "I stabbed her with one of these."

"Good." The anger behind that one word wasn't a surprise.

Amelia hoped the woman used that anger to be smart. "Free as many of the others as you can and find somewhere to hide if you can't escape. And shut the doors behind you. We can't let anyone know we've escaped. Are there video cameras in the rooms?"

"I don't think so, but there could be." The woman looked around nervously. "I know they have them outside in the courtyard."

"Okay, thanks . . . What's your name?"

"Bonnie."

"I'm Amelia. We're going to get out of this, okay?"

Bonnie nodded, though doubt and fear lived in her bright green eyes.

Seeing one of Collette's victims, knowing what she'd done to countless others, Amelia felt no guilt about what she'd done to the woman. She moved back to the door and peeked out again. The hallway was still empty, so either there weren't cameras or someone wasn't monitoring them. She glanced over her shoulder. "I'm going now. Be careful."

She hurried down the hallway as fast as she could. At the corner she paused and listened. She heard male voices from somewhere. They weren't agitated and she couldn't gauge how far away they were.

Sweat bloomed across her forehead as she peeked around the next hallway. Clear.

She followed Bonnie's instructions and went to the first doorway. Surprisingly it was unlocked. She twisted the handle and stepped into what was clearly an office.

Raw hope bloomed inside her until she heard a clicking sound. When she turned, the doctor was standing by a filing cabinet, a gun in his hands.

Pointed directly at her.

Chapter 21

Tango: NATO Phonetic Alphabet representation of the letter *T.* In military and law enforcement operations, tango often means target/terrorist.

"Second level, section B is clear," Nathan said quietly into his comm. The facility was basically a giant square shape with a courtyard and parking area in the middle of it. Because of the structure, there was no outside visibility even without the giant privacy fences around the private property. "Moving onto third level, section B."

The other teams all murmured affirmatives.

Dax, Freeman, and Bell all fell in behind him as they moved back to the stairwell. Elliott had scrambled the video capabilities, so while the enemy couldn't see them, they couldn't see the enemy either. One of the other teams had already found ten women, each in individual rooms. They'd been terrified but were now just sobbing messes. And no one knew how many guards there were.

Nathan and his guys had already secured three armed men, but none of them were talking. And he wasn't waiting on them to go after Amelia.

He thought about how eerily quiet the place was as they moved up the stairwell in a well-trained unit. Taking point, he eased open the door when they reached the next level. Just like with the last level, it opened up into a long hallway. Their job was to sweep individual sections of each level.

M4 raised, he motioned that it was clear and he was moving forward. As he stepped out into the hallway, a blur of motion from one of the doorways caught his gaze.

A blond, pregnant woman stepped into the hall, saw him, and darted back into the room she'd come from. So far all the rooms had been locked.

"Potential civilian sighting three-quarters of the way down," he murmured, moving to the first door. He didn't have to worry about instructions; they all knew what to do. He started the clearing of rooms at the beginning, and the other three fanned out down the hallway. Then they'd move inward, meeting at the middle.

As he progressed from room to room, he didn't have to pick any of the locks. They were all unlocked. The back of his neck tingled as he reached the third door. Something was wrong. These rooms were empty but clearly had been lived in.

His gut tightened. Everything was too damn quiet tonight. What if the women had been moved? What if Amelia was gone?

He shoved back that thought as he eased open the next door. For a moment, he froze. Collette Mercado was lying on her back with blood pooling around her body. She'd been stabbed right through the heart with a piece of glass. He moved inside and cleared the bathroom before checking her pulse. It was clear she was dead, but he checked anyway.

"Primary tango down. Body's cold."

Burkhart's voice came over the line. "Repeat."

He repeated what he'd said to confirm it. "I'm marking the door with a red X." They all carried two sticks of chalk with them to mark off cleared areas. On silent feet, he stepped back into the hallway and marked the door.

Dax pointed to the door Nathan had seen the blonde come out of earlier. Keeping alert of his surroundings, Nathan hurried down the rest of the hall as both Freeman and Bell confirmed that they'd cleared their rooms.

When Nathan reached the room, Dax pointed at Nathan's weapon. Then he motioned for him to hold it down. After he did, Dax opened the door. Ten pregnant women were all huddled in the room, sitting or standing and looking at them as if they were monsters. He scanned the faces, looking for Amelia. When he didn't see her, he had to shelve that disappointment.

"We're here to help you." He kept his voice low as he stepped inside. He was dressed in fatigues and armed with an extra pistol, ammo, grenades, and tear gas. He knew his presence likely wasn't going to comfort them, but there was no way around it.

When he stepped farther inside, some of the women cowered back in fear. The sight twisted him up inside. He held up his hands. "I know this has to be terrifying, but we are here to help you. Right now we're still securing the facility, so we need you to stay put. My man here"—he motioned to Dax—"is going to stay with you until we've secured every one of those monsters who works here." He couldn't keep the heat out of his voice.

His words seemed to have a calming effect. Surprisingly.

The blonde he'd seen earlier stood from where she'd been perched on the edge of the bed. "There's another woman on this floor. She's new, I think. She killed . . . she helped us escape. She gave me a key and told me to free the others while she went to find help. I told her where I thought the office on this floor is. Her name's Amelia, but we haven't seen her again."

Amelia. His heart rate kicked up. "Where's the office?"

After she gave quick directions, he nodded at Dax. "I'm going after her. Keep these women safe." In the hallway he looked at Bell. "Stand guard." Because no one was getting through that door. Then he nodded once at Freeman. "With me." He was going to find Amelia no matter what.

"Who knows you're here?" the doctor, whose name Amelia still didn't know, asked her with a growl as he shoved his gun into her ribs.

"I don't know." She didn't bother to keep her voice down as he pushed her through a swinging door into what was a midsized cafeteria.

"Don't lie to me." He wrapped his fingers around her upper arm in an unforgiving grip.

She winced, tears stinging her eyes. "I really don't know."

He looked around the empty cafeteria, his eyes wide, a frantic light to them. "Then why can't I get in touch with anyone in the building? And why's the security been shut off? You're working with someone," he muttered, tightening his grip and dragging her across the floor.

Maybe if he thought she was working with someone, he'd have a reason to let her live. She still couldn't figure out why he was keeping her alive—and she didn't plan to ask. It was possible he wanted to use her as a human shield.

"No one's letting me take the fall for this," he muttered to himself as he pulled her between bench tables and plastic chairs.

There was another door across from them with a red EXIT sign above it. Amelia didn't want to go with him but couldn't see another choice. But if they did escape, this guy would have no reason to keep her alive.

She didn't want to die. God, the thought of never seeing Nathan again, of never getting to tell him that she loved him, had pretty much never stopped . . .

"Drop your weapon! All your people are in custody and you have nowhere to go," a male voice said from the right of her.

Moving lightning quick, the doctor grabbed her arm and shoved her in front of him so that she was facing the armed man who looked as if he'd stepped off the cover of *Soldiers-R-Us*. "You drop your weapon or I shoot her in the back!" As if to prove his point, he dug the gun into her spine.

Sweat trickled down the sides of her face even though she was icy-cold with terror.

The other man didn't flinch. "Don't be stupid. You have no exit, nowhere to go. If you kill her, we'll kill you."

"Put your fucking gun down!" The gun dug tighter against her spine.

She barely felt it, though. There was no way the armed man would do it—

"All right, I'm putting my weapon down. We can talk about this." He held up one gloved hand, his other one still around the big gun as he started to crouch down with it.

Amelia didn't want him to put his gun down. She didn't want to freaking die.

"On the floor. Now!" the doctor shouted in her ear.

She automatically winced as she watched the man gently set his weapon on the floor. If he was here, he had to be working with Nathan. Or she assumed so. Oh God, where was Nathan? Another burst of hope bloomed inside her. Maybe that was why this guy was giving up his weapon.

The doctor wavered as the man started to slowly stand up; she could feel it. He was more relaxed now that a gun wasn't trained on him. But what if he'd rather die than go to prison? Anything could go wrong, and her rescuer had just given up his gun. Fear slid through her veins, making her even more numb. No way was this going to end well for her.

Suddenly the gun fell away from her back. Before terror could gain even more footing inside her, she fell forward, as if the doctor had shoved her. On instinct she dove for the floor and covered her head. She tensed, waiting for a gunshot to rip through her, when the doctor screamed in pain behind her. A shot blasted through the room, echoing loudly as one of the chairs toppled over from the impact. Before she could react, the gun skittered across the floor. She rolled over.

Nathan!

He had the doctor on his back and was pummeling him in the face, over and over. The middle-aged man was no match for Nathan. The way he looked right now, no one was.

She jumped up and moved to him. "Nathan, stop!" What if he killed an unarmed man? She stepped forward to stop him, but had barely moved. Then the other armed man flew past her.

He grabbed Nathan's arm, stilling him from beating the unconscious doctor anymore. "Don't do this. He's not worth it."

Nathan looked up at the guy before his eyes locked on hers. Too many emotions swirled inside them as he stood. She'd never seen him look truly angry before. Not like this. As if he could truly kill the man on the floor and not regret it.

She was barely aware of moving until she threw herself into his arms, wrapping her own around him as she buried her face in his neck. "You came for me," she said on a sob, the words broken and desperate sounding.

His grip on her was solid, the most reassuring thing she'd ever felt. "Amelia." Just her name, a shuddered declaration.

"I should have trusted you." The words tore from her throat. "Seventeen or not, I should have trusted you." Everything seemed so clear now.

He just murmured soothing sounds as he rubbed

a hand up and down her back. "Get this piece of garbage out of here," he murmured to the other man.

She didn't look up as his teammate dragged the doctor away. With tears stinging her eyes, she pulled back so she could look at him. She cupped his face, needing to touch him. "It was Collette. I killed her and—"

"I know. You're safe, though. That's all that matters." He reached up and tapped something on his earpiece, turning it off, she guessed. His lips skated over hers, the gesture a reassurance she needed. "I don't care about the past, Amelia. Just tell me there's a future with us."

She tightened her fingers behind his neck. "I love you, Nathan. And I'm not letting you go. I don't care who you work for or anything else, just that you come home to me every night."

He didn't say a word, just crushed his mouth over hers with an intensity she felt all the way to her core.

They still had a lot of stuff to work out and she had plenty of questions about how he'd found her and how all the other women were doing, but right now all she cared about was that the man she loved had come for her and wanted a future together.

Nothing else mattered.

Chapter 22

Black operations: covert ops not assigned to the organization performing them.

Two days later

Stretched out on her couch, Amelia smiled lazily as Nathan lifted her legs and propped them on his lap as he settled next to her.

"Have you gotten off this couch since I left this morning?" His lips twitched slightly.

"Unfortunately yes. A few friends stopped by to drop off food, which is pretty awesome. The fridge is stocked if you're hungry. And a bunch of people from both restaurants came by too."

Nathan frowned, but she shook her head. She knew he hadn't wanted her to let anyone in while he was gone, but she couldn't live her life like that. "The threat has passed. I can't just ignore everyone in my life." It had been pretty stunning how many calls and drop-ins she'd received once the news broke this morning. Yesterday she'd filled out tons of fun paperwork for the Miami PD and answered a bunch of questions about what had happened.

The state's attorney wasn't going to press charges for her killing Collette—obviously—but knowing it for sure eased any residual tension. Unfortunately she'd been bombarded with phone calls from reporters requesting interviews, but she was ignoring all of them. Her name shouldn't even have been leaked, but shit happened and there was nothing she could do about it now.

"We need to talk."

The serious note in Nathan's voice made her sit up. "That sounds ominous."

"It's not. I just . . . I need to tell you who I work for and what I do for a living. The truth. I had to get permission first."

"Okay." She reached for his hand and linked her fingers through his. After the last two days she didn't want to let go of him.

"I work for the NSA, usually in an undercover capacity. Black ops. We . . . are not honest about some of the things we do, but it's for the right reasons. When my boss got a tip about the missing women, he wanted to cut through the red tape and find them. It's why I told you I was with the FBI. I'm not saying it's right or wrong or asking you to agree with what I do. I'm just saying I sleep fine at night and I'm okay with what I do. If that changes, I'll find a new profession. I'm going to be cutting back on undercover work and I've asked for a transfer to the Miami office. I'll still travel for work, but it won't be as much as I used to. And there will be some things I simply can't tell you. If—when—we get married,

I'll be able to tell you more, but some things will always be a matter of national security. And you'd prefer not to know most of the time anyway, trust me." He finished in a rush, as if he'd practiced his speech.

Which, knowing Nathan, he had. She loved that about him. "Are you done?"

He nodded, his body language rigid, as if he expected her to what . . . disapprove? She nearly snorted at that.

"Well, first, I guessed who you worked for. Originally I thought it must be the CIA when I realized you weren't with the FBI, but the night of . . . the other night after the Miami PD got called in by your boss and started clearing out all the women, I recognized him from that awful Westwood bombing. Second, I'm glad you're transferring to Miami, but I would have moved anywhere you were. Just for the record. And third, when we get married? That's a lame proposal if I ever heard one and I expect better."

He blinked, as if in surprise. Seriously, did he think he'd told her anything to get mad about? Or maybe he was just as freaking nervous about everything as she was. Things had gotten serious with them pretty fast. Or at least things were serious for her. With Nathan in her life, there would never be anyone else. It was as simple as that.

"I'll do better, then. You don't care about what I do for a living?" He squeezed her hand once as he watched her.

"You saved not only my life, but dozens of other women." Including Tessa and Danita. Tessa was luckier than most since she hadn't been in captivity long. And

Danita would be staying with a friend, her former land-lord, as long as she needed. Amelia couldn't even think about the nightmare some of them were going through right now. Most were pregnant and having to figure out what to do with their lives. Thankfully Maria's father was setting up a fund to help them all get on their feet and start fresh. The donations already pouring in were stag-gering. She cleared her throat, suddenly feeling nervous. "Where are you going to live when you move to Miami?"

"Here."

"Good answer." A smile tugged at her lips, but just as quickly dimmed. She needed to get on the full-disclosure honesty train too.

"What is it?" He tugged her closer, pulling her into his lap.

She loved that he wouldn't allow any barriers between them. "I'd planned to tell you this and I guess now's as good a time as any." She took a deep breath, feeling ashamed about some of the things she'd done to get started. "When I first started my restaurant I got in a little over my head. I learned quickly what I was doing wrong, but . . . I had some debt. Not a lot, but enough that it made my first year really hard. I turned to a loan shark for a quick loan to cover some of it, and in return he wanted me to do some favors for him. Nothing huge, but . . . I occasionally let him set up meets in my place for drops. Not drugs or weapons," she said quickly when he didn't respond.

"It was mainly jewelry and other stolen goods. I know because I looked in his packages a couple times. I was up-front with him in the beginning that he could never use my place to run drugs, but I checked just to make sure." Amelia narrowed her gaze at Nathan. "And you're not even surprised by this. You knew?"

His lips twitched. "Yeah. I was hoping you'd trust me enough to tell me. I'm glad you did."

She brushed her lips over his, wanting to turn it into something deeper, but she pulled back before she jumped him. "What's going to happen with Iker? It didn't sound like he was involved, but what if he figures out you aren't who you say you were? Or that I killed his daughter?" So far that hadn't leaked to the media. The only thing they knew was that Amelia had been kidnapped. She gnawed on her bottom lip, not liking the thought of any of that.

"Don't worry about him."

"Kinda hard not to." Because she knew that even if Nathan wasn't going to be doing as much undercover work, it would be impossible not to worry.

"Let's just say he's got his hands full right now. After Collette's many crimes came to light, he's being scrutinized by almost every law enforcement agency. DEA, FBI, some I don't even want to think about. I think he'll try to run or flip on some of the people he does business with. He won't ever find out you killed his daughter. We . . . tweaked the final reports. He's not a problem for either of us."

Relief and pure happiness slid through her veins. She shifted and straddled him. "Good."

His expression went white hot. "I used to think I'd built up what we had in my mind, but now I realize that the life we're going to make together is even better. I love you, Amelia."

"I love you too." More than she'd ever thought possible. And this time when she kissed him, she didn't stop.

Epilogue

Two months later

"I'm never going to remember all these people," Amelia murmured to Nathan under her breath during a break in the receiving line.

"Yeah, you will," he said just as quietly as Dax and Hannah approached. Nathan watched as Amelia's face lit up when she saw Hannah.

The two women had become friends over the past two months, with Hannah giving advice on planning a quickie wedding. Amelia had wanted to wait a year, but Nathan had been insistent on one thing. He'd wanted his ring on her finger and wanted her to have his last name as soon as possible. Partially for completely caveman reasons, but he'd also wanted to be able to tell her more about what he did when off on assignments. Married couples had more freedom.

"You look stunning," Hannah said, grasping Amelia's hands in hers.

"I probably shouldn't say this, but *I know.* The stylist you recommended is amazing."

The stylist had nothing to do with it, but Nathan bit his tongue. His wife—would he ever get used to that?—looked damn amazing. Her long white dress was simple and formfitting and he couldn't wait to take it off her.

"How's it feel to be married?" Dax asked, drawing Nathan's attention to him. With a glass of champagne in hand and his tie already loosened at his collar, he looked relaxed.

"Kinda the same." As he said it, the answer surprised him. He'd expected to feel different, but they'd already been living together and had figured out a schedule that worked for them. He loved her even more each day. The ring just made everything official—something he needed.

Dax laughed. "I know what you mean." He gently took Hannah's elbow and started guiding her away. "I know you've still got a lot of people to greet. We'll see you guys out on the dance floor."

The rest of the day was a blur of talking to people, eating, toasting, and dancing. Neither of them had any immediate family, but they ended up having about a hundred friends at the wedding. Some of whom he'd fought and bled with.

It was the happiest day of his life.

"What are you thinking about?" Amelia's fingers were linked behind his neck as they slowly danced. Couples surrounded them as the night wound down, but he only had eyes for her.

He leaned down, his mouth skimming her ear. "That I can't wait until you're naked."

She snorted. "You're such a guy."

"I'm glad you realize that."

Amelia snickered, slightly tipsy from the champagne, and leaned closer into his embrace. "I can't wait to get you naked either."

She wasn't as quiet as she clearly thought she was, because over his wife's head he saw one of his old friends, Jack Stone, and his pregnant wife, Sophie, grin at him before turning away.

The most primitive part of Nathan couldn't wait to see Amelia pregnant with his child. But for a while, at least, he planned to simply enjoy being married to the woman who'd stolen his heart when he was a seventeen-year-old kid. They had a lot of years to catch up on, and he was going to make every second count.

ACKNOWLEDGMENTS

As always, I owe a big thanks to my editor, Danielle Perez, for all her wonderful insight into this book. To the team at New American Library—Christina Brower, Jessica Brock, Ashley Polikoff—thank you for all the behind-the-scenes work that you do; it's very appreciated. To my agent, Jill Marsal, thank you for your continuing guidance. For Kari Walker, I'm so incredibly grateful that you read the early draft of *A Covert Affair* (and all my early drafts!). You make reaching the finish line of a book a whole lot easier. To my patient family, I owe gratitude to my husband and son for living with me when I'm on a deadline. You guys are my rocks. For Sarah, thank you for all the behind-the-scenes stuff you do that gives me more time to write. "Thank you" doesn't seem like enough. And I definitely owe thanks to my Deadly Ops readers. Thank you, guys, for reading this series and for reaching out to let me know how much you're enjoying it. I hope you love this latest book. Last, but never least, I'm thankful to God for so many opportunities and blessings.

Don't miss the first exhilarating novel in
the Deadly Ops series,

TARGETED

Available now from Headline Eternal.

Chapter 1

Black Death 9 Agent: member of an elite group of
men and women employed by the NSA for covert,
off-the-books operations. A member's purpose is to
gain the trust of targeted individuals in order to
gather information or evidence by any means
necessary.

Jack Stone opened and quietly shut the door behind
him as he slipped into the conference room. A few
analysts and field agents were already seated around
the long rectangular table. One empty chair remained.

A few of the new guys looked up as he entered, but
the NSA's security was tighter than Langley's. Since
he was the only one missing from this meeting, the
senior members pored over the briefs in front of them
without even giving him a cursory glance.

Wesley Burkhart, his boss, handler, and recruiter
all rolled into one, stuck his head in the room just as
Jack started to sit. "Jack, my office. Now."

He inwardly cringed because he knew that tone well.
At least his bags were still packed. Once he was out in
the hall, heading toward Wesley's office, his boss briefly

clapped him on the back. "Sorry to drag you out of there, but I've got something bigger for you. Have you had a chance to relax since you've been back?"

Jack shrugged, knowing his boss didn't expect an answer. After working two years undercover to bring down a human trafficking ring that had also been linked to a terrorist group in Southern California, he was still decompressing. He'd been back only a week, and the majority of his time had been spent debriefing. It would take longer than a few days to wash the grime and memories off him. If he ever did. "You've got another mission for me already?"

Wesley nodded as he opened the door to his office. "I hate sending you back into the field so soon, but once you read the report, you'll understand why I don't want anyone else."

As the door closed behind them, Jack took a seat in front of his boss's oversized solid oak desk. "Lay it on me."

"Two of our senior analysts have been hearing a lot of chatter lately linking the Vargas cartel and Abu al-Ramaan's terrorist faction. At this point, the only solid connection we have is South Beach Medical Supply."

"SBMS is involved?" The medical company delivered supplies and much-needed drugs to third-world countries across the globe. Ronald Weller, the owner, was such a straight arrow it didn't seem possible.

"Looks that way." His boss handed him an inch-thick manila folder.

Jack picked up the packet and looked over the first document. As he skimmed the report, his chest tightened painfully as long-buried memories clawed at him with razor-sharp talons. After reading the key sections, he looked up. "Is there a chance Sophie is involved?" Her name rolled off his tongue so naturally, as if he'd spoken to her yesterday and not thirteen years ago. As if saying it was no big deal. As if he didn't dream about her all the damn time.

Wesley shook his head. "We don't know. Personally, I don't think so, but it looks like her boss is."

"Ronald Weller? Where are you getting this information?" Jack had been on the West Coast for the last two years, dealing with his own bullshit. A lot could have changed in that time, but SBMS involved with terrorists—he didn't buy it.

"Multiple sources have confirmed his involvement, including Paul Keane, the owner of Keane Flight. We've got Mr. Keane on charges of treason, among other things. He rolled over on SBMS without too much persuasion, but we still need actual proof that SBMS is involved, not just a traitor's word."

"How is Keane Flight involved?"

"Instead of just flying medical supplies, they've been picking up extra cargo."

Jack's mind immediately went to the human trafficking he'd recently dealt with, and he gritted his teeth. "Cargo?"

"Drugs, guns . . . possibly biological weapons."

The first two were typical cargo of most smugglers, but biological shit put Keane right on the NSA's hit list. "What do you want from me?"

His boss rubbed a hand over his face. "I've already built a cover for you. You're a silent partner with Keane

Flight. Now that Paul Keane is incapacitated, you'll be taking over the reins for a while, giving you full access to all his dealings."

"Incapacitated, huh?"

The corners of Wesley's mouth pulled up slightly. "He was in a car accident. Bad one."

"Right." Jack flipped through the pages of information. "Where's Keane really at right now?"

"In federal protection until we can bring this whole operation down, but publicly he's in a coma after a serious accident—one that left him scarred beyond recognition and the top half of his body in bandages."

Jack didn't even want to know where they'd gotten the body. Probably a John Doe no one would miss. "So what's the deal with my role?"

"Paul Keane has already made contact with Weller about you—days before his accident. Told him he was taking a vacation and you'd be helping out until he got back. Weller was cautious on the phone, careful not to give up anything. Now that Keane is 'injured,' no one can ask him any questions. Keane's assistant is completely in the dark about everything and thinks you're really a silent partner. You've been e-mailing with her the past week to strengthen your cover, but you won't need to meet her in person. You're supposed to meet with Weller in two days. We want you to completely infiltrate the day-to-day workings of SBMS. We need to know if Weller is working with anyone else, if he has more contacts we're not privy to. Everything."

"Why can't you tap his phone?" That should be child's play for the NSA.

His boss's expression darkened. "So far we've been

unable to hack his line. I've got two of my top analysts, Thomas Chadwick and Steven Williams—I don't think you've met either of them." When Jack shook his head, Wesley continued. "The fact that's he's got a filter that *we* can't bust through on his phone means he's probably into some dirty stuff."

Maybe. Or maybe the guy was just paranoid. Jack glanced at the report again, but didn't get that same rush he'd always gotten from his work. The last two years he'd seen mothers and fathers sell their children into slavery for less than a hundred dollars. And that wasn't even the worst of it. In the past he hadn't been on a job for more than six months at a time and he'd never been tasked with anything so brutal before, but in addition to human trafficking, they'd been selling people to scientists—under the direction of Albanian terrorists—who had loved having an endless supply of illegals to experiment on. He rolled his shoulders and shoved those thoughts out of his head. "What am I meeting him about?" *And how the hell will I handle seeing Sophie?* he thought.

"You supposedly want to go over flight schedules and the books and you want to talk about the possibility of investing in his company."

Jack was silent for a long beat. Then he asked the only question that mattered. The question that would burn him alive from the inside out until he actually voiced it. The question that made him feel as if he'd swallowed glass shards as he asked, "Will I be working with Sophie?"

Wesley's jaw clenched. "She *is* Weller's assistant."

"So yes."

Those knowing green eyes narrowed. "Is that going to be a problem?"

Yes. "No."

"She won't recognize you. What're you worried about?" Wesley folded his hands on top of the desk.

Jack wasn't worried about *her*. He was worried he couldn't stay objective around her. Sophie thought he was dead. And thanks to expensive facial reconstruction—all part of the deal in killing off his former identity when he'd joined Wesley's team with the NSA—she'd never know his true identity. Still, the thought of being in the same zip code as her sent flashes of heat racing down his spine. With a petite, curvy body made for string bikinis and wet T-shirt contests, Sophie was the kind of woman to make a man do a double take. He'd spent too many hours dreaming about running his hands through that thick dark hair again as she rode him. When they were seventeen, she'd been his ultimate fantasy and once they'd finally crossed that line from friends to lovers, there had been no keeping their hands off each other. They'd had sex three or four times a day whenever they'd been able to sneak away and get a little privacy. And it had never been enough with Sophie. She'd consumed him then. Now his boss wanted him to voluntarily work with her. "Why not send another agent?"

"I don't *want* anyone else. In fact, no one else here knows you're going in as Keane's partner except me."

Jack frowned. It wasn't the first time he'd gone undercover with only Wesley as his sole contact, but if his boss had people already working on the connection between Vargas and SBMS, it would be protocol

for the direct team to know he was going in undercover. "Why?"

"I don't want to risk a leak. If I'm the only one who
knows you're not who you say you are, there's no
chance of that."

There was more to it than that, but Jack didn't question him. He had that blank expression Jack recognized all too well, which meant he wouldn't be getting
any more, not even under torture.

Wesley continued. "You know more about Sophie
than most people. I want you to use that knowledge
to get close to her. I don't think I need to remind you
that this is a matter of national security."

"I haven't seen her since I was eighteen." And not
a day went by that he didn't think of the ways he'd
failed her. What the hell was Wesley thinking?

"It's time for you to face your past, Jack." His boss
suddenly straightened and took on that professorial/
fatherly look Jack was accustomed to.

"Is that what this is about? Me, facing my past?" he
ground out. Fuck that. If he wanted to keep his memories buried, he damn well would.

Wesley shrugged noncommittally. "You *will* complete this mission."

As Jack stood, he clenched his jaw so he wouldn't
say something he'd regret. Part of him wanted to tell
Wesley to take his order and shove it, but another
part—his most primal side—hummed with anticipa-
tion at the thought of seeing Sophie. She'd always
brought out his protective side. Probably because she'd
been his entire fucking world at one time and looking
out for her had been his number-one priority.

He'd noticed Sophie long before she'd been aware of his existence, but once he was placed in the same foster house as her, they'd quickly become best friends. Probably because he hadn't given her a choice in being his friend. He'd just pushed right past her shy exterior until she came to him about anything and everything. Then one day she'd kissed him. He shoved *that* thought right out of his mind.

"There's a car waiting to take you to the flight strip. Once you land in Miami, there will be another car waiting for you. There's a full wardrobe, and anything else you'll need at the condo we've arranged."

"What about my laptop?"

"It's in the car."

When he was halfway to the door, his boss stopped him again. "You need to face your demons, Jack. Seeing Sophie is the only way you'll ever exorcise them. Maybe you can settle down and start a family once you do. I want to see you happy, son."

Son. If only he'd had a father like Wesley growing up. But if he had, he wouldn't have ended up where he was today. And he'd probably never have met Sophie. That alone made his shitty childhood worth every punch and bruise he'd endured. Jack swallowed hard, but didn't turn around before exiting. His chest loosened a little when he was out from under Wesley's scrutiny. The older man might be in his early fifties, but with his skill set, Jack had no doubt his boss could take out any one of the men within their covert organization. That's why he was the deputy director of the NSA and the unidentified head of the covert group Jack worked for.

Officially, Black Death 9 didn't exist. Unofficially, the name was whispered in back rooms and among other similar black ops outfits within the government. Their faction was just another classified group of men and women working to keep their country safe. At times like this Jack wished the NSA didn't have a thick file detailing every minute detail of his past. If they didn't, another agent would be heading for Miami right now and he'd be on his way to a four-star hotel or on another mission.

Jack mentally shook himself as he placed his hand on the elevator scanner. Why was Wesley trying to get under his skin? Now, of all times? The man was too damn intuitive for his own good. He'd been after him for years to see Sophie in person, "to find closure" as he put it, but Jack couldn't bring himself to do it. He had no problem facing down the barrel of a loaded gun, but seeing the woman with the big brown eyes and the soft curves he so often dreamed about—*no, thank you.*

As the elevator opened into the aboveground parking garage, he shoved those thoughts away. He'd be seeing Sophie in two days. Didn't matter what he wanted.

Sophie Moreno took a deep, steadying breath and eased open the side door to one of Keane Flight's hangars. She had a key, so it wasn't as though she was technically breaking in. She was just coming by on a Sunday night when no one was here. And the place was empty. And she just happened to be wearing a black cap to hide her hair.

Oh yeah, she was completely acting like a normal,

law-abiding citizen. Cringing at her stupid rational-
ization, she pushed any fears of getting caught she had
to the side. What she was doing wasn't about her.

She loved her job at South Beach Medical Supply, but
lately her boss had been acting weird and the flight logs
from Keane Flight for SBMS's recent deliveries didn't
make sense. They hadn't for the past few months.

And no one—meaning her boss, Ronald Weller—
would answer her questions when she brought up
anything about Keane Flight.

Considering Ronald hadn't asked her over to dinner
in the past few months either, as he normally did, she
had a feeling he and his wife must be having problems.
They'd treated her like a daughter for almost as long
as she'd been with SBMS, so if he was too distracted
to look into things because of personal issues, she was
going to take care of this herself. SBMS provided
much-needed medical supplies to third-world countries, and she wasn't going to let anything jeopardize
that. People needed them. And if she could help out
Ronald, she wanted to.

She didn't even know what she was looking for, but
she'd decided to trust her gut and come here. Wearing
all black, she felt a little stupid, like a cat burglar or
something, but she wanted to be careful. Hell, she'd
even parked outside the hangar and sneaked in
through an opening in the giant fence surrounding
the private airport. The security here should have been
tighter—something she would address later. After
she'd done her little B&E. God, she was so going to get
in trouble if she was caught. She could tell herself that
she wasn't "technically" doing anything wrong, but

her palms were sweaty as she stole down the short hallway to where it opened up into a large hangar.

Two twin-engine planes sat there, and the overhead lights from the warehouselike building were dim. But they were bright enough for her to make out a lot of cargo boxes and crates at the foot of one of the planes. The back hatch was open, and it looked as if someone had started loading the stuff, then stopped.

Sophie glanced around the hangar as she stepped fully into it just to make sure she was alone. Normally Paul Keane had standard security here. She'd actually been here a couple of weeks ago under the guise of needing paperwork, and there had been two Hispanic guys hovering near the planes as if they belonged there. She'd never seen them before and they'd given her the creeps. They'd also killed her chance of trying to sneak in and see what kind of cargo was on the planes.

When she'd asked Paul about them, he'd just waved off her question by telling her he'd hired new security.

One thing she knew for sure. He'd lied straight to her face. Those guys were sure as hell *not* security. One of them had had a MAC-10 tucked into the front of his pants. She might not know everything about weapons, but she'd grown up in shitty neighborhoods all over Miami, so she knew enough. And no respectable security guy carried a MAC-10 with a freaking *suppressor*. That alone was incredibly shady. The only people she'd known to carry that type of gun were gangbangers and other thugs.

So even if she felt a little crazy for sneaking down here, she couldn't go to her boss about any illegal activities—if there even were any—without proof.

SBMS was Ronald's heart. He loved the company and she did too. No one was going to mess with it if she had anything to say about it.

Since the place was empty, she hurried across the wide expanse, her black ballet-slipper-type shoes virtually silent. When she neared the back of the plane, she braced herself for someone to be waiting inside.

It was empty except for some crates. Bypassing the crates on the outside, she ran up inside the plane and took half a dozen pictures of the crates with the SBMS logo on the outside. Then she started opening them.

By the time she opened the fifth crate, she was starting to feel completely insane, but as she popped the next lid, ice chilled her veins. She blinked once and struggled to draw in a breath, sure she was seeing things.

A black grenade peeked through the yellow-colored stuffing at the top. Carefully she lifted a bundle of it. There were more grenades lining the smaller crate, packed tight with the fluffy material. Her heart hammered wildly as it registered that Keane was likely running arms and weapons, using SBMS supplies as cover, but she forced herself to stay calm. Pulling out her cell phone, she started snapping pictures of the inside of the crate, then pictures that showed the logo on the outside. In the next crate she found actual guns. AK-47s, she was pretty sure. She'd never actually seen one in real life before, but it looked like what she'd seen in movies. After taking pictures of those, she hurried out of the back of the plane toward the crates sitting behind it.

Before she could decide which one to open first, a loud rolling sound rent the air—the hangar door!

Ducking down, she peered under the plane and saw the main door the planes entered and exited through starting to open. Panic detonated inside her. She had no time to do anything but run. Without pause, she raced back toward the darkened hallway. She'd go out the back, the same way she'd come in. All she had to do was get to that hallway before whoever—

"Hey!" a male voice shouted.

Crap, someone had seen her. She shoved her phone in her back pocket and sprinted even faster as she cleared the hallway. Fear ripped through her, threatening to pull her apart at the seams. She wouldn't risk turning around and letting anyone see her face.

The exit door clanged against the wall as she slammed it open. Male voices shouted behind her, ordering her to stop in Spanish.

Her lungs burned and her legs strained with each pounding step against the pavement. She really wished she'd worn sneakers. As she reached the edge of the fence that thankfully had no lighting and was lined with bushes and foliage behind it, she dove for the opening. If she hadn't known where it was, it would be almost impossible to find without the aid of light.

Crawling on her hands and knees, she risked a quick glance behind her. Two men were running across the pavement toward the fence, weapons silhouetted in their hands. She couldn't see their faces because the light from the back of the hangar was behind them, but they were far enough away that she should be able to escape. They slowed as they reached the fence, both looking around in confusion.

"Adónde se fue?" one of them snarled.

Sophie snorted inwardly as she shoved up from the ground and disappeared behind the bushes. They'd never catch her now. Not unless they could jump fences in single bounds. Twenty yards down, her car was still parked on the side of the back road where she'd left it.

The dome light came on when she opened the door, so she shut it as quickly as possible. She started her car but immediately turned off the automatic lights and kicked the vehicle into drive. Her tires made a squealing sound and she cringed. She needed to get out of there before those men figured out how to get through the fence. She couldn't risk them seeing her license plate. Only law enforcement should be able to track plates, but people who were clearly running weapons wouldn't care about breaking laws to find out who she was.

She glanced in the rearview mirror as her car disappeared down the dark road, and didn't see anyone in the road or by the side of it. Didn't mean they weren't there, though. Pure adrenaline pumped through her as she sped away, tearing through her like jagged glass, but her hands remained steady on the wheel.

What the hell was she supposed to do now? If she called the cops, this could incriminate SBMS and that could ruin all the good work their company had done over the past decade. And what if by the time the cops got there all the weapons were gone? Then she'd look crazy and would have admitted to breaking into a private airport hangar, which was against the law. Okay, the cops were out. For now. First she needed to talk to her boss. He'd know what to do and they could figure out this mess together.